HER
OCEAN
GRAVE

BOOKS BY DANA PERRY

The Silent Victim
The Golden Girl

DANA PERRY

HER
OCEAN
GRAVE

Bookouture

Published by Bookouture in 2021

An imprint of Storyfire Ltd.
Carmelite House
50 Victoria Embankment
London EC4Y 0DZ

www.bookouture.com

ISBN: 978-1-80019-385-7
eBook ISBN: 978-1-80019-384-0

For Laura Morgan

PROLOGUE

Most crime stories have a beginning and an end. They start with the crime, then the investigation by law enforcement authorities, and finally the solving of the case. But that's not the way it works all the time. Especially with missing person cases. Sometimes all we have left is unanswered questions.

A veteran detective told me once that unsolved missing person cases were the toughest ones for a police officer to deal with.

In even the most tragic murder, there is still closure for the family and loved ones of the victim. But when someone goes missing, there is nothing but uncertainty. Are they dead or alive? Will anyone ever find out for sure? It is that wondering – that uncertainty – which is the most terrifying thing of all.

"The worst missing person cases are the ones that make no sense whatsoever… no reason, no evidence, nothing about why the person disappeared," the detective said. "It's like a flying saucer simply swooped down one day and scooped them up. One minute they're there, and the next minute they're gone forever."

I've been thinking about that a lot recently.

About all the people out there who have disappeared without a trace.

Poof… and they're gone.

Just like Samantha Claymore…

CHAPTER 1

The first time I ever went to work in a police station was at the 13th Precinct in New York City.

The 13th Precinct is located on East 21st Street in the heart of Manhattan, right by the Police Academy where I had just graduated as a new recruit. Dressed in my blue police uniform with my name badge on my chest and my recently issued Sig Sauer P226 weapon on my hip, I felt a sense of excitement like I'd never experienced before.

Abby Pearce.

NYPD.

This was where I wanted to be. This was where I belonged.

Things are different now.

And the police station where I work these days is different too.

"The boss is looking for you, Abby," Meg Jarvis said to me now as I walked into the Cedar Cliffs, Mass. police station on Martha's Vineyard on a hot August day at the height of the tourist season.

"Chief Wilhelm?"

"He's the only boss we have. Said I should tell you to come see him right away. He said he had a case he wanted you to work on. Oh, and he also said to tell you that you were late."

I sighed.

"I had a long night."

"Big date?"

"Just me and Oscar."

"Oscar?"

"My dog."

Meg smiled. She was somewhere in her 60s, and she'd served as the department's administrative clerk for most of her life. She'd been through more than a half dozen police chiefs during that time, and she was still here. Everyone said Meg Jarvis was the person who kept the department running. It was important to stay on her good side. So far, I had done that. She seemed to like me.

"A pretty young woman like you should be spending her nights with a man, not a dog."

"I'm not that young. I just turned thirty-three."

"That's still plenty of time for you to settle down and get married."

"I've already done that, remember?"

"Right. To the state trooper back in New York. Well, maybe it's time for you to find someone new. Someone nice."

"Oh, it's time all right. But it's tough to meet nice guys. Especially in a small town like this and on an island. I suppose I could go into Boston and meet some guy at a singles bar, or hook up with someone on Tinder or through one of those other dating services. But I'm not really into that."

"Oh, no, Abby – that could be dangerous," Meg said. "You never know who you're meeting that way. Those are men just looking for someone to bed down for the night. Or worse. Of course, you're probably safer than most women. I mean no one's going to get too out of line with a policewoman who has a gun."

"I guess not," I said. "Of course, I generally don't shoot mashers with it on the first date."

The Cedar Cliffs Police Department where I'm a detective now – actually I'm the only detective – is housed in a small building across from the ferry docks where thousands of vacationers descend on the island of Martha's Vineyard every day during the summer.

On the other side is a famous carousel for children to ride. The rest of the area is filled with beach stores, ice cream parlors and outdoor cafes. The Cedar Cliffs Marina where all the fancy boats are anchored – some of them so big they could be called yachts – is right across the street.

I'd grown up on Martha's Vineyard, and now I was back, after ten years working on the New York City police force – first as a patrol officer on the street and then as a homicide detective. Going from being a cop with the NYPD to working here on the tiny Cedar Cliffs force was… well, a helluva adjustment to make.

Most of the police work done on this island has traditionally consisted of lost dogs, stolen mopeds, traffic problems, and maybe a rowdy beach party or two when the drinking and the drugs get out of hand.

In fact, there have only been two major crimes as far as I know in the history of Martha's Vineyard.

One was the famous Chappaquiddick drowning death of Mary Jo Kopechne in a car with Senator Ted Kennedy during the summer of 1969, which derailed his presidential aspirations.

The other was that of a seventy-two-year-old woman named Clara Smith who was mysteriously found beaten and strangled to death in her bed back in 1940. The murder was never solved, and I didn't figure there was much chance of me or anyone else solving it eighty years later.

Police Chief Barry Wilhelm was in his 50s, stocky, with close-cropped grey hair, dressed in his crisp blue uniform. He looked like a cop. Or at least what a lot of people thought a cop was supposed to look like. I think he really worked on that look. Probably posed in front of a mirror every morning before he came to work. Getting that tough police chief look just right.

Only problem is he was here running a tiny police force on an idyllic island where crime hardly ever happened. I'd heard that

Wilhelm once hoped to move up to a big city police force, but instead he was still here as a small-town cop. Maybe that's why he didn't like me very much. I'd been a big city cop once.

"So what's going on today?" I asked him when I sat down in front of his desk. "What's the case you want me to check out?"

He picked up a picture from his desk and handed it to me. It was a young girl in her teens. Pretty, with long blonde hair and smiling for the camera.

"That's Samantha Claymore, Valerie Claymore's daughter. Sixteen years old. She didn't come home last night."

"Valerie Claymore, the cosmetics queen?"

"Right. The Claymores have been staying here for the summer. Samantha went out for a bike ride yesterday, headed for Edgartown. They haven't heard from her since. She was supposed to be back for some barbecue last night, but she didn't show."

'Maybe she found something better to do than be with her family. There's a lot of stuff for a teenage girl to do between here and Edgartown. Beach parties, bars… it's probably something like that. A kid just having some fun."

"That's what I tried to tell Mrs. Claymore. But she is still worried. And she'll continue to be until the girl comes home again."

"You don't figure this is anything serious?"

"No. That's why I want you to go out and talk to Mrs. Claymore. Tell her we're taking all the necessary steps to look for her daughter, but mostly convince her not to worry."

"Sure, Chief. I'll head out there now."

Wilhelm fiddled nervously with some paperwork on his desk. I could tell he had something else he wanted to say.

"How is everything in your life these days, Pearce?" he finally asked me.

"Such as?"

"Well, that problem…"

I sighed.

"If you want to know about my drinking, I'm fine. I haven't had a drink since my trouble that night in East Chop."

"And that's the truth?"

"It's the truth."

"How can I be sure about that?"

"I understand, Chief. And you're right. Because even if I was drinking again, I'd probably lie to you about it. So, I can see why you might be concerned."

"But you're not drinking?"

"No, I'm not drinking."

CHAPTER 2

The house where Samantha Claymore's mother was staying on Martha's Vineyard turned out to be a little bigger than my apartment in New York City. Not just *my* apartment, but the entire building. It had more bedrooms than I could count; a living room the size of a football field; a spacious workout room with gym equipment; an outside swimming pool; and private decks wrapped around the whole house with ocean views of Nantucket Sound from the front and Sengekontacket Pond from the back.

The place was about a five-minute drive south of the center of Cedar Cliffs, not far from Beach Road, which ran all the way down to Edgartown on the south side of the island. There was a bike path along the entire six-mile route, which was probably the way Samantha had pedaled her bike away from the house the previous day.

I stood there now, watching other bikers and cars and Jeeps passing by, hoping Samantha might possibly be one of them and that she'd soon show up at the house with an explanation of where she'd been. But she didn't do that, of course. So, I went up to the house and rang the bell.

"Are you the detective?" Valerie Claymore asked when she opened the door.

"Yes, I'm Detective Abby Pearce."

"You don't look like a detective."

People have always said that about me. I have long black hair, which I usually wear in a ponytail or a bun held in place by a plastic hair clip. I'm pretty much average size – 5 foot 5, 105 pounds or so. I know men find me attractive because a lot of them have told me so. Which is all good. It's just that when people meet me for the first time – especially since I don't wear a uniform – they sometimes figure me for a businesswoman or a real estate broker, maybe even a media person or soccer mom. Not a cop. Which I've sometimes been able to use to my advantage by catching people off guard. But that wasn't the situation here.

I took out my badge and showed it to Valerie Claymore. It wasn't as impressive as the NYPD shield that I used to carry, but it did the job. She nodded and motioned for me to come inside the house.

"I hope you can help me find my daughter, Detective Pearce," she said as I followed her down a long hall.

"That's what I'm here for, Mrs. Claymore."

Valerie Claymore had to be at least fifty, according to the math I had done on her before coming here. But she looked more like someone my age. Perfectly coiffured blonde hair, flawless facial features, dressed in a fashionable, expensive-looking sundress and sandals – and a body so tight it must have been the result of daily workouts in the gym and pool.

I guess when you run a cosmetics empire like Valerie Claymore, it's important to look good. And it's a lot easier to do that if you are worth the kind of money she was.

"The most important thing to remember is that your daughter is very likely safe and in no danger," I said as we sat on a plush white couch in the living room. "If she was in an accident, we would have found her bike or her belongings by now. There's no sign of any of that. And there's no record of Samantha – or anyone fitting her description – at the hospitals nearby and seeking medical care. So, it looks as if she simply chose to go someplace without telling you."

I asked her to tell me everything about the last time she saw the girl – and anything else she remembered leading up to that point.

"It was a normal day," she said. "We've been up here since July. There was nothing different about yesterday. Samantha got up early – she always gets up earlier than me – and sat out on the deck getting some morning sun. That's where I found her when I woke up. Then she was on her computer and her iPad and her phone and all the rest of it for a few hours. You know how teenagers are addicted to their electronics. She ate breakfast at some point, but a very light one, because she said she wanted to stop for lunch later during her bike ride. Said she was going to eat at a place in Edgartown called the Chicken Shack. She loves the chicken wings there."

"Tell me what else she said about the bike ride."

"Not much else to tell. She likes to ride her bike, and it is so much easier to do here than back in New York City where we normally are. She wanted to buy a blouse at a store in Edgartown. She'd seen it there one day, and decided to go back and buy it."

"Do you know the name of the store?"

"Yes. It was called Sunflowers."

"And, as far as you know, she never got there?"

"That's right. I called the store. No one there had seen her or had any record of her buying anything yesterday."

"And you checked others places too?"

"Yes, I called the Chicken Shack and some other places I know she'd gone to in the past. Not only in Edgartown but all around the island. No one had seen or heard from her. I'm sure she was going to Edgartown though, and not anywhere else. That's what she told me. And I saw her from the deck pedaling away from the house. It was south on Beach Road, taking the bike path that leads to Edgartown. Maybe she stopped somewhere along the way. But I don't know where that might be."

I thought about one possible spot Samantha Claymore might have stopped. I raised it as delicately as I could.

"It was nice weather yesterday," I said, "and there are open beaches all along that bike path your daughter was on. Do you think she might have gotten off her bike at some point? Maybe she wanted to go for a dip in the ocean and…"

I didn't finish the thought. It was an ominous one.

If she'd gone in the water without people around – and somehow got pulled out to sea by a rip tide or something else – no one would have seen what happened. Of course, that didn't explain the missing bike or the belongings she presumably would have left behind on the beach. But, even though I didn't want to say it out loud to Mrs. Claymore, it was the most logical theory I could come up with about how or why she'd disappeared.

Except her mother quickly dismissed that idea.

"Are you saying she might have drowned? That's ridiculous. Samantha would have never gotten off her bike to go into the water."

"How can you be sure of that?"

"Because Samantha hated the water. She was terrified of it."

"She never went swimming?"

"Never. Wouldn't go into the ocean. Not even into our pool here. She sunbathed and nothing else. Samantha had a tremendous fear of the water. I know my daughter. And one thing she would never do is put herself in a situation where she might drown."

I thought about how strange it was that she brought her daughter to an ocean island for the summer if the girl hated being around water. But I wasn't here to grade this woman on her parental choices.

"What about Samantha's father? Would he have any more insight into what her plans were when she set out on that bike trip yesterday?"

"Samantha's father is dead."

"Oh, I'm sorry. When did he die?"

"Several years ago. I'm remarried now."

"Maybe your current husband would know something."

"Bruce is in New York City. He rarely comes out to the Vineyard."

I nodded like I understood. I didn't really. I figured it wasn't a good sign that they were spending most of the summer in different places. But, if he wasn't here, he couldn't tell me anything more about Samantha. I moved on with my questions.

"How would you describe your relationship with your daughter, Mrs. Claymore?"

"Close. Extremely close."

"I see. Well, that's good."

I waited for her to say something more, but she didn't. So, I looked down at the checklist of questions I'd made in my notebook to see where to go next.

"Tell me about some of her friends?"

"What do you mean?"

"I thought I'd talk to some of her friends on the island. See what they might know. She might have confided in them. Can you give me a list of the young people here she spent time with?"

She looked baffled.

"I don't know anyone like that."

"You don't know anyone she was friends with here?"

"No, I'm sorry."

"What about back in New York City? She might have called a friend back home to tell them what she was planning to do. If you could give me any names at all…"

Another shake of her head.

"I don't know any of her friends in New York."

"Any romantic interests?"

"You mean boys?"

"Yes, did she have a boyfriend?"

"She was only sixteen."

"Lots of sixteen-year-old girls have boyfriends."

"I never knew of anyone. I mean, she never talked to me about a boyfriend. She never talked to me about boys at all. Sorry. I'm doing the best that I can. But I can't help you with this."

"I understand."

Yep, sounded like a real tight mother-daughter relationship.

"Can you tell me what she was wearing when you last saw her?"

"I think it was some kind of T-shirt with shorts or maybe jeans. That's what she usually wore."

"Do you remember what color they were?"

She shook her head.

"Any significant jewelry? Earrings? Necklaces?"

"Why does that matter?"

"Someone might remember a girl wearing a specific type of jewelry. It could help us in our search."

She thought about it.

"She would have been wearing her ring, that's all I can tell you."

"What kind of ring?"

"A big, black onyx ring. She wears it on her left index finger. Never takes it off. Her father gave it to her before he died. It's very important to her. She always wears it in his memory. That's all I can think of, Detective. Is there anything else?"

I had a few more questions for her, but I didn't learn anything useful. Then I reassured her that the Cedar Cliffs police force was doing everything possible to find her daughter, and that I would be in touch as soon as I had more information.

I tried to sound as optimistic as possible about the outcome.

But I already had a bad feeling. About Valerie Claymore's marriage. About her seemingly dysfunctional relationship with her daughter. And, most of all, about the fate of Samantha Claymore.

CHAPTER 3

Ask any cop – the first forty-eight hours of a case are the most critical.

When I was a homicide detective in New York, everyone knew about this rule for murder cases. If we didn't come up with a lead, a suspect or an arrest within those first forty-eight hours after the murder was committed, then the chances of solving the crime dropped by fifty percent.

It's been proved time and time again in countless murder investigations over the years.

And the "first forty-eight hours" rule is even more important in a missing person case, where the chances of a successful solution plunge dramatically the longer that someone is out there missing.

Maybe the most glaring example of this was the murder of JonBenét Ramsey, the six-year-old pageant beauty queen who went missing – and was then found murdered – in her Boulder, Colorado home on Christmas Day, 1996.

We all remember that haunting picture of little JonBenét Ramsey dressed up and dancing on stage before she died. Who would want to kill such a lovely little girl?

But crucial mistakes made during the first forty-eight hours after she went missing made it impossible for investigators to crack the case. The initial crime scene was compromised; evidence was mishandled; full statements weren't taken immediately from key people. As a result, JonBenét's murderer was never apprehended

— and most people believe they will never be found after all these years.

I picked up the picture of Samantha Claymore that her mother had given me. The photo had been taken on the docks near the Cedar Cliffs Marina. Samantha was wearing cut-off jeans and a tank top, and was smiling for the camera. It was a haunting look. A young woman filled with so much life when this picture was taken — and with so much to live for. What happened to her on that bike ride? And where was she now?

I put the picture down and went to work.

It had already been nearly twenty-four hours since Samantha Claymore was last seen.

The clock was ticking.

I had gained access to Samantha's computer and iPad, which were in her bedroom at the house. She had seemingly taken her phone with her on her bike ride. Neither the computer or the iPad was password protected, so I was able to look at her files, emails and social media posts. That was the good news. The bad news was they didn't tell me much.

She had accounts on Twitter, Facebook and Instagram. But she didn't seem to be a particularly prolific poster on any of them. Just stuff here and there about sights she'd seen or a TV show she was watching. I found out she was a fan of *Game of Thrones*, *Ozark* and *Bosch*. Which showed she had good taste in her TV choices, but was of no help to me in any other way.

There were lots of files she'd downloaded and saved. Most of them seemed to be pretty mundane, like her social media posts.

I scrolled through as many of them as I could. But there was one folder I couldn't get into. It was simply labeled "Mandell" and it required a password. I thought it might auto fill the password saved on the site, but that didn't work. I couldn't access it. So, I wrote down "Mandell" in my notebook for later.

From Samantha's emails and friends list on Facebook, I was able to put together a list of people she communicated with regularly. I wrote down their names and contact info. Then I reached out to some of them over email, asking them to get back to me or the Cedar Cliffs police force as soon as possible. I stressed that Samantha wasn't in any trouble, we only needed to locate her. I wasn't sure if that would work, but I figured it was worth a try.

One of the friends on Samantha's list – who she seemed to communicate with frequently – had an unusual last name. Bridget Feckanin. From their exchanges, it appeared as if she was a friend on Martha's Vineyard, not in New York City. I looked up "Feckanin" and found a listing for a Jonathan Feckanin in Vineyard Haven. I called the number and asked to speak to Bridget.

"Sam's missing?" she exclaimed when I told her what the call was about. "What happened?"

"That's what we're trying to determine, Bridget. All we know is she left on a bike ride to Edgartown yesterday, and she hasn't been heard from since. Her mother has asked us to look into the matter. We don't want to cause any trouble for her. All we want to do is get Samantha home safely," I said.

"Who?"

"Samantha. The young woman we're talking about."

There was a silence on the other end.

"Oh, you mean Sam," she said finally.

I realized now she had called the missing woman Sam, not Samantha.

"Sam hated the name Samantha," Bridget said. "None of us ever called her that. We always knew her as Sam. And no one who really knew her ever called her Samantha. It was a big deal with her. Do you know what I mean?"

I sure did.

Except her mother had called her Samantha.

Just another example of that really close mother-daughter relationship.

"When was the last time you heard from her?"

"Uh, a few days ago… I was going to call Sam today…"

We talked awhile longer. But she didn't seem to know anything about Samantha Claymore's disappearance. I told her to call me if she heard from Samantha or remembered anything else that might be significant in the search.

When the going gets tough, the tough hit the street. That's what cops say sometimes when they've run into a roadblock on a case. Meaning old-fashioned shoe leather can be better than computers and all the other fancy accoutrements of modern-day crime fighting.

I decided to retrace Samantha's steps along her bicycle route. Or at least the route she would have taken if she had followed through in her plan to take the bike trail on Beach Road all the way to Edgartown on the bottom tip of the Vineyard.

I didn't ride a bicycle like she would have done. I drove instead. But I drove very slowly, trying to imagine that I was her on that bike.

It had turned into a terrific beach day on the island – sunny, with temperatures in the 90s. Beach Road – and the bike path that ran alongside it – was packed with people, most of them tourists here for the high point of the summer season in August.

Every once in a while I stopped. The first stop came at a bridge a mile south of the Claymore house, where about fifty young people were crowded together and jumping – one by one – into the water below. This was an island tradition, and the bridge was always filled with kids doing this in the summer. Could Samantha Claymore have decided to try it? And then been injured in the fall and drowned? No, that didn't make sense. The place was always crowded, someone would have noticed her. I got out of the car and showed her picture to as many of the people on the bridge as I could, but no one remembered Samantha being there.

After that came miles of beach, up and down the highway, where anyone could sit down near the water. She could have done that, I suppose. But then what? She didn't drown because she didn't like to go in the water. She could have been attacked or abducted by someone on the beach. But who? Things like that hardly ever happened on Martha's Vineyard.

Eventually, I made it into Edgartown. Edgartown was the largest town on the island, populated by lots of stores and businesses. I started with Sunflowers, the one where Samantha had said she was going to buy a blouse, but they repeated what they had already told Valerie Claymore. Her daughter had not shown up there yesterday. I showed Samantha's picture around other places nearby too without any success.

After that, I wound up at the Chicken Shack, the place where Samantha had told her mother she planned to eat lunch. It's a restaurant in the heart of Edgartown with an outdoor rooftop bar and dining area. Sitting up there you get a beautiful view of the boats in Edgartown Harbor.

The guy behind the outdoor bar recognized me and came over. His name was Jim. Or Jack. Something like that, I wasn't sure. I'd been drinking the last time I was here, and things got fuzzy when I did that. But he knew me. He took a bottle of Heineken out of the cooler, brought it over and put it down on the bar.

"Good to see you, Detective Pearce. It's been awhile."

"Yeah, I've been busy."

"Working hard, huh?"

"Right. Working hard."

I looked down at the Heineken. It was still there. He pushed it towards me now.

"On the house," he said.

"No thanks," I said quickly. "I don't want it. I'm on duty."

He nodded, but didn't take the Heineken away. I could see ice melting down the side of the bottle. The sun was beating down on me, and I was really hot. Damn, that Heineken sure looked good. But I didn't drink any of it. Instead, I asked the bartender about Samantha Claymore and showed him her picture.

"I know her," he said. "I've seen her here eating. Too young to drink, of course. But I've seen her come in for the chicken wings. I remember she really liked them."

That sounded like her.

"But not yesterday?"

"No."

"You're sure."

"Yes, I was here all day."

"Who was she with when you saw her here in the past?"

He shrugged. "Friends usually. Why? What's going on with her?"

"She's missing."

He said he'd keep an eye out for her – and pass the word to other bartenders and waitresses in the place.

I thanked him, gave him my card and told him to contact me if he heard anything at all.

By the time I got back to my car, the seats and the steering wheel were hot from sitting out in the blazing sun. I turned up the air conditioner full blast and let the cool air hit me in the face. On the street around me more people headed into the restaurant and the other shops around it.

I looked at them all, hoping for a miracle.

I wanted Samantha Claymore to suddenly show up. I wanted to take her home to her worried mother and have a happy ending to this case.

There was something else I wanted too.

I wanted to drink that goddamned beer I left behind on the bar.

Except I didn't do that anymore.

CHAPTER 4

I was living in a house near the town of Chilmark. That's about a twenty-five-to-thirty-minute drive west from Cedar Cliffs, although it can take longer in the summer because of the glut of cars, Jeeps and bikes on the road.

Driving there after leaving the station at the end of the day, I played over in my head everything I knew – or, to put it more accurately, didn't know – about the case.

The forty-eight-hour mark was rapidly approaching, and I was no closer to finding the missing girl than I was when I started.

Oh, I'd done all the by-the-book investigative moves when I got back to the station after leaving Edgartown, including checking with the airlines at Martha's Vineyard Airport to see if Samantha might have taken a flight off of the island. But there was nothing.

Of course, she could have boarded one of the ferries that leave from Cedar Cliffs and Vineyard Haven every hour or so, and there was no registration needed for that.

But all I could do right now was keep looking for her here on Martha's Vineyard.

Except so far, I clearly hadn't been looking in the right places.

My place in Chilmark was more of a cottage than a house. It sure was a far cry from the house where the Claymores were staying.

It had two bedrooms, a small living room and a kitchen. There was no ocean view, but every place in Martha's Vineyard is only a short distance from the water. And I did have a back porch that looked out onto several miles of beautiful woods. It was pretty remote; the closest business was the Chilmark General Store five minutes away.

Even a place like this would normally cost a lot at this time of the island's tourist season. More than a Cedar Cliffs detective could afford. But because I lived here year-round, I was able to rent it for a much lower rate.

I grew up in the larger town of Vineyard Haven. My father ran a restaurant there. My mother had lived in the same house until recently. But then, after my father died, she had moved into an assisted living facility on Cape Cod. I was just glad that I didn't have to go back to my parents' house anymore.

That place held too many memories for me.

It was six months ago that I made my decision to leave the NYPD and return to Martha's Vineyard. I hadn't lived on the island – or even been back here – for more than a decade. Still, I thought maybe getting away from New York City and all that happened to me there might help me get my life back on track.

Living in the house in Chilmark was certainly a big transition from my old apartment in the heart of Manhattan. But I'd discovered a lot of the simple joys of island living again, things that I couldn't do when I was in New York City.

Things like gardening, biking – and even sailing.

The gardening was a surprise to me. In New York, I hardly ever had plants in my apartment. It was just too much trouble to water and take care of them regularly. But here I started planting daffodils, begonias, sunflowers, irises and even roses. I enjoyed it so much I decided to try my hand at vegetables too. So now I have a garden in my backyard where I grow tomatoes, lettuce, carrots and a few stalks of corn. There is something incredibly satisfying about preparing – and eating – a salad made from ingredients that I grew myself in my own garden.

Lots of people ride bicycles in New York City, but it's completely different to bike riding here. You spend more of your time weaving in and out of traffic on city streets, dodging taxis and trucks, and yelling at people to get out of your way. Here it is much more peaceful. There are bike trails everywhere, to the beaches and through the woods. Thus far, I've taken only ten-mile round trips on my bike but I am working up to longer treks. My goal is to bike from Cedar Cliffs on the east shore of the Vineyard all the way to the western coast, which is more than twenty-five miles away. And fifty miles round trip. I'm not quite ready for that yet, but maybe someday soon. I enjoy the bike riding. It's fun to look at the trees and the water from a solitary road as I pedal around the island after a long day on the job.

As for the sailing, that was something I'd always wanted to do when I was growing up here but never did. People always said that if you lived on the island, you needed to learn how to sail. So, I finally decided to learn. I took sailing lessons twice a week – first on ponds and lakes, then out on the ocean waters of Nantucket Bay. My goal is to one day sail by myself to the neighboring island of Nantucket and to the Cape Cod mainland.

Another thing I've spent a lot of my free time doing is revisiting places on the island I remember from my youth here. The beaches, the movie theaters, the hangouts, the schools that I'd attended. I'm not sure exactly what I've been looking for. Maybe I'm trying to make the memories of those days come out with a happier ending than they did. But most of the places are different now. And the people I remember from back then are long gone. Very few young people who grew up on Martha's Vineyard stayed here. And even fewer came back here again.

When I got home, I was greeted by my dog Oscar. He's a five-year-old black and tan dachshund. But not one of those tiny dachshunds you see around a lot. Oscar weighed around thirty-five pounds and looked more like a basset hound. Me and my husband Zach – well, my ex-husband – had two dogs when were together in New York City. Both dachshunds. We named them Oscar and

Felix. Right, like the *Odd Couple*. I got Oscar when we divided everything up after our split.

One of the good things about having a dog when you live alone is that it gives you someone to talk to. Okay, it's kind of a one-way conversation. But I knew someone who insisted animals loved it when you talked to them, even if they didn't understand what you were saying. Apparently they picked up on your feelings and emotions.

So I wound up talking a lot to Oscar.

"Where in the hell is the Claymore girl?" I asked him now.

He licked my face.

"Is she safe?"

Another lick.

"What do you think I should do next to try and find her?"

This time he ran over to his dish to show me he was ready to eat. No help at all.

I fed Oscar, took him outside for a short walk and then made my own dinner. I'd bought a takeout order of those wings from the Chicken Shack before I left Edgartown. I heated them up in my microwave and poured myself a big cup of coffee to drink. Then I decided I wanted a Diet Coke. But that didn't do the trick for me either, so I wound up drinking bottled water with my meal instead.

What I really wanted now was a drink. A real drink. But, like I told Chief Wilhelm, I wasn't drinking. At least for the moment.

I thought about Zach, my ex-husband. He'd moved on with his life, had a new girlfriend back in New York. But me, well... I guess I hadn't quite gotten over Zach yet. I'd met him while working on a case as part of a joint task force between the NYPD and the New York State Police, where he worked as an investigative trooper. Zach and I solved the case, fell in love and got married. I thought he was the love of my life. Maybe he was. But, in the end, he left – like so many other men before him. It was the drinking that came between Zach and me. I'm not a pretty sight when I drink.

The truth is I drank a lot during my time with the NYPD. First, as a patrol officer on the street, and then later as a homicide detective. But that didn't stop me from breaking big cases and becoming a kind of a media star for it. I was on the front pages of the tabloids and the TV news channels a few times. One time when I subdued a bank robber to foil a holdup. Another time when I did the perp walk with a suspect I'd arrested for a high-profile murder. People liked the idea of a young woman like me cracking big cases. Sort of like a modern-day *Cagney & Lacey*.

I was younger then, of course, and I felt indestructible. I was able to balance my drinking with the demands of my job. I could handle it. That's what I told myself anyway, and it seemed to be true.

Until the time came when I couldn't handle it anymore.

After my partner, Tommy Ferraro, died in my arms.

That's when it all fell apart.

I dream about Tommy a lot. The dream is always the same. Tommy and I are on the street. There's the glint of a gun. Then a shot. Tommy falls to the ground. And I just stand there watching it all play out – knowing what the outcome will be, no matter how many times I relive it.

But I didn't dream about Tommy on this night.

Instead, I dreamt about Samantha Claymore.

I saw her face – so young and innocent – just like she was in her mother's picture.

But she wasn't missing anymore.

I'd found her.

Outside a mansion on Martha's Vineyard, walking towards the door and getting ready to open it.

I screamed at her: "No, Samantha, don't go in there!"

She turned around and looked at me.

Except she wasn't Samantha Claymore anymore.

The young girl standing outside that house was me.

CHAPTER 5

Before I left the station house the night before, I'd asked the Edgartown police to do a massive search in town for any evidence Samantha had been there at all. I was especially interested in her bike. I found out the next day that my move had paid off.

"We just found Samantha Claymore's bicycle," Chief Wilhelm told me.

"Where?"

"At a bike rack in Edgartown."

"Was there any…?"

"No. No sign of the girl. But it definitely looks like her bike. Fits the description that you got from the mother. And there was still a receipt in the basket from the rental place where she must have got it. The receipt was made out to Samantha Claymore."

"Who's with the bike now?"

"Teena Morelli. You better get there quick."

Teena Morelli. Of all the people on the Cedar Cliffs police force, I sure wish Teena Morelli wasn't the one on the scene with the damn bike. I mean I was glad to get a break on the case, but I wasn't looking forward to having to deal with Morelli.

Morelli was standing next to the bicycle when I got there, in an area which had been roped off with tape to keep onlookers away. Morelli herself was a physically imposing woman – curly dark hair, six feet tall, muscular from hours of workouts at a health club in Cedar Cliffs. Standing there now in her perfectly creased blue uniform and with a gun on her hip, she looked like how most people think a cop is supposed to look. Probably more like one than I ever did.

"We'll need to get someone here to dust for fingerprints on the bike," I said to her. "To see if anything turns up besides the girl's own prints. That might give us some kind of a lead."

"I've already called. That's why I've been keeping the area protected so no one else touches it until forensics gets here."

"Okay. Well since I'm here now to watch the bike, why don't you start going place to place to see if anyone in this area saw or remembers anything about Samantha and the bike."

"That's already in motion. I asked the Edgartown police for help. They've got officers questioning store owners, customers and everyone else they can find for several blocks around here."

I nodded. "Good work, Morelli."

"Just doing my job. Of course, I'm not a hotshot detective like you. But then I was the one who found the bike you were looking for, wasn't I?"

There were fifteen full-time members on the Cedar Cliffs police force, plus another five temporary officers added during the summer tourist months. I got along pretty well with all of them except for two people. Chief Wilhelm and Teena Morelli. I knew with Wilhelm it was because he resented my big city success, and I had a pretty good idea about Morelli too. It was because I had the job she thought should have been hers.

There's only one full-time detective in Cedar Cliffs. When the man doing that job died, it was about the same time I made my decision to return to Martha's Vineyard. Teena Morelli had been in line for the job. But there was a lot of publicity about the possibility of an NYPD homicide cop coming home to work for the small-time island police force, including a front-page story in the local newspaper. That led the Cedar Cliffs mayor and other local officials to tell Wilhelm they wanted me – and not Morelli – in the job.

Our relationship had been tense ever since.

It was kind of a shame because I might have really liked Teena Morelli under different circumstances. She was tough. I was tough. Maybe we could have even been friends. But there wasn't much chance of that happening now.

I looked around where we were standing. The bike rack was in front of a place selling newspapers, magazines and various other sundry items. Had Samantha Claymore left the bike parked here to go in there? Then what happened? There were other stores – food, clothing, antiques – all around us where she could have gone too. A few blocks down the street was the entrance to the ferry for Chappaquiddick Island. Samantha might have gone there to get to Chappaquiddick, I suppose. But she would have brought her bike along on the ferry. And the easiest way off of Chappaquiddick is to come back again by the same ferry.

Where the hell was she?

I put on a pair of gloves and examined the bike myself. There was no blood. No damage. No sign of any physical struggle. It simply looked like she'd parked her bike, locked it to the rack, walked away – and then never come back.

I picked up the receipt for the bike and looked at it. It said the bike had been rented from Island Bicycle Rentals in Cedar Cliffs in July – and that the rental was good until the end of the summer. So that was of no help. Samantha must have put the receipt in the basket when she rented the bike, and never bothered to take it out. There was nothing else in the basket – no cell phone, no handbag, no nothing. But then she would have taken all that stuff with her wherever she was going, right? Unless something else happened.

"Any idea how long the bike has been here?" I asked Morelli.

"No. Who pays any attention to a bike sitting at a rack like this?"

"I can make an educated guess how long it's been here," I said.

"Go ahead."

"Well, the mother said she saw Samantha riding the bike down Beach Road in the late morning. That's about a thirty-minute ride, maybe an hour tops – depending on whether or not she stopped along the way. Which means the bike must have been here since early afternoon the day she disappeared. Sitting here until we found it."

"Weren't you down here in Edgartown yesterday, Pearce?" Morelli asked now. "Why didn't you bother to check out the bike racks while you were here? It's called basic police work."

I'd had it with Teena Morelli.

"Look, don't lecture me about police work," I snapped at her. "I know how to do my job. I spent ten years with the NYPD – the biggest and best police force in the country – working the streets…"

"Yeah, and your partner on those streets with you wound up dead, didn't he?"

I felt my face flush red with anger.

"That's a cheap shot, Morelli."

"It is. But you're the one who started talking all that NYPD crap of yours so…"

My phone rang. I looked down at the screen. It was a call from Valerie Claymore. Probably asking for an update. Well, at least I could tell her we'd found her daughter's bicycle. I'd put the best possible spin on it. Tell her there was no blood or any sign of a crime. And then I'd placate her fears the best I could, even if my own fears about Samantha Claymore were growing bigger with every minute she was gone.

But I never got the chance to tell her any of that.

Because she had something to tell me.

Something much more important.

"I just got a ransom note for Samantha," Valerie Claymore said.

CHAPTER 6

The ransom note was very strange.

On many levels.

First off, it hadn't been delivered to Valerie Claymore directly, but to a neighbor instead. The neighbor found the envelope taped to her door when she went out to walk her dog that morning. The envelope had Valerie Claymore's name on it, so she simply brought it to her without looking at what was inside.

I found out that though the Claymores' house had a security camera above the front door, which would have picked up surveillance video of anyone approaching, the neighbor's house didn't. Which meant that whoever left the note was possibly familiar with both houses. Or else was watching them both. Or maybe just put the note on the wrong house by mistake.

The writer of the letter also seemed to have taken no special steps to conceal their identity. It wasn't typewritten. It wasn't block letters cut out and pasted on from a newspaper like you see on TV or in the movies. It was plain handwriting, which could be matched to a suspect whenever one was found.

The letter itself was written on plain white paper and placed inside a standard-sized business envelope. Nothing unusual there. But there was something strange on the outside of the envelope. On the back flap, someone had drawn a symbol. It looked like some kind of lightning bolt.

The words in the letter were bizarre too. At times disjointed, at others almost eloquent. As if two different people had written it. Or, as seemed more likely, someone who wanted to make it seem that way for a reason.

The letter read:

> *Mrs. Claymore: We have your daughter. She is safe and unharmed. But you must follow our instructions carefully if you want to see her again.*
>
> *Have $583,000 ready in cash to deliver to us. The money should all be in $100 bills. When the money has been withdrawn from your accounts, put it in an attaché case and await further instructions.*
>
> *If you don't pay, your daughter dies.*
> *If you alert the police, your daughter dies.*
> *If you do exactly as we say, she will be returned home safely.*

After this, the letter switched tone and became almost philosophical.

> *You don't always know what you've got until it's gone.*
> *Like your daughter Samantha.*
> *Hopefully this will be a positive learning experience for you – and worth the money it will cost to get your daughter back.*

But the words soon became threatening again.

> *Your company has gotten rich by underpaying workers and abusing animals in your test laboratories. Change is coming.*

It ended like this:

> *Do you really want to know the pain of your daughter being dead? Do everything we say and you'll get her back. Withdraw the money and await our next communication.*

At the bottom of the letter was the same symbol as on the back of the envelope.

It was larger – and clearer – here than on the envelope. And I could see now that it was actually the number seven, repeated three times. One on top of each other. Three sevens in a pattern that looked like a lightning bolt.

"Why $583,000?" I asked Chief Wilhelm as we read the note again together – trying to decipher some clues about the sender. "What's that number about?"

"It's the ransom amount."

"I know. But why $583,000? Not $500,000, not $50,000, not $5M. Seems like a strange and exact number to come up with for a ransom."

Wilhelm shrugged. He seemed truly stunned, and maybe a bit overwhelmed, by this shocking new development in Samantha Claymore's disappearance. Sure, he always dreamed of being a tough cop working on big city crime cases like I did in New York City. But the reality, I guess, was he was just a small-town police chief. He'd never handled a case of this magnitude before. But I had, and I was ready to take on this case. I think Wilhelm knew that too, even if he wouldn't admit it.

"There's also this thing about the change in tone midway through the letter," I said. "It goes from talking about this being a learning curve to becoming a political diatribe."

"More than one person involved in it, you think?"

"Maybe. Or just one person who wants to make it sound like there is more than one person involved. To confuse us."

"Why?"

"I have no idea."

I pointed to the symbol on the back of the envelope and again at the end of the ransom note.

"At first, I thought it was a lightning bolt. Now I see it's a series of the number seven – three sevens written on top of each other. I remember now that three sevens is some kind of occult or pagan symbol. Sort of like 666 for the devil. It came up in a case I handled back in New York. That's the kind of craziness we might be dealing with here, Chief."

"Jesus."

"Yeah, I know."

More than ever before, I realized that Chief Wilhelm was overwhelmed by the enormity of this case.

My reaction was completely different.

I spent ten years on the New York City police force and I loved every minute of it – until I didn't love it anymore. That's why I made the difficult decision to return to Martha's Vineyard. I needed to take control of my life again. But something had been missing for me here. My job felt unfinished. I needed to do something to erase the memories and regrets of those last days in New York. I needed something more. I needed... well, redemption.

Sitting there in Wilhelm's office, I remembered my glory days on the NYPD – the arrests, the awards, the acclaim I got in the media that, back then, I thought would never go away.

I remembered too my marriage to Zach and how wonderful it was in the beginning. Before I ruined it all.

And, most of all, I remembered my partner Detective Tommy Ferraro lying dead in the street on a New York City night, and me standing there with my gun still in my holster.

I looked down at a new picture of Samantha Claymore I held in my hand. Her mother had given it to me before I left her house earlier. It was from Samantha's sixteenth birthday celebration. The girl in the picture had bright eyes and a smudge of chocolate on her chin from a gaily decorated birthday cake. She looked young and beautiful in her flowered party dress. Now she was missing – and someone was demanding a ransom for her life.

Wilhelm had never handled a case like this before. He simply wasn't ready for it. But I was. I felt exhilarated, I felt renewed, I felt more alive than I had in a long time.

Because I knew this was my one chance – maybe my last chance – to find the redemption I was looking for.

I had to find Samantha Claymore and get her home safely.

CHAPTER 7

Teena Morelli and a Cedar Cliffs officer named Vic Hollister were at the home of Valerie Claymore – waiting to hear from the writer of the letter for whatever was going to come next.

I had no idea what that would be.

Normally the ransom pickup instructions came quickly. I mean that was the whole point of the abduction, right? Get the money fast and make a getaway.

But so much about this kidnapping was different to any other I had ever been involved in or heard about.

I also kept thinking about the logistical obstacles facing a kidnapper on a small island like Martha's Vineyard. How do you get a victim off the island without someone seeing what you're doing?

We were watching all of the ferries, and that kind of escape would be difficult to pull off with so many tourists on each vessel. Someone would get suspicious if it looked like a teenage girl was being taken against her will, and would report it to the police. And there had been no information from any of the scheduled passenger flights off the island. A private plane? Maybe – but we'd checked the records of the private pilots who'd recently departed, and they were all people who flew in and out regularly. A private boat? Possibly.

But it seemed more likely that Samantha Claymore was still somewhere on the island.

As I went back to talk with Valerie Claymore again, after my meeting with Wilhelm, I saw a Cedar Cliffs officer named Dave Bowers sitting in a car outside the Claymore's house. I'd assigned him to stake out the outside of the house, in case the letter writer returned. It wasn't likely, but I didn't want to take any chances.

Bowers was sitting in an unmarked car out of sight from anyone directly approaching the house. We didn't want to spook the kidnapper who could be watching the house from somewhere nearby. Of course, unless this was the stupidest kidnapper ever, they couldn't help but have noticed the streams of police officers that had been going in and out of the house since the letter arrived.

"Anything happening, Dave?" I asked as I approached the open window of his car.

"Nothing. Not here, and not inside neither."

"I didn't figure there was much chance someone would ring the doorbell and ask for the ransom, but you never know."

"Detective Abby Pearce on the case." Bowers smiled.

"You bet!"

"I'm serious, Abby. I'm really glad you're here for this one. None of us have ever had a case this big on the island and this is new for us. But you've done this before, you've been a big city cop and you've handled big cases. So like I said, I'm glad Detective Abby Pearce is on the case."

He smiled again. Bowers liked me. Maybe a little too much. He was a good-looking guy, around thirty, and I had a feeling he was interested in a relationship with me. But he knew, like I did, that it just wasn't possible in the workplace.

I wasn't thinking about that now though.

I was thinking about the missing Claymore girl.

I told Bowers to keep watching the house, and I went inside.

Teena Morelli was sitting on the couch in the living room with Valerie Claymore, who was holding a phone in her hand. Not talking into it, not listening either – just holding it. I guess she was waiting for *the* call. Hey, we all were.

Standing nearby was Hollister. Though he'd been on the force for thirty years, he looked stunned by the enormity of this case, the same as Wilhelm and Bowers had been. Hollister smiled at me as I came into the room. I got along with him, and was glad to see him there.

Teena Morelli didn't smile at me. She got up off the couch and walked over to where I was standing.

"Glad you could make it, Pearce. Nice of you to drop by."

"What's that supposed to mean?"

She shrugged.

"I figured you'd stopped off for a drink along the way."

'I don't drink anymore."

"Really? I heard you like the sauce a lot."

I knew this woman was trying to get under my skin, and she was doing a damn good job of it.

"What is your problem, Morelli?" I asked.

"I don't like you. I'm a better cop than you. And I should have been the one to get your job. That's my problem."

'Look," I said, doing my best to not let her get to me, "you and I are the only two women on the force. It would be nice if we could be civil."

She snorted.

"Hey, I'm too busy for this. We've got a missing girl out there. Go talk to the mother."

"That's what I plan to do."

"You're going to need a stiff drink after you spend time with her. She's a handful."

Morelli was right about that. Valerie Claymore was clearly very agitated and upset.

"No one's going to call," she said to me. "They warned me not to call the police and now whoever it is knows you're here. I should have done this on my own. Now I'll never get Samantha back."

I sat down on the couch beside her.

"No one actually thinks that a victim's family won't call the police, Mrs. Claymore. That's only something you see on TV. You had to call the police. Even if it's just to facilitate the paying of a ransom. The kidnapper knows that. You haven't put your daughter in any greater danger by getting us involved. You did the right thing."

"But they haven't called yet."

"There's a lot of possible reasons for that."

"Like?"

"Well, maybe they want you to sweat a bit. Make you worried and anxious so you'll pay without any argument."

"Well, I *am* worried and anxious."

"See, they accomplished their goal."

"Why else could they be taking so long?"

"They could be giving you time to get the money together. After all, that's a lot of money. Especially in the $100 denominations they're demanding. They understand you're still trying to accomplish that, and when the money is ready, that's when they'll call. That scenario makes sense too, doesn't it?"

She didn't say anything.

"Mrs. Claymore?"

"Do you really think we should be doing this, Detective?"

"Doing what?"

"Paying the ransom. That's a lot of money. And we don't have any assurance this will get Samantha back. We don't even know for sure if they have her. I mean she could just be off somewhere like you said earlier, but maybe someone heard about her disappearance and came up with a phony ransom demand. I have a lot of enemies – people who don't like what I do or the cosmetics industry. It could be one of them trying to make trouble. And we'd be giving all that money away for nothing."

Damn, this woman was all over the place.

"We hope – and believe – that no ransom will ever be paid. But we need to go through the motions to make it seem real. The kidnapper has to be convinced we're really prepared to pay the ransom money and so we need to actually take the money out of the bank. But we'll use the ransom money to smoke out the kidnapper – and catch them before they get away with the money. That is the best way for us to accomplish both goals – get your daughter home safely and apprehend who did this to her. This is totally by the book, Mrs. Claymore, right out of the manual for dealing with kidnappings. And it is by far the best plan of action."

She nodded.

"Now tell me more about the situation with the money."

"My husband is getting it together now in New York. He'll be bringing it here in a private plane."

"Good. Now if the kidnappers call before it arrives, you tell them the same thing. That it took time to get the money together in those $100 denominations. Do you understand?"

Another nod.

I couldn't tell if she was in shock, worried about her daughter, concerned about losing the money – or maybe a combination of all three.

I took the opportunity now to ask her some questions that had come up during my discussion with Wilhelm about the letter.

"Does the number mean anything to you, Mrs. Claymore? $583,0000 exactly. Any idea why the kidnapper would want that specific amount?"

"No. I have no idea… why would I?"

I pointed out too the part in the middle of the letter about the cosmetics industry. I asked her if she had any enemies in New York who might do something like this as a political act. She gave me the name of a security chief for Claymore Industries that she said kept a file of threats against the company. I wrote down the name to check later.

"Has anything unusual happened to your daughter while she was here? Encounters with strangers? Suspicious phone calls? Anyone stalking her on social media?"

"Not that I know of. Well, except for the flowers. That was strange. But there didn't seem to be anything dangerous or suspicious about it."

"Someone sent her flowers?"

"On her sixteenth birthday. Last month, right after we got here. It was a really big, beautiful bouquet of roses. Along with a 'Sweet Sixteen' birthday message. But it wasn't signed. We assumed that whoever sent her the birthday roses forgot to sign the card."

Or left their name off deliberately to remain anonymous, I thought.

Was Samantha Claymore being stalked?

It seemed like a long shot. Nothing else had happened since then and up to Samantha's disappearance now, according to Mrs. Claymore.

I asked her a few more questions and eventually, we got back to the issue of the money. She said her husband was flying in that night with the money in an attaché case. I said we'd meet him at the airport to provide security, but she said his own security guard would be with him.

I still wasn't sure exactly who her husband was or what he did. I made a note to check on him later.

"What is your husband's relationship with your daughter?" I asked just to make conversation.

"What does that have to do with anything?"

"I was just asking."

I waited.

"How would you characterize their father-daughter relationship?"

"Bruce is not Samantha's father," she said. "He's her stepfather."

"I know, but…"

"Samantha's father is dead," she snapped.

I didn't figure she was going to give me any more information about Samantha Claymore's relationship with her stepfather.

But that was all right.

She'd already answered the question for me.

CHAPTER 8

Valerie Claymore's husband, Bruce Aiken, arrived a few hours later, carrying the money in an attaché case and accompanied by security. The security guy looked familiar to me, but I couldn't quite remember why.

Bruce Aiken had slicked-down brown hair and was wearing what looked like a very expensive suit. He was good looking, I suppose. But I didn't like him from the first moment I laid eyes on him.

Aiken said something to his wife – no kiss, only a brief hug – and she pointed at me. He walked over to where I was standing in the living room.

"Are you the detective in charge here?" he asked.

"I am," I said.

"I'm a little surprised. You look too young to be running a big operation like this."

He meant it as a compliment, but I took it as an insult. I didn't say anything though. I kept it as professional as possible.

"You've got the money there with you?" I asked, glancing at the attaché case he had brought with him.

"Yes, the full amount. $583,0000. In $100 bills. Like the letter demanded."

"I think we should keep that for safekeeping in a bank until we need it. I've already made arrangements with the main bank in Cedar Cliffs—"

"That won't be necessary. We will hold onto the money."

"But that's a lot of money. I can guarantee you that it will be safe and secure in a bank here."

"Mr. Malone here can protect my money better than a bank," he said.

I looked over at Mr. Malone. He glared at me, I guess trying to show me he was a tough guy. I glared back at him to show him I was tough too.

I pointed to the attaché case Malone was holding.

"I really recommend you store that in a bank, Mr. Aiken. But, if you choose to keep it with you, and that's your choice, make sure it's available at short notice for whenever we need it. It's the key to the whole plan to catch whoever did this and – most importantly, of course – make sure Samantha gets home safely."

"What exactly is this plan?"

"Excuse me?"

"What is your plan to get my wife's daughter home?"

My wife's daughter?

This family sure seemed like a dysfunctional one!

"You do have a plan, don't you, Detective?"

"I do."

"Well, let's hear it. I want you to tell me everything. Please don't leave a single detail out."

"Okay," I said slowly. "Here's the complete plan. We wait until someone contacts us, then we use this money to try to smoke them out and save the girl. And that's it. I think I told you everything."

Aiken stared at me.

"I don't care for your attitude, Detective Pearce."

"I don't care whether you do or don't, Mr. Aiken. What I do care about is getting Sam" – I made a point of saying the name her friend Bridget told me she liked – "home safely. I will do everything in my power to achieve that. And, along those lines, I have some questions I'd like to ask you now."

"Such as?"

"Do you think her abduction could be linked in any way to the enemies of your wife or yourself?"

"Of course not."

"Well, your wife has already told me she has a lot of enemies as a result of her cosmetics business. Looking at you and your associate here, I figure you might have some enemies too. What exactly is it you do for a living, Mr. Aiken?"

"I'm a real estate investor. And no, I can't imagine my business – or my wife's – has anything to do with what happened here."

"What about the other Mr. Claymore?"

"Who?"

"Valerie's husband before you. Did he have any enemies?"

"I have no idea. He's dead. Are we done here? I hope that this 'plan' of yours works. Otherwise, there's going to be repercussions because I'm, well…"

"A very powerful man," I said.

"That's right. I'm a powerful man."

"Good to know."

After that, we waited. And waited. And waited some more.

The phones were hooked up with recording devices, of course.

And Mrs. Claymore held onto the receiver most of the time, staring at it as if she could will the kidnapper's call to come.

But there was nothing, except for one telemarketer and a few social calls that Mrs. Claymore ended quickly. She made hurried excuses to the callers about being busy, but not telling anyone why she needed to keep the phone line open. This hadn't gone public yet, and the longer we kept the ransom note for Samantha Claymore under wraps the better our chances were of finding her.

At least as far as I was concerned.

At some point, Valerie Claymore began to close her eyes and nod off to sleep. I'd seen her pop a number of pills during the day. Bruce Aiken told her she should go to bed. They'd wake her up if anything happened. She nodded sleepily. I figured Aiken would take her up to the bedroom himself. But instead he turned to the security guy Malone. Maybe that was part of Malone's duties for his boss. Tuck his wife in for the night.

Wow, this was a screwed-up family.

I felt badly again for Samantha Claymore, wherever she was.

Because whatever had happened to her now, she'd also had to deal with this growing up.

And I couldn't help but wonder if all of it – the mother, the stepfather, the dead father – was somehow a catalyst for this kidnapping.

CHAPTER 9

While we waited, I decided to find out more about the key players in this case so far.

I googled them all: Bruce Aiken, Valerie Claymore, her first husband and Samantha Claymore too.

I started with Samantha because I didn't know much about her except for the fact that she was very rich and missing.

She'd been born sixteen years ago to Ronald and Valerie Claymore at a hospital in Manhattan. Growing up, she split her time between the Claymores' townhouse on Sutton Place and a house in Sag Harbor. She attended the Spencer Academy, a private school in Upper Manhattan, and was a good student there. She played tennis, volleyball, and was on the swim team too.

Wait – the swim team?

That was strange, since her mother had told me she was terrified of the water. It became even stranger when I found out she also belonged to a sailing club in Sag Harbor and had even done some scuba diving there.

I was still puzzling over this when I turned to the information on her father, Ronald Claymore.

Ronald Claymore had started Claymore Cosmetics International in the '90s and turned it into a billion-dollar worldwide business. With his newfound wealth, Claymore acquired interests in media, real estate, retail outlets and even had controlling interest in one of the Atlantic City casinos.

He married Valerie – who was then Valerie Garrett. She'd been a fashion model who met Claymore when she did an advertising job for one of his products. After they were married, she became the face of Claymore Cosmetics. She was featured in newspapers, magazines, commercials and on billboards around the world. She also gave interviews and made numerous appearances representing the company.

There was no indication that she had made any business decisions while Ronald Claymore was alive, even though he gave her the title of CEO. He called the shots until his death – which happened right here in Martha's Vineyard during another Claymore summer vacation five years ago. Now Valerie was ostensibly in charge of everything and everyone in the company. But, after seeing her interactions with her new husband, I had a feeling it was Bruce Aiken who was really pulling the strings these days.

There were a number of articles about Ronald Claymore's death on the Vineyard, since he had been such a high-profile business figure. But they all pretty much said the same thing. He drowned when his fishing boat capsized a few hundred yards off the shore of Nantucket Sound, not far from Cedar Cliffs. He had apparently tried to swim for shore, but never made it. After a massive search by law enforcement and coast guard officials, he was declared dead at sea. There was no sign of any crime, just a tragic boating accident.

The most interesting thing I found out though was who was with him on the boat the day he died.

His daughter Samantha was aboard too.

Samantha Claymore was eleven years old at the time, but – because she was a good swimmer – had managed to swim to shore. But then she almost died too. Her lungs were filled with water and had to be pumped out by Emergency Rescue crews on the beach. She spent a long time in hospital afterward recovering from the ordeal.

Well, that explained her fear of the water.

She'd seen her father drown.

And then she'd almost died herself.

I still didn't understand why Valerie Claymore had taken her to an ocean island – particularly the same island where her father had died – for the summer if she had such an aversion to water. But then I didn't understand a lot of things about Valerie Claymore.

Meanwhile, I remembered now where I'd seen the security guy with Aiken. His name was Muzzy Malone. I'd run across him in Brooklyn a few years ago on an extortion case where store owners were being threatened with violence unless they paid a protection fee. Malone was never convicted because everyone was afraid to testify against him. But it was clear he was the muscle behind the threats. He was the enforcer. He was… well, he was the Mob.

So, what did that say about Valerie Claymore and her husband?

When I checked on Aiken himself, I discovered he'd been involved in a suicide case several years ago. His wife – a wealthy patron of the arts and a philanthropist from a monied background – had plunged off the balcony of their Park Avenue penthouse. It was ruled an accidental death by suicide.

But not everybody believed it was really a suicide.

His wife's family had a lot of questions about her death.

And, according to people I checked with in New York, the homicide detectives who investigated the case suspected Aiken might have murdered her – but never had enough evidence to charge him.

Then, only a few months after Ronald Claymore's death, Aiken met, wooed and married another wealthy woman – Valerie Claymore.

He sure liked rich women.

No crime in that.

Unless you kill them.

Was Valerie Claymore in danger now too, just like her daughter?

*

On my way home that night after work, I didn't drive directly to Chilmark. Instead, I kept driving west until I got to the other end of the island. I finally pulled over at a big house overlooking the ocean. I'd been inside this house before. A long, long time ago.

Ever since I'd moved back to Martha's Vineyard, I'd avoided coming back to this place. Because I didn't want to confront the memories of what happened to me here.

I sat there in my car staring at the house – big and beautiful, but also forbidding and dark. It looked just like I remembered it.

From when I was a teenage girl.

And from my dream the other night.

It was the same house that I had tried to stop Samantha Claymore from going into.

I was now more determined than ever to find Samantha before it was too late.

On the ride back to Chilmark, I felt revved up and excited about this case. The first big case I'd handled in a long time. And a case I felt a strong personal connection to. I identified with Samantha Claymore. Because of the bad stuff that had happened to me when I was a teenage girl like her on Martha's Vineyard. I suddenly wanted to talk to someone about all this. About being back on Martha's Vineyard. And about the new life I was trying to create here.

I thought about calling my mother. But I'd barely spoken to her since she sold the house here on the Vineyard and moved to an assisted living facility in Cape Cod. I knew I should speak to her at some point, but I kept putting it off. Not that I'd get much support from my mother if I did talk to her. I never had in the past.

I remembered a time a few years ago when I'd called her about my drinking.

"I need help," I told her when she answered the phone.

"How much do you need?" she asked.

"It's not about money, Mom."

I told her about the pressures of my job as a police officer; about my not so perfect love life; about my fears and insecurities; and, for the first time, about my drinking. I explained how everything seemed to revolve around my drinking.

"So why don't you just stop?" she said.

"I can't."

"Then you should try harder."

Terrific advice.

I didn't even bother with my father then. We hadn't enjoyed any kind of father-daughter relationship in years. All he cared about was his damn restaurant, which took up more and more of his time. The only person I had ever been able to confide in about my problems, especially as a teenager, was my father's partner in the restaurant. His name was Stan Larsen. I called him Uncle Stan, but really, he was a second father to me. The dad I always wanted. Once I even brought him to a father-daughter day at school, because my own father said he was too busy. But then, when I was in high school, he and my father got into a big argument and he quit the restaurant and left the island. After that, I had nobody for a long time.

Eventually I reconnected with Stan Larsen. I tracked him down in California, called him up and told him who I was. We talked a lot that day about me and my life, just like we did when I was a little girl. It was nice to talk to Uncle Stan again. I'd called him many times since then for advice or just to talk to someone I could trust. So why not now?

I punched in his number on my cell phone and listened as it went to voice mail. "Hey, this is Abby," I said to the recording. "Your favorite girl from Martha's Vineyard. No big deal, I'd just like to talk to you about some stuff going on in my life. Give me a call back when you can."

CHAPTER 10

The next morning, when there was still no word on the ransom payment, Chief Wilhelm said we needed to come up with a different approach to the waiting game we were currently playing. I didn't disagree.

"I don't like this," Wilhelm said. "It's been too long since that first note. Someone should have been in contact with the mother by now. What else would they be holding onto the Claymore girl for?"

"We're not even certain she's been abducted," I pointed out.

"I thought about that too."

"There was no evidence to confirm they had her. No lock of hair, no piece of clothing or anything with the note. All we know for sure is that whoever wrote that note knew she was missing. I mean, we've been asking around in Edgartown and talked to Samantha's friends, and people probably have noticed the police going in and out of the house. That's not even taking into account who Mrs. Claymore and her husband might have talked to about it. It wouldn't be hard for someone to find out the girl was gone and try to make a big score from the Claymore family by pretending they knew the girl's whereabouts."

"Then why haven't they made a move for the money?"

"Cold feet maybe. Or maybe the note was a joke from the beginning. A sick joke for sure, but not serious. I have no idea. But if she's not being held by anyone that means she could be anywhere. Hurt. Dead. A runaway. Everything's on the table again if you take the ransom note out of the equation. If she's alive, she's probably somewhere on this island. If she's dead, we have to find her body."

"We can't be sure she's still on the island."

"I think it's a pretty good bet. We've checked all of the departing flights and ferries for any sign of her. I suppose she could have boarded a ferry before anyone realized she was missing. But she left her bike in Edgartown, on the other side of the island from both ferry terminals. We checked the fingerprints on the bike and there was only one set, presumably hers. I think we have to assume that – either dead or alive – she's still on Martha's Vineyard. We need to search everywhere. The beaches, woods, going house-to-house – whatever it takes. Which means we'll have to go public with this some point soon."

We had made the decision early on to keep a lid on the news that Samantha Claymore was missing. Especially after the ransom note showed up. If we were going to use the note to get the girl back and capture whoever took her, we wanted to keep it secret to avoid any possible complications.

But – if the ransom note was not in play and the girl was somewhere on the island – the public attention could help. Someone might have seen her, heard something, or know something that could give us a clue to Samantha Claymore's whereabouts.

"We'll need more people for the search parties. Maybe the state police or volunteers," Wilhelm said.

"Any help we can get," I agreed.

Thus far, the Samantha Claymore investigation had been handled in the straightforward way any missing person case, even a possible kidnapping, was done. The local police – in this case us in Cedar Cliffs – had jurisdiction. Depending on the circumstances, local police might ask for assistance from forces in adjoining towns, from the state police or even the FBI. But the FBI would only get involved in a kidnapping where there was evidence the victim had been carried across state lines.

"I'll check with the island's other local police forces to see how much help they can give us in terms of search parties," Wilhelm said.

We'd been dealing with the island's other police forces already on Samantha Claymore. Especially in Edgartown, where her bike was found. But now we needed a concerted joint operation.

"I'll also see how many people the state police can provide us with," he said.

The mention of state troopers suddenly reminded me of my ex-husband, who was with the state police. Of course, he wouldn't be involved here – he worked for the New York state police. But the state police were a good option for us. They could probably lend us a number of people from their units on the Cape.

"And I'll coordinate with the FBI," Wilhelm said. "See if there's any evidence at all that she might have been taken out of the state."

"We've got to find her," I said. "And quickly. The longer this goes on, the more danger she's in. Whatever that danger is."

"Of course, once we go public there's no going back. There's going to be all sorts of attention on everything we do here. It could turn into a real circus. Especially given the prominence and wealth of the Claymore family. I'll run it past the FBI, state police and the other chiefs on the island. See how they want to handle releasing all this information to the media."

"Let me know as soon as you decide."

As it turned out, we didn't have to make any decisions on how to go public with the disappearance of Samantha Claymore. Events were moving too quickly.

I found this out when Dave Bowers, who was still outside the Claymores' house, called me.

"You're never gonna believe what's happening right now," Bowers said.

"Tell me."

"Are you near a TV?"

"Yeah, I'm back in the station at my desk."

"See for yourself then. Turn on the TV. Channel 6 out of Boston."

I picked up a remote and aimed it at a big TV not far from where I sat. Suddenly, I saw the Claymore house on the screen. A good-looking male reporter – is there any other kind on TV? – was standing there with a microphone and talking to the camera in an excited, almost breathless voice.

"I am outside the house where cosmetics queen Valerie Claymore has been staying this summer on Martha's Vineyard. I have learned exclusively that her sixteen-year-old daughter is missing. And that the family has received a ransom note demanding more than half a million dollars for her safe return. We are trying to find out further details now. Stay tuned for more on this breaking story. This is Lincoln Connor in Cedar Cliffs, Channel 6 News."

"There are already more people starting to show up here," Bowers said to me. "People from around the island. Others traveling down Beach Road to see what's going on. I think there's more press that just got here too. This is going to be a media spectacle, Abby."

So much for our decision about going public.

That decision had been made for us.

Good or bad, Samantha Claymore was now going to be big news.

Along with me and the entire Cedar Cliffs Police Department.

CHAPTER 11

The press conference we held was everything I feared it would be.

Media from all around the country had descended on Martha's Vineyard following the breaking news flash that cosmetics heiress Samantha Claymore was missing – and presumed kidnapped.

There was Channel 6 from Boston, with Lincoln Connor – the reporter who broke the story – sitting in the front row of the press conference, clearly loving his moment in the spotlight. Other Boston stations were there too, along with the cable news channels and newspapers.

There were important people from Martha's Vineyard there too.

One of them was the mayor of Cedar Cliffs, Peter Randall. Randall was more than just the mayor. He was a big wheel with the chamber of commerce, local business groups and state politics. He had a lot of money and clout on the island. In fact, Randall was the reason I got the detective job over Teena Morelli. I never knew him when I grew up here – he came after I left – but I guess he liked the idea of a high-profile NYPD detective being on his town's police force. He pushed me for the job over the objections of Wilhelm and his concern about my drinking. I guess I owed Randall for that, and now it was time to repay him by solving the biggest crime in the island's history.

I wasn't surprised to see Randall at the press conference. But I was surprised to see one of the island's other VIPs, Melvin Ellis. Ellis was the richest man on Martha's Vineyard. He was very reclusive, and normally didn't attend public events like this. Ellis had lived on Martha's Vineyard for a long time, and I remembered him well – too well – from my childhood here. I remembered his family too. Especially his son, Mark Ellis. Those weren't happy memories for me.

Randall stood up now to announce that he, Ellis and several others had joined forces to put up a $100,000 reward for anyone providing information that led to the return of Samantha Claymore.

I thought it was a bit strange that they needed to give money to help someone as rich as Valerie Claymore. I wondered if she and Bruce Aiken would offer a reward. But it was a nice gesture by Randall and Ellis – and I knew from experience that rewards always helped get people to provide potentially important information.

Then it was time for the Cedar Cliffs police force to tell everyone what they knew about the missing Samantha Claymore.

Wilhelm began the briefing, clearly uncomfortable talking to the press in such a high-pressure situation. Wilhelm had probably never had to do this before on any case here on the Vineyard. Not that I had much media experience either – people higher up than me on the chain of command handled it when I was with the NYPD. But I was sitting there next to Wilhelm now, and he quickly turned it over to me, saying: "Abby Pearce, the detective handling this case, will tell you all the details of the investigation at the moment."

Of course, there wasn't much to tell.

I went through everything we did know. The disappearance, the discovery of the bicycle in Edgartown, the arrival of a ransom note for Valerie Claymore. I went through the efforts we'd been making to find out more information: talking to people in Edgartown and those along the bicycle route Samantha would have traveled; reaching out to friends of hers; and how we were going to be conducting a massive search of the island for any evidence.

I didn't give any specific details about the ransom note. I only said someone had asked for a large amount of money in exchange for Samantha's safe return, but that we hadn't heard anything else since.

Everything I said was true and accurate. But that wasn't what the media wanted. They wanted meat. They wanted a sensational story. So, they quickly began hammering me with questions.

"Do you believe Samantha Claymore has been kidnapped?"

"I don't know that for sure."

"What about the ransom note? Is that real?"

"We are operating under the theory that it was a legitimate demand from someone who has Samantha Claymore."

"Do you have any leads at all on who might have sent it?"

"I don't know any more about the note other than what I've told you."

"Do you expect to hear from the person who wrote it again soon?"

"I don't know."

"What do you know then, Detective Pearce?"

That last question – and the edge it had to it – came from Lincoln Connor, the guy from Channel 6 who broke the story. He had a smug look on his face. He was happy to be in the media spotlight right now and he was going to milk every moment of it. Even if it involved going after the police.

"What I do know, Mr. Connor, is that my department will do everything possible to get answers to your questions. I know that our number one priority is to find Samantha Claymore and get her home safely. And I know that every minute I stand here talking with you is a minute I am not out there and doing that job. That is what I know."

Valerie Claymore and her husband Bruce Aiken were at the press conference too, they insisted on it. Valerie Claymore was used to dealing with the media, and she seemed very comfortable with them. A lot more comfortable than when I'd last seen her at the house with her husband. This was the public Valerie Claymore, the cosmetics queen from TV and their beauty advertisements.

She was dressed very fashionably. Her hair was perfectly in place, she was wearing plenty of makeup (presumably her own brand), and she looked terrific. Not much like a worried mother. That is until one of the reporters asked her a question, and then she became very emotional. Her lip trembled, her voice shook and she seemed to tear up around her eyes as she stared at the TV cameras and said:

"Oh, please, whoever out there has my daughter – or knows anything about her – come forward and tell us. Sam and I are much more than mother and daughter, we are best friends too. We've always been so close, Sam and I. All I want is to get her home again. I'll do anything, I'll pay anything – just don't hurt her. I think of how scared she must be and I want to hold her in my arms again…"

At this point, she broke down completely into tears.

The cameras picked up every moment.

It was a great shot for the news.

It was certainly incredibly moving.

But I couldn't help wondering one thing as I watched Valerie Claymore sobbing about her lost daughter: how much of this was real?

I mean she'd told me the whole "close mother-daughter" story that first day too, but I quickly found out it wasn't true. I also noted that she called her "Sam" here – not Samantha like she had in the past. Before I'd mentioned that Samantha's friend Bridget said she liked to be called Sam, Valerie hadn't seemed to know that. But now, here she was calling her Sam at a national press conference. All of this made me wonder about Valerie Claymore.

Bruce Aiken put his arm around her and comforted her as he walked Valerie back to where she was originally sitting.

Sure, it was touching – a mother's grief.

If you believed it.

Me, I wasn't sure what I believed about any of them anymore.

There were more questions shouted at me after that. And I answered them all the best I could. Finally, when the questions began getting repetitive, I thanked everyone for coming and walked off the podium. Wilhelm did too. The press conference was officially over, as far as we were concerned.

But the media wasn't going away.

I knew that all too well.

They had descended on this island for a big, sensational story – and they weren't going to leave until they got it.

Oh, we'd had press here before when Presidents Clinton and Obama came to the Vineyard for their vacations. Those had turned into real media circuses too. A two-week period – usually around August – where you couldn't go anywhere without bumping into a reporter on the hunt for a story.

But eventually Clinton or Obama would go back to Washington, and things would return to normal on Martha's Vineyard.

But this was different.

Lincoln Connor and the rest of the media were here to stay.

Until we found Samantha Claymore.

CHAPTER 12

It turned out to be the biggest law enforcement search ever to take place on Martha's Vineyard.

We were able to confine the search to the island, which gave us some specific boundaries. That was because we were still operating under the assumption Samantha Claymore had been not been taken off the island. At least that was our theory for now.

But – whether or not she was still here – the area that had to be covered by the search teams was still formidable in both size and terrain.

It's nine miles from the north side of Martha's Vineyard to the south, and twenty-six miles from its east coast at Edgartown to the cliffs of Gay Head on the western side. Much of this is undeveloped territory: woods and rugged areas; miles of open beaches; and lakes and ponds scattered throughout.

Samantha Claymore – or her body – would be extremely difficult to locate in one of these places.

All of the police units on the Vineyard – from Cedar Cliffs and the other towns – had been mobilized to conduct the search. We also had a lot of volunteers from the island who joined us in looking for Samantha. The other big boost came from the state police who sent a contingent of troopers who fanned out over the island.

Now that the news of Samantha Claymore's disappearance had been made public by Lincoln Connor, we received a lot of tips and potential leads from residents. Possible sightings, various pieces of information, even a few callers who thought their neighbors might be capable of kidnapping a teenage girl.

Most of them meant well, but not all. One anonymous caller to the hotline we'd set up even "confessed" to murdering her – and told us where he left the body. There was no body at that location, of course. We eventually tracked the call to a mental facility in Boston where one of the patients had seen the TV story about Samantha Claymore and decided to make up the stuff about the murder.

In the end, none of the calls or tips that came in brought us any closer to finding out what had happened to her.

We ran checks on Samantha Claymore's cell phone records; credit card usage; social media postings. There was nothing. Which seemed ominous in itself. What sixteen-year-old girl wouldn't use her cell phone or credit cards over a period of several days? There were only two explanations I could think of: she was being held against her will, or she was dead.

We also checked out the "Mandell" file I'd found password protected on her computer. We got some tech people to bypass the password. But the file itself didn't reveal much. Just the names and addresses of people named Mandell around the country. We reached out to all of them, hoping for some kind of lead – but they claimed they knew nothing about the girl or why their names were in her file. So, the meaning of the file remained a mystery. But then there was no indication either that it had anything to do with Samantha Claymore's disappearance.

While Bowers and Hollister and Morelli went back and started re-interviewing storekeepers, neighbors and anyone else who might have had contact with Samantha, I tried to find out more about her life in New York City.

I mean she was only in Martha's Vineyard for the summer. If there were any clues about what happened to her, those would be more likely found in New York. She would presumably know more people and have more friends there too. Of course, her mother did not know who any of them were. But there had to be people in her life back in the city.

I talked to the head of Spencer Academy in Manhattan. His name was Brian Solters, and he was shocked to have heard on the news that one of his students was missing. But he didn't know much that could help me. He told me that Samantha was an excellent student, but she seemed to have problems socializing with other kids. He said he assumed she was self-conscious because of her family's enormous wealth. As a result, she kept mostly to herself.

"The best way to describe Samantha was socially awkward," he said. "But that happens with teenagers. We try to help as much as we can within the framework of the school. But that kind of emotional support really has to come from the people at home. I hope I'm not talking out of turn, but – from what Samantha told us on a few occasions – I don't think she had a great rapport with her family."

Just as I suspected. It made me even more interested in the Claymores' home life.

I checked with some people I knew in the NYPD to make sure they didn't have any records on Samantha. It meant I had to get into an awkward conversation about how I was doing in Martha's Vineyard and whether or not I missed being in New York, but I wanted to make sure I touched every base.

I didn't expect Samantha Claymore to have any kind of criminal record. But she did. Well, not really a criminal record. But there was a file on her. She'd been taken into custody during a protest a few months earlier.

"No big deal," the NYPD guy I was talking with told me. "They wrote her a ticket for unlawful assembly and blocking traffic – then let her go."

"What kind of protest was it?"

He read through the file while I waited.

"Here it is. A protest over the use of lab animals for testing by the cosmetics industry."

Damn.

"Let me get this straight: Samantha Claymore, heiress to the Claymore Cosmetics empire, was part of a protest against the same industry that her family is part of?"

"Better than that, guess where the protest was?"

"Where?"

"Outside Claymore Cosmetics headquarters in Manhattan."

After I hung up, I looked again at the picture I had of Samantha Claymore. I was seeing a whole new side of her that I hadn't even known existed.

Socially awkward.

Confused.

Angry at her family.

She reminded me of someone else I once knew.

A sixteen-year-old Abby Pearce.

"She's exactly like I was at sixteen years old," I said to Dave Bowers after I told him everything I'd found out.

"You were socially awkward? I can't imagine that."

"Oh, definitely. I had a lot of trouble relating to the other kids."

"You weren't popular in high school?"

"Well, I was funny. But no, I was never popular with the kids I wanted to be popular with. Boys generally."

"You didn't date in high school?"

"No one ever asked me out. I was too tall and my nose was too long. But then something happened."

"What?"

"I got pretty."

"Just like that?"

"It happened the summer before my senior year. I just matured physically. Suddenly, boys were falling all over themselves trying to talk to me."

"So, things got better for you then?"

"Different, not better."

I looked down again at the picture of Samantha Claymore, and saw myself there at sixteen.

Lost and looking for answers.

"Where are you, Samantha?" I said out loud. "Where in the hell are you?"

CHAPTER 13

There's a pizza place right across from the Cedar Cliffs police station. Later that night, when I finally decided nothing was likely to happen immediately, I took a break and went there to get something to eat. I was sitting at an outdoor table working on a large piece with extra cheese, mushrooms and sausage when I heard someone call my name. I looked up to see Lincoln Connor.

"I'm starved," Connor said. He eyed my pizza hungrily. "Mind if I have a piece?"

I shrugged and he grabbed a slice. Then he sat down in the chair across from me.

"So, this is what the taxpayers pay you to do all night? Eat pizza?"

"Do you think I should give my paycheck back?"

"Nah."

"Good to hear."

"If you did that, I might have to pick up the check for this."

He flashed me a smile and bit into the slice he was holding. It was a charming smile. Hey, he was a charming guy, and he knew it. He probably used that smile to open a lot of doors for himself – both in the media for a story and with women he met too. He was good looking, no question about it. Longish dark brown hair, brown eyes, a little bit of a beard like a lot of TV presenters seemed to be sporting on air these days. He was big, or at least formidable looking – maybe six foot or so, two hundred pounds, and in good shape. If I had to guess his age, I'd say around thirty-five. A lot of women would go for a guy like Lincoln Connor. But I wasn't one of them. Well, I might have been in another time and place, but not now.

"You remember me, right?" Connor said.

"You're the annoying reporter from the press conference."

"I'd prefer 'insightful.'"

"And you're the one who has made my investigation much more difficult by going public with the story before we were ready."

"Hey, I was just doing my job."

"Let me do mine."

He took a big bite of the pizza.

"So, what's happening?" he asked.

"With the case?"

"Sure."

"No comment."

"You can't tell me anything?"

"I could, but I won't."

"Why not? Are you still mad at me because I put you on the spot at the press conference? C'mon, you handled it well. You shot right back at me and zinged me in return. How about we move forward with a clean slate? What do you think about that, Detective Pearce?"

I sighed.

"Look, Connor, I know what you're all about. I met a lot of guys like you when I was in New York. You're after a big story. You think if you get a lot of attention on this Claymore story, it will eventually get you a job with one of the networks or cable news channels. And you figure that you can use me to do that. But it won't work. I can smell phonies a mile away. So, stop wasting your time with me, okay?"

I thought that might make him mad enough to walk away. I was sort of hoping for that, I suppose. But he only smiled – that same charmer of a smile – and grabbed another piece of pizza.

"Well, you got me figured out," he said. "And all it took was a few minutes of eating pizza together. You're a damn good detective, Pearce."

I didn't say anything.

"We could talk about Samantha Claymore off the record, if you want?"

"You mean you promise not to put anything I say on the air? I'd have your word on that?"

"Of course."

"Okay."

"So – off the record – what can you tell me about the case?"

"No comment," I said.

"That's your 'off the record' answer?"

"That's all you're going to get from me about the investigation, no matter how hard you try. Like I said, your tricks won't work on me. I'm not buying what you're selling, Connor. Now go away and let me eat in peace."

Connor laughed. He was a tough guy to insult.

"Okay, but what if we talk about something else besides the Claymore case?"

"Like what?"

"Well, we could talk about you having dinner with me one night."

I looked around at the pizza place where we were sitting.

"We are having dinner," I told him.

"No, I mean a real dinner. In a real restaurant."

"Why?"

"You're an interesting woman. I was impressed with you at the press conference. In more ways than one. Very cool. Very good at your job. And very attractive too. Hell, I even kind of liked the way you sassed me back when I asked that question. I'd like to get to know you better, Abby Pearce."

"Why would I want to get to know you?"

"I'm a nice guy. You'd like me if you knew me. So, what about us having that dinner?"

"Are you asking me out on a date?"

"You could call it that."

"A date," I said again.

"Sure, it would be fun."

I just laughed. No way was I going to get personally involved with some ambitious journalist trying to score a big scoop on Samantha Claymore.

"Is that a yes or no?" he asked.

"No."

"Okay, I have another question for you then. I don't understand what you're doing here in Cedar Cliffs. You should be on some big city police force. You spent more than a decade with the NYPD. Lots of big arrests and awards – hell you were promoted to homicide detective before you were thirty." He grinned. "Yeah, I checked up on you. Everyone says you're supposed to be a really great cop."

"Thanks. I'll put you down as a reference on my resume."

"Why are you working in this small-town police force, Detective Pearce?"

I reached for my pizza. It was cold now. I pushed the plate away.

"It's a long story." I sighed.

"Tell it to me."

"No comment," I said.

When I checked my phone after leaving the pizza place, I saw there was a message from Stan Larsen. He was returning my call. I punched in the number and he answered right away.

"Hello, there, Abby, my girl. How are you? What's it like being back on Martha's Vineyard?"

"Not quite what I expected, Uncle Stan."

"Sun, sand, surf… what could go wrong on an island paradise like that?" He laughed.

I told him about my place in Chilmark and my dog; about my job on the Cedar Cliffs police force; and about Samantha Claymore's disappearance. I even went through some of the details of the case with him.

It felt good to have an old friend to talk to like this.

"What about you?" I asked him at one point. "Why don't you come back to the Vineyard? You could reopen the restaurant, the one that you and my father used to own…"

"No way," he said. "I'm happy here in California. Just a little bit south of San Francisco, you know. The weather is good, I have my own restaurant here – and it's doing really well."

He asked me about a few people and places on the Vineyard, then said: "By the way, Abby, I was really sorry to hear about your father's death. Please give my belated condolences to your mother."

I wasn't sure when I was going to see my mother again.

And I didn't want to talk about my father.

Neither of them were a part of my life anymore.

But I sure was glad to reconnect with my Uncle Stan.

"Can I call you again?" I asked him now.

"About your big case?"

"About that and… well, just about me too."

"Sounds good, Abby." He laughed. "Talk to you again soon."

CHAPTER 14

Chief Wilhelm wanted to see me.

"Have you been drinking again, Pearce?" Wilhelm asked me as soon as I walked into his office.

"What?"

"You heard me. Yes or no?"

"No."

"What if I told you someone saw you in the Black Dog Bar one night this week. What would you say to that?"

"I'd say they were right."

"But you said you hadn't had a drink since that night in East Chop."

A few months earlier, not long after I returned to Martha's Vineyard from New York, I stopped off for a drink at the Black Dog Bar in Cedar Cliffs after I left the station house. Just one drink, I told myself. But then I had another. And I kept drinking after that.

I woke up in my car and in a ditch on the side of the highway near a small town called East Chop on the north side of the island, nowhere near Chilmark. I have no idea how or why I drove there. When someone found me, I was bleeding from a cut on my head, and an ambulance took me to a hospital for stitches. I passed out in the emergency room, and when I woke up the doctors told me that my alcohol level was so high they wanted to keep me overnight for observation. Somehow, I talked my way out of the hospital and a DUI charge – showing them my police shield – and slept if all off at home instead.

But, when I got to the station the next morning, Chief Wilhelm suspended me for two weeks. He also put me on formal notice that any other drinking incidents would result in my dismissal from the force.

That really scared me.

I hadn't drunk a drop of alcohol since then.

I couldn't let that happen.

Being a police officer was all I had.

If I lost that, I'd have nothing.

"Chief, I was in the Black Dog this week. But I wasn't drinking alcohol. Only club soda. Look, I like bars and everything about them. The atmosphere. The ambience. The crowds. The music. I especially like the Black Dog. So even if I'm not drinking, I like hanging out in them sometimes. It was a long day, and I wanted to unwind before I went home."

He seemed to accept my explanation. But he added a warning: "You're the face of the Claymore investigation, Pearce. The entire media has their eyes on us. If you screw up this time, it's going to be big news. 'Top Cop on Samantha Claymore Kidnap Case is a Drunk.' That would be a serious black mark against the Cedar Cliffs police force. And against me. So, if I find out you have been drinking again, you're off this case. Understood?"

"I'm fine with that."

He asked me about Samantha Claymore. I bought him up to date on the latest news. The status of the search teams, the stuff I'd found out about Samantha's life – and what I planned to do next.

"I'm going to talk to her best friend, Bridget Feckanin. The one I was on the phone with that first day. I'm hoping she can tell me more about Samantha's state of mind in the days before she disappeared. We've been reaching out to a lot of other kids on the island too, trying to find any teenagers that might have known her. One of them told us Samantha had a boyfriend. Or at least a boy she was friendly with. A kid named Eddie Haver. I don't know how serious their relationship was – she'd only been on the Vineyard for a few weeks – but I want to find out what he knows. And, of course, we'll keep the search teams out there until they turn up something."

Wilhelm agreed that it sounded like a good plan.

Before I left, I asked him one question. Even though I knew he wouldn't give me an answer.

"Who told you I was in the Black Dog?"

"I'm not at liberty to reveal that information."

"Was it Teena Morelli?"

"Like I said…"

"She wants my job. And she'll do anything she can to get it. Even if it means spreading lies behind my back."

"Teena is a good police officer."

"I didn't say she wasn't."

"Then try to work with her."

"I will. But you tell her to keep her nose out of my personal business."

"What happened in there?" Meg asked me when I came out. "The chief seemed pretty upset earlier."

I told her about my conversation with Wilhelm. Including his warning about taking me off the Samantha Claymore case if he found out I was drinking again.

"He didn't say it outright but I presume he would also try to get me fired from the force if that happened."

Meg shook her head sadly.

"I haven't known you long, Abby, but I know that this job means everything to you. You're not drinking, are you?"

"Don't worry, Meg. I'm not drinking."

I had a question for her.

"Has Teena been to see Wilhelm recently?"

"Yes… I think she was here yesterday."

"That explains it then."

"What do you mean?"

"Someone told Wilhelm about me being in a bar the other night."

"Maybe she was talking with him about something else. They talk a lot. She and the chief are very friendly."

Yep, it must have been Teena who reported seeing me at the Black Dog. I mean, what better way to get my job than to have me thrown off the force for drinking?

CHAPTER 15

Bridget Feckanin had a summer job working at a place called the Ice Cream Emporium. It was within walking distance of the Cedar Cliffs police station and located in a small arcade at the marina. They had more than thirty flavors to choose from. Apparently, there were a lot of decisions I had to make.

"Cone, cup, sundae or shake?" she asked me when I approached the counter.

"Cone."

"Waffle, wafer, pretzel or sugar cone?"

"Uh, wafer."

"One scoop or two?"

"Two."

"And what flavor would you like?"

"Chocolate fudge," I said.

She made the cone and handed it to me.

"You're Bridget Feckanin, aren't you?" I said as I paid her.

I took a lick of the cone. It tasted good.

"That's right. Do I know you?"

"My name is Detective Abby Pearce. I'm with the Cedar Cliffs Police Department. We talked on the phone a few days ago about your friend Samantha Claymore."

I showed her my badge.

"Has there been any news?" she asked.

Bridget was a pretty girl, with dark brown hair and a slender figure. In just another year or two, she'd be a grown-up woman.

"Not yet. That's why I wanted to talk to you. I was hoping you'd know something about her that might help us in the search."

"Of course. Anything I can do to help. Sam is my best friend. I hope she's all right."

"Do you have a few minutes to go over some of it now?"

"I'm the only one on duty. The other girl who works here is on a break. But she'll be back in ten minutes. Do you want me to come over to see you then at the station?"

"No, I'll wait here until you're free."

I walked over to a bench inside the arcade, sat down and worked on my ice cream cone. Being in places like this always brought back memories for me. This arcade – and even the ice cream parlor in it – had been around when I was growing up here. I remembered biking here in the summer with the other kids to get ice cream.

Bridget Feckanin was waiting on a line of other customers now. She seemed happy. I figured her to be sixteen years old, the same age as Samantha Claymore – and this was probably Bridget's first summer job. I got my first summer job when I was sixteen too, working at a Mad Martha's fudge store not far from this arcade. I liked fudge when I started the job, but never could stand it afterward. I wondered if Bridget would soon feel the same way about ice cream. Still, your first ever summer job was a big deal.

Ten minutes later, another young girl showed up and went behind the counter. Bridget took off her apron, walked over to me and sat down on the bench.

She seemed familiar to me, but I couldn't quite place why. Maybe I'd seen her in the arcade or around Cedar Cliffs before.

I ran through what we knew – or, more accurately, what we didn't know – about Samantha Claymore's case and then asked Bridget some questions.

"Did she ever tell you she felt in danger from anyone?" I asked.

"Danger from who?"

"I don't know. That's what I'm trying to find out. Did she ever express any concern about her well-being to you?"

There was a slight hesitation, I thought, before she replied. But then she answered me definitively.

"No, nothing like that."

"You're sure?"

"Absolutely."

"Okay, then. Let me ask you something else. Do you think there's any possibility she could have left on her own?"

"Wasn't there a ransom note?"

"Yes, but we're not sure if it was legitimate or just someone trying to cash in on her disappearance. I'm trying to look at all the possibilities. Any ideas?"

Another slight hesitation, but then she said, "No, there's nothing at all I can think of."

I had the feeling she knew more than she was telling me, but I didn't want to push her too hard. I wanted her to feel that I was on the same side as her. That I cared about Samantha Claymore as much as she did.

Bridget then talked about how she'd met Samantha that summer.

"We were standing in line at the doughnut shop, and we struck up a conversation. She told me she had just arrived here for the summer, I told her about my job at the ice cream place – and we kind of hit it off. I mean we haven't known each other that long, but we became best friends. People said we were like sisters. I mean we even look sort of alike. Except my hair is darker than hers, of course."

I realized now that's why she looked familiar to me. Because of the pictures I'd seen of Samantha Claymore. There was a real resemblance.

"I'd never had a best friend before. Sam hadn't either. She said most of the kids at school in New York were snooty and spoiled.

That's when I found out who she was – I mean about all her money. But Sam wasn't like you'd think a rich kid would be. She was the real deal. We spent a lot of time together after that. And, when she wasn't with me, she was with Eddie."

"Eddie Haver?"

"Yes, her boyfriend. We used to giggle when she talked about kissing him."

I was about finished with my ice cream cone. I used a napkin to wipe chocolate fudge from my hands and my face too.

"Have you talked to Eddie?" she asked.

"That's where I'm going next," I said.

CHAPTER 16

Eddie Haver lived near Vineyard Haven, the same town where I grew up.

Growing up on Martha's Vineyard is a unique experience. Much of the time you see the same people wherever you go – stores, school, the movies, restaurants. The year-round population on the island is only sixteen thousand people. And Martha's Vineyard Regional High School – the school Eddie Haver attended, like I once did – had a total enrollment of only seven hundred students, one of the lowest in the state.

All changed in the summertime when tourists swelled the population to over a hundred thousand people. For the two months of July and August, new faces packed the beaches, towns and everywhere else on the island.

It's a bizarre existence for a young person, and most kids move away from the island when they're old enough – to go to college or find a job somewhere else. Like I did.

Samantha Claymore had been part of that influx of summer tourists who came here in July, so she hadn't known Eddie Haver for very long. Several weeks at most. I wasn't sure what the relationships of sixteen-year-old boys and girls consisted of these days. But I figured he must have some information that might help me find out what happened to Samantha.

I found Haver at a baseball field near the high school. He was playing a pickup game with a few other kids. I'd checked with his parents first, who called him to tell me I was coming. I think his parents were a bit nervous about why a police officer wanted to talk to their son. But, after I explained about the disappearance of Samantha Claymore, they were happy to cooperate.

Eddie seemed nervous too. Talking to a police officer can do that to you. He was a decent looking kid with blond hair, wearing a T-shirt, jeans and a Boston Red Sox baseball cap. I could see why a sixteen-year-old girl like Samantha Claymore would be interested in him. I told him why I was there – and asked about their relationship.

"I met her at the beach early last month," he said. "Down at South Beach, near Edgartown. That's where I like to hang out, the waves are so good there. Anyway, she was there with Bridget, and I was there with some guys. Sam and I wound up hanging out together. She was nice. I liked her."

I realized he was talking about Samantha Claymore in the past tense. But I didn't really think that meant anything. She was gone, and a lot of people presumed at this point she was dead. I also noted he called her "Sam" and not "Samantha." Which confirmed for me that he knew her well.

"I understand she was afraid of the water," I said after he told me about their meeting at South Beach.

"Oh, God, yes. She wouldn't go near the water when we were at the beach. I kept trying to take her into the waves. I said I'd make sure she was safe. But she would never go in."

"What else did the two of you do together?"

"We took walks, went bike riding, to the movies – sometimes we played video games at that new arcade in Cedar Cliffs. We had fun."

"How close were the two of you?"

"What do you mean?"

"Were you boyfriend and girlfriend?"

He looked embarrassed. "Uh, well… I wanted to be her boyfriend. And I think she liked me. So…"

I asked him about drugs and alcohol then. That got him really defensive, until I told him I wasn't looking to bust him – it was all about getting information on Samantha Claymore.

"We smoked weed a few times. That's even legal now, isn't it? But neither of us did much of that. Only at a party or something when someone was passing a joint around. And no other kinds of drugs either. We weren't really into that."

"What about drinking?"

"It's really hard to get alcohol when you're sixteen. I think there were a couple of times we had some beers. But that's all. Sam and I just liked spending time together. We liked each other. At least I liked her. And I hoped she liked me. You know what I mean?"

I did. It seemed – at least on the face of it – to be a normal relationship between two sixteen-year-olds trying to figure stuff out as they were growing up.

The only difference here was that one of those sixteen-year-olds was the heiress to a multimillion-dollar cosmetics fortune.

And she now was missing.

I asked him about the roses sent to Samantha on her birthday. They had been bothering me ever since Valerie Claymore told me about them.

"Was that you?" I asked.

"Roses? No, I don't know anything about any roses."

"You didn't give her anything for her birthday?"

"Her birthday was in July. We'd just met. I think I kissed her for the first time on her birthday. But there were no roses or anything else from me. That's the truth."

I believed him. Besides, a dozen roses – especially as big and beautiful as Valerie Claymore described them – was not the kind of thing Eddie Haver could afford on his allowance. No, the roses must have come from someone else. An adult probably. Not a kid.

"When is the last time you saw her?" I asked Haver.

"It must have been the day before she disappeared. We went to that new hamburger place in Cedar Cliffs. Ate some lunch, then walked in the park nearby and sat on one of the benches overlooking the harbor."

"Did she talk about biking to Edgartown the next day?"

"No."

"What did you talk about with her?"

"You know, lots of stuff."

"Can you remember anything specific?"

"Well, just about her father. She'd been talking about him a lot recently."

I wasn't sure where this was going. Valerie Claymore had indicated that Samantha had a troubled relationship with her stepfather, Bruce Aiken. Had Aiken done something to Samantha? Something that led to what happened to her the following day on her bike?

"We're talking about Bruce Aiken here, right?" I said to Eddie Haver.

"No, not him – her real father."

"Ronald Claymore?"

"Yes."

"The one who died years ago in the boating accident?"

Haver nodded.

"That was the weird part. Sam kept saying she believed it wasn't an accident. That her father had been murdered."

"Murdered? Murdered by who?"

"She blamed her mother for it."

CHAPTER 17

The accidental death of Ronald Claymore five years earlier didn't really have anything to do with the disappearance of his daughter, Samantha. Or at least that's what I thought when Valerie Claymore had mentioned her late husband that first day.

Now I wanted to find out more about Ronald Claymore's death.

The quickest way was to search for information online. For support, I radioed Dave Bowers to come back to the station, and we sat at the computers on our desks looking for info.

Of course, this also meant I had to make conversation with Bowers – who seemed more interested in my personal life than Ronald Claymore's death. Like I said, I knew Dave Bowers was interested in me. But so far it just involved a lot of flirting.

"I saw you eating pizza with that TV guy," Bowers said now.

"Lincoln Connor."

"Interesting choice for a dinner companion."

"He just stopped by my table."

"And you think that was an accident?"

"Huh?"

"I noticed him. He was waiting for you to leave the station. Then he followed you to the pizza place. He planned it all."

I shrugged. "Good for him."

"Did this Connor guy get what he wanted from you?"

"Why not ask him?"

"You know, Abby, I'd love it if you and I could do something like that one night. What do you think?"

"We're still talking about pizza here, right?"

"Man does not live on pizza alone." Bowers grinned.

"Let's focus on Ronald Claymore's death, huh?" I said.

There were a number of articles written about it. 'Multimillionaire New York businessman dies in boat accident while vacationing on Martha's Vineyard.' It was pretty big news at the time.

"Were you here when it happened?" I asked Bowers.

"No, I came to the Vineyard afterward. All I know is what I've heard about it."

"Me too."

"Why are you so interested in Claymore's death?"

"It's come up a few times in the investigation."

"Do you think there's any sort of connection with the girl's disappearance?"

"Probably not. But worth checking out."

Bowers began reading aloud now from one of the articles on his computer screen: "Ronald Claymore chartered a small fishing boat in Cedar Cliffs, where he and his family had rented a home for the summer. They left the dock at six in the morning and spent approximately two hours ocean fishing for stripers, blues and sea bass. They were supposed to return at ten. But something went wrong. A fire broke out in the engine of the boat. They weren't able to put out the blaze. The captain of the boat then tried to get the boat to shore before the fire worsened."

"The captain?"

"That's right."

"Ronald Claymore wasn't piloting the boat himself?"

"No, he wasn't a boat guy, from what I can see here. He just liked to fish. He hired a fishing boat with a captain to take him and the girl out that day."

"What happened to the captain?"

"He survived."

Interesting. Now that captain was someone I'd like to talk to. If I could find him.

"Anyway," Bowers continued, "the boat was a few hundred yards away from shore when the fire spread to the engine. There was an explosion. Everyone on board was either blown off the boat or jumped into the water to escape the fire. You know the rest of what happened. The girl made it to shore and was taken to a hospital with water in her lungs and burns from the fire. They found the captain on shore too. But Ronald Claymore died. It was ruled an accidental death."

We did some more checking online – and came up with a few interesting things. But I wasn't really sure how any of it fit Samantha's case.

"Ronald Claymore was a very strong swimmer, according to this piece," Bowers said, as he went through another newspaper article. "He was on the swim team at Harvard, he swam regularly in the pool the Claymores had at their house here – and he was the one who taught Samantha to swim."

That raised a red flag. Why couldn't he swim to shore like the other two? But the explanation was that something probably prevented him from being able to swim. Either he was injured by the blast – or else maybe knocked unconscious.

"Was there any evidence of an injury on his body?" I asked.

"No."

"No evidence?"

"No body."

"They never found him?"

Bowers shook his head.

"It's the ocean. Not a pond or lake. Sometimes bodies wash up on shore, but often they go out to sea. So, at first he wasn't officially listed as dead. He was just missing at sea."

"Missing? So technically he's still missing?"

"No. Valerie Claymore went to court and had him officially declared dead a few weeks later."

"That's pretty quick to take that kind of legal action."

Bowers shrugged.

"Just out of curiosity, when did she marry Bruce Aiken?"

He checked that information online.

"Six months later."

"Not a very long mourning period for Valerie Claymore, was it?"

"There's no law that states how long a person should mourn for."

I thought about the captain of the fishing boat who survived along with Samantha Claymore.

"What was the boat captain's name?" I asked.

"Robert Malone," Bowers said quickly, without having to look it up.

"How'd you know that so fast?"

"There's a separate article about him here that I just read. Got his picture and everything."

Robert Malone.

There was something familiar to me about that name.

But I wasn't sure why.

It wasn't until I looked at the picture on Bowers' computer screen that I realized who he was.

I didn't know him as Robert Malone though.

I knew him by another name.

Muzzy.

Muzzy Malone.

CHAPTER 18

The Black Dog Bar was packed with people when I got there on my way home. That was good. I liked it that way. Whether or not I was drinking. Just like I'd told Chief Wilhelm. I still loved the atmosphere.

I took an empty seat at the end of the bar. The bartender, whose name was Wally, noticed me and brought over my usual drink. Or at least my drink at the moment. A glass of club soda and ice.

"Good evening, Detective Pearce," he said.

"You can call me Abby, Wally."

"Okay, Abby. How you doing?"

"I've been better."

"Still trying to find that missing girl?"

"That's my problem."

"No idea yet what could have happened to her?"

"We've got some leads we're pursuing…"

I took a sip of the club soda. It tasted good. Not as good as a cold beer or glass of vodka. But it would do for now.

"Quite a treat for me tonight," Wally said. "I have two of Cedar Cliffs' finest in my place."

"Huh?"

He pointed a finger towards a table in the corner. Teena Morelli was sitting there. Still in her police uniform. Talking to some guy. She didn't see me.

Terrific, I thought to myself, Ms. Tattle-Tale will see me here again.

But I didn't care.

I had nothing to hide.

I wasn't drinking that first night.

And I wasn't drinking now.

I sat there for a while, nursing my club soda and going over all the new – and somewhat baffling – information I'd learned about Samantha Claymore and her family. Her claim to Eddie that her father had been murdered. Blaming her mother. The details about the death of Ronald Claymore. And, most puzzling of all, the fact that Muzzy Malone was the captain of the fishing boat that went down that day. And now Malone was working for Bruce Aiken – Valerie Claymore's new husband – and carrying the ransom money for Samantha. I tried to connect the dots between these things.

I was having trouble concentrating though. I kept thinking about Teena Morelli sitting at the other end of the bar. Probably getting ready to report me to Chief Wilhelm again.

I decided to confront her. I walked over to where she was sitting. The guy she'd been talking to was gone, and she was alone now. Drinking a beer.

She looked surprised to see me.

"What are you doing here, Teena?" I said. "Spying on me again? Are you going to march into Wilhelm's office in the morning and tell him you saw me here? Maybe embellish it a bit? Have me buzzing beers, doing shots and maybe even dancing on the bar. I'm sure you'll come up with enough details to make it interesting for him. Only problem is, I'm not drinking. This is club soda. Check it out."

I showed her my drink.

"I don't care what you're drinking, Pearce."

"Then why did you tell Wilhelm about the last time I was here? You probably figured I was drinking then too. But I wasn't drinking. Then or now. Tell that to Wilhelm since you two are so buddy, buddy."

"I didn't tell Wilhelm anything about you."

"Well, someone did."

"Maybe so, but it wasn't me."

"Really?"

"Really. I'd tell you if it was. I don't stab people in the back. I go right at them full frontal. If I'm bad-mouthing you, you'll know it. Believe me…"

I actually did believe her. If she'd been responsible for reporting me to Wilhelm, she would have told me by now. Maybe even bragged about it. I'd jumped to a conclusion about her because of our rocky relationship. But it was the wrong conclusion. I realized that now.

"I'm sorry," I said.

"You should be."

"No, I mean it. I really do apologize for accusing you of being a snitch."

"If you're really sorry, there's a way you can make it up to me."

"How?"

"Buy me another beer."

When the beer came, I wasn't sure if I should leave or not. But that seemed awkward. So, I drank some more club soda and decided to bring up what was on my mind.

"What do you think about Bruce Aiken?"

"The father?"

"Stepfather."

"All I know about him is that he brought the ransom money. Why?"

"I'd like to keep an eye on him. See what he's doing here."

"Why the interest in Aiken?"

"I don't like him."

"I don't like you, but that doesn't mean I'd investigate you. What's going on, Pearce?"

I hadn't told anyone about my suspicions yet. Not Wilhelm, not even Bowers when he asked why I was looking into Ronald

Claymore's death. I wasn't sure why. Maybe I was afraid they would think I was crazy. I figured Teena Morelli would too. But I told her anyway. But she surprised me.

"Damn," she said when I finished running though the developments involving Ronald Claymore. "That is interesting. But what does it have to do with Samantha going missing?"

"Well, let's say there is something suspicious about the way Ronald Claymore died. And the girl found out about it. Maybe she didn't remember at the time, maybe she lied about what she knew for some reason – but anyway maybe she wanted to now reveal something about that fateful day at sea. Maybe the people responsible for Claymore's death found out about it. Maybe that's why she disappeared. She ran away, she was killed – or someone is holding her hostage until they decide what to do. Makes sense to me. How about you?"

"What about the ransom note? The one that never got followed up. Where does that fit in?"

I shrugged. "I didn't say I had all the answers."

CHAPTER 19

For me, the toughest part about giving up drinking is that it's forever.

I can go a day, a week or even a month with no problem at all. You summon up all your willpower and determination and resolve each day to simply say no to drinking. That's what my whole "one day at a time" thing is all about. You don't worry about the next day or the next month or the next year. You just worry about today. And that's how you try to get through the rest of your life.

It doesn't always work like that though.

I thought about this on my way home from the Black Dog.

This was the crunch time for me. It was easy for me to not drink when I was with people in a bar. I could distract myself talking to them, laughing with them and making jokes. But now, driving home, I was alone. Now no one would know if I had a drink or not.

Except me.

I was the one who'd have to answer for it in the morning.

I don't have many vices. I don't do drugs. I never smoked cigarettes. I like animals and children. I don't rob banks and I've been known to help an old lady across the street once or twice. Basically, I'm a pretty good person. Except for the drinking.

I took my first drink when I was a teenager, and I've been drinking pretty much ever since. Oh, there've been breaks, of course. I've tried to stop before. The longest I've ever gone without a drink was after I married Zach. I stayed sober for the first year and a half of our marriage. But then one day I started drinking again.

I'd like to say there was some dramatic reason for this decision to fall off the proverbial wagon, but there really wasn't. I wasn't depressed, or worried about my job, or unhappy in my marriage, or upset about anything else.

All I remember is that there was this little bar that I used to pass every night on my way home from work. It seemed so cozy and inviting. Exactly the kind of place I used to love. I didn't know anyone in this bar, so I realized I could slip in there for a quick one without my friends being any the wiser. But I resisted this temptation for a long time. Each night I summoned all my resolve and willpower and kept walking past that bar. Until one night I stopped walking.

At first, I'd been able to keep it under control. Two drinks, no more – twice a week. I even did it on the same nights every week, Mondays and Fridays. One to start the week off and one to end it. Then one night I went in on a Wednesday. No problem, I told myself. I'll skip Friday to make up for it. But I didn't. Pretty soon, I was drinking every night of the week. The two-drink limit fell by the wayside too.

I kept it a secret from Zach for a while. I've always been good at hiding my drinking. I'd walk around the block a few times before going home to get my head straight. I'd chew gum and eat breath mints to make sure I didn't smell of booze.

I always had an excuse for Zach too about where I'd been and why I was so late, as if I'd been cheating on him with someone else. Which I suppose, in a sense, I was.

Several times Zach confronted me and asked if I'd been drinking. I always denied it, of course. But then he found the empty vodka bottle in the trash one morning. I'd drunk it after he went to sleep the night before, and passed out without throwing it down the incinerator.

He tried harder than anyone else ever did to get me to stop drinking. He talked to me. He pleaded with me. He begged me to get help. Then he got angry. And finally he left. I remember feeling empty, like I'd lost something irreplaceable. But I took a drink of vodka to ease the pain. It made me feel better. Vodka made everything better.

When I got home to Chilmark, I received my usual enthusiastic greeting from Oscar.

He wagged his tail frantically, jumped up and licked my face.

That's the great thing about a dog. Their love for you is unquestioning. Even if you do something bad, a dog is always there for you.

After I walked and fed Oscar, I had my own dinner. I took some tomatoes, carrots, green onions and cucumbers – all of which I grew in my vegetable garden outside – and made myself a salad. I cut up some pieces of chicken I had in my refrigerator and mixed them in too, and then added a balsamic Dijon dressing on top. I was really proud of myself. Eating a healthy salad that I made with my own ingredients and drinking a glass of water with it. It almost made me forget about how much I'd love a real drink. Almost.

When I finished eating, I watched a *Big Bang Theory* rerun on TV; played video games for a while; and read a book I'd bought recently about sailing on the open ocean. (I was still determined to sail from Martha's Vineyard to Nantucket or Cape Cod one day soon.)

But, no matter what I did, I couldn't stop thinking about drinking.

And about Zach.

I took out an old scrapbook of pictures I'd kept of me and Zach together over the past few years. We looked so happy. At the beach. At the theater. At a Yankees game. Zach dressed up in his full-dress state trooper uniform for an awards ceremony – with a big smile on his face and me on his arm. Zach loved the beach.

He loved going to the theater. He loved baseball. And, most of all, he loved being a cop. He just didn't love me anymore.

At some point, going through that scrapbook, I realized I'd lost track of time. I glanced over at the clock. It was 12:06. In a few hours, it would be morning.

I'd made it through another day without a drink.

CHAPTER 20

The mayor, Peter Randall, wanted to see me. I wasn't sure if it was good news or not. He probably wanted an update on where we stood in the search for Samantha Claymore. But why not get that from Chief Wilhelm? Still, Randall was the one who'd pushed to bring me here as a detective in Cedar Cliffs, so I figured it was a good idea to keep him happy. With people like Barry Wilhelm and Teena Morelli around, it was nice to have someone in town on my side.

One of the good things about working in a small town like Cedar Cliffs is that it doesn't take you very long to get around. In New York City, it could take a good forty-five minutes to get downtown to City Hall or Police Headquarters from the precinct uptown – maybe even longer depending on traffic. But the Cedar Cliffs municipal building was around the corner from our station. I was able to walk there in less than a minute.

Mayor Randall had silver-grey hair, an effusive smile and a dynamic personality that made you understand why he had been so successful in politics on the island. Oh, I'm sure he'd done some not so nice things over the years, but he was damn charismatic and that helped him get away with it. The people of Martha's Vineyard liked him. I liked him. And, more importantly, he seemed to like me.

"How are you enjoying Martha's Vineyard?" he asked when I sat down in front of his desk.

"Not as uneventful as I expected." I smiled.

He shook his head. "None of us can remember a crime of this magnitude happening on the island. I'm glad you're here though.

That's one of the reasons I pushed for you. To have an experienced law enforcement professional – someone who can handle big crimes like this – working for the Cedar Cliffs police. God knows, we needed someone like that."

"Well, there is Chief Wilhelm…"

"Wilhelm isn't up to a job like this. You know that as well as I do. I need you to be the lead on this investigation. I want that media spotlight on you – not Barry Wilhelm. You have a bright future here, Abby. I could see you being police chief one day."

There was a picture on Randall's desk of him and his family. His wife, a pretty blonde woman, and three children – two boys who looked to be in their early teens, and a younger girl. I figured the picture was a few years old, but Peter Randall sure seemed to have a happy family who loved him. I wondered what it was like to have a family like that. To be surrounded by people who cared about you. I had nobody like that in my life. Nobody except Uncle Stan.

I brought Randall up to date on the search for Samantha Claymore. I ran through everything we'd been doing. I also said there were a number of puzzling questions I had about the case. I didn't get specific – I wasn't ready to do that with him yet – but I did ask one question.

"Were you mayor at the time Samantha's father disappeared at sea five years ago?" I asked. "I know you lived here so you must have been aware of the circumstances of his death. But were you involved at all in the official investigation?"

"No, I wasn't mayor yet. But, yes, I knew all about it. Ronald Claymore's death was a big deal. The biggest thing to happen on the island at that time."

"Don't you find it all a little curious?"

"What do you mean?"

"That Ronald Claymore died here in a boating accident five years ago. And now his daughter is missing."

"Do you think there's a connection between the two things?"

"I don't know. But I suspect that Samantha Claymore's disappearance is a lot more complicated than we think. I have plenty of questions – about her life, her family and her past. And I feel like if I can get answers to my questions about her father's death, maybe they will lead to answers of what happened to Samantha Claymore too."

"What does Chief Wilhelm think about all this?"

"I haven't really told him yet."

"What do you think he will say when you do?"

"That I should concentrate on finding Samantha."

"But you're going to pursue these other angles anyway, aren't you?"

"It's the only way I know how to run an investigation," I said. "Looking at all the evidence. And then going wherever that evidence takes me."

Randall nodded.

"Here's what I want you to do. I want you to run this investigation in whatever way you think best. You're the most qualified police officer we have. And then I want you to report directly to me. Don't worry about Wilhelm. I'll handle everything from here."

"You want me to go over Wilhelm's head?"

"Let's just say we'll remove him from the equation. How does that sound to you?"

"Not good at all."

"Why not?"

I shook my head. "Look, it's very important to follow the chain of command. Wilhelm is my commanding officer. I report to him. Then he reports to you. I'm sorry, Mr. Mayor – but that's the only way I'm going to operate here."

I thought he might be upset by my reaction, but he wasn't. Instead, he gave me a big smile.

"First off, you don't have to call me Mr. Mayor. It's Pete."

"Okay, Pete, but—"

"And I hear what you're saying. I respect your loyalty and sense of decorum. I guess I should have expected that kind of a reaction from you."

"It's not my style."

"But remember this. If you do need someone higher than Wilhelm to help you get the answers you need, I'm here. My door is always open. Don't hesitate to ask for my help. Okay?"

"Okay," I said.

When I left Peter Randall's office, I wasn't exactly sure what this all meant.

But I knew it had to be good.

It was good to hear that the mayor was on my side.

You never know when a friend in high places might come in handy.

"You've got a visitor," Meg told me when I got back to the station. "That Boston TV reporter. Asking questions about Samantha Claymore."

"Tell him to talk to Captain Wilhelm."

"I did. But he insists on seeing you."

"Where is he?"

"I put him in the break room and gave him some coffee until you got back."

I started heading there.

"Abby?"

"What?"

"He's kinda cute."

"Really? I hadn't noticed."

"I think he's interested in you too."

"Well, there's absolutely no interest on my part."

"You could do worse."

"I have," I said.

Lincoln Connor put down his coffee when I walked into the break room and flashed me a smile. The same smile he'd used on me the other night. Oh yeah, I'm sure it opened up a lot of doors for him.

"What can I do for you, Mr. Connor?"

"Mr. Connor? I thought it would be Lincoln by now."

"I'm really busy so if you could tell me why you're here."

"I have a question for you. Actually, three questions."

"What's your first question?"

"Tell me what's happening in the search for Samantha Claymore."

"We're holding another press conference later today. Any updates will be given at that time. Next question."

"What do you think about me doing an on-air profile of you? The detective handling this sensational case. I'd interview you about your time with the NYPD and talk about why you decided to come back here to your hometown. It would be a terrific story."

"Not interested. Third question?"

"Have you thought any more about my dinner invitation?"

"I have."

"And?"

"Three strikes and you're out, Mr. Connor."

"Lincoln." He smiled.

"We're done here," I said.

"So far, my boss is threatening to fire me if he catches me drinking," I said to Oscar when I got home that night. "The mayor wants to promote me, maybe even to chief. The other woman on the force thinks she should have my job. And the hotshot TV reporter from Boston wants to jump my bones and get an exclusive on Samantha Claymore – not necessarily in that order of priority. How can a woman get herself in such a confused mess on what is supposed to be a peaceful island paradise?"

Oscar listened intently as always. Staring at me and interested in every word I said. Or maybe he was more interested in the meal I was preparing for him on the kitchen counter. Science Diet Beef Chunks was the choice today. I hoped that it met with his culinary approval.

"Here's my plan for dealing with all of this, Oscar," I said.

"A. Don't drink – so Wilhelm can't take me off the case.

"B. Keep Peter Randall in my back pocket in case I need him to do anything Wilhelm wouldn't approve of.

"C. Avoid pissing off Teena Morelli any more than I already have – and maybe even see if we can build some kind of relationship. Teena is a damn smart cop. I could use her help.

"D. Stay as far away as possible from Lincoln Connor. That guy is nothing but trouble."

I put the plate of Science Diet Beef Chunks down on the floor.

"That's my plan, Oscar. What do you think? Pretty good, huh?"

Oscar wagged his tail happily, raced to the dog dish and began to wolf his meal down.

I took that as a yes.

CHAPTER 21

One of the things I've learned over the years is that when you're at a dead end in an investigation, go back to the beginning and do the same moves over again. Check out every bit of evidence, every clue, everything you've done again. Sometimes you find something you missed the first time. That's what I decided to do with Samantha Claymore.

The best piece of evidence we had so far was her bicycle in Edgartown. That seemed to pinpoint her last known location. Now we had to figure out what happened after she parked that bicycle. We'd gone through security videos from stores and businesses in the area where the bike was found, looking for some sign of her. There wasn't any. But that didn't mean there wasn't more security footage we hadn't seen yet.

I told Teena to work with the Edgartown police to track down every security video made that afternoon in Edgartown.

And it worked – we got lucky.

"We just found a security video that shows Samantha Claymore on the afternoon she disappeared," Teena Morelli told me now.

"Where?"

"A few blocks away from where she left her bicycle."

"I thought we had checked all the security cameras from that downtown area?"

"We thought we did. But this time we found an extra camera. It's not on the street or inside any of the stores where we looked. It's in a little mini-mall area a few steps off of Main Street in

Edgartown. Nothing inside that mall was connected with any of the stores we thought Samantha was interested in. Which is probably why no one bothered to check it. But it definitely looks like her on the video."

I was impressed at how Teena had tracked this video down.

Maybe she and I could work together after all.

Me, Morelli, Hollister and Bowers gathered around a screen a short time later to watch the video. Bowers hit the play button and an image came up on the screen. It was a hallway containing several small shops selling T-shirts, jewelry and other tourist items. A printed date and timeline across the bottom of the screen read: "August 11. 2:30 p.m."

"The day she disappeared," Hollister noted. "This is what we've been looking for, all right."

"And now we know that she was safe until 2:30 p.m.," I said. "That gives us a better timeline. Whatever happened to her came after this."

The video showed a few other people in the hall for a few seconds – people who weren't Samantha Claymore – but then she came into view.

I'd seen pictures of her, but this footage made her seem so much more real. She had strawberry-blonde hair and was wearing a pair of plaid shorts and a white T-shirt that said "Hi, I'm Sam" on the back. She was walking away from the camera on the screen, looking into shop windows. It all looked perfectly normal for a summer afternoon on the Vineyard. She'd taken a bike ride down to Edgartown, parked her bike, stopped off at some stores and… then what?

In the video, she stood peering into the window of a jewelry store. Not expensive jewelry. More summer stuff, not the kind of thing you'd expect a wealthy heiress to be interested in. She wore an expensive looking ring on the index finger of her left hand. That was the ring her mother had told me she'd gotten from her father and wore everywhere. The black onyx ring. Yep, this was Samantha Claymore. Right before she vanished.

I watched to see if she went inside the jewelry store. But she didn't. Instead, she browsed in a few other store windows. It was all very casual, very relaxed – a teenage girl enjoying herself. Finally, as she got to the front of the mini-mall, she walked through the door and disappeared. That was the last image of her on the security video.

We fast-forwarded the video to see if she reappeared on it. But she was gone.

"Let's check the security cameras outside this area on Main Street to see if we can find anything," I said.

"We already did that," Teena pointed out. "There was no sign of her on any of that video. She must have gone into a spot that was blacked out from the cameras. What exactly are you looking for?"

"Something else."

"What?"

"I don't know. But maybe there's something else out there that could help us figure out what happened to her after this. Let's start going through the rest of the outside security videos from that area of town. From that entire day."

"That's a big job," Hollister said.

"You got a better idea?"

It took a long time to collect all the outside security videos we wanted – and even longer to watch them all.

Especially since none of us, including me, had any idea what we were looking for.

All I could do was hope I'd know what was important when I saw it.

When what I was looking for finally did appear on screen, I almost missed it.

There were crowds of people on the streets in the video. But then I recognized someone. Or at least I thought I did. Even though it didn't make any sense.

"Freeze the video," I said to Bowers.

He did.

The time stamp read: "August 11, 1:30 p.m." An hour before those images of Samantha Claymore we'd seen on the day she disappeared.

The man's face I was looking at gradually came into focus as Bowers followed my instructions to enlarge it on the screen.

No one had noticed the man before.

No reason to.

But I recognized him right away. I'd met him recently at Valerie Claymore's house.

"My God," I said. "That's Samantha's stepfather. Bruce Aiken."

"But Aiken didn't show up on the island until he brought the ransom money from New York after Samantha disappeared," Teena said.

"Apparently he was already here."

"What the hell is he doing in Edgartown right before his stepdaughter disappeared?"

It was a good question.

And Aiken was with someone. Standing on the street and talking with another man. The second man had his back to the camera at first. But then he turned around so we could see him. And we all recognized him right away.

"That's Melvin Ellis!" Teena yelled.

"Oh, Jesus," I said out loud.

CHAPTER 22

No question about it, Melvin Ellis was the wealthiest man on Martha's Vineyard.

But Ellis – and, to be more exact, his family – had been significant to me for a long time for other reasons too.

I'd never forgotten about Melvin Ellis or his family or their big house.

No matter how hard I tried.

But I was shocked to find out he might be connected to Samantha Claymore's disappearance.

Ellis had made a fortune with his business years earlier in New York, Washington, Los Angeles, London and other places around the world – then moved full-time to Martha's Vineyard where he continued to run his corporate empire. He had many holdings on the island itself including miles of valuable real estate; investments in commercial buildings, stores and tourist attractions; and he even owned a big chunk of the Cedar Cliffs Marina, which was right across the street from our police station.

And he was also one of the prominent Martha's Vineyard residents – along with Mayor Peter Randall – who were at the initial press conference offering a $100,000 reward for Samantha Claymore's return.

At the time, it seemed like a noble gesture on Ellis' part.

But now I wondered if there was some other connection between him and the Claymore family that made him so interested in this case.

"What in the world was Bruce Aiken meeting with Melvin Ellis about?" Bowers asked, saying what we were all thinking.

"Why was he even on Martha's Vineyard when he was supposed to be in New York City? That is, until he showed up with the ransom money," Hollister asked.

"And how does he happen to be in Edgartown with Ellis on the same day – and nearby – where Samantha was last seen on video?" Teena wanted to know.

They were all good questions, and I was the one who was supposed to have the answers. But I didn't have a clue.

I watched the security videos over and over. Both videos. The one with Aiken and Ellis, and the one of Samantha Claymore window-shopping before she disappeared. There was something about the Samantha video I thought I was missing, but I couldn't figure out what it was.

I watched especially closely at the end of the video when she left the mini-mall and went out onto the street, hoping I might see something there. Like another image of Bruce Aiken. Or Melvin Ellis. But I didn't. Only Samantha Claymore walking out the door. And then disappearing.

The bottom line was that there were only two possible reasons for Bruce Aiken being in Edgartown at the same time she went missing there. One, he was somehow involved in whatever happened to his stepdaughter or, two, it was a bizarre coincidence. Since I learned a long time ago as a law enforcement officer not to believe in coincidences, that left me with just the first option.

"Let's talk hypothetically for a minute," I said. "Let's assume Aiken – and by extension Ellis – were there in Edgartown because of Samantha. Hypothetically, that means Aiken could have had something to do with her disappearance. Now what could be his motive for snatching his own stepdaughter?"

"Maybe it had something to do with the questions Samantha was asking about her father's death five years ago," Teena said.

"Maybe Samantha was about to reveal information about what happened to Ronald Claymore that day. Maybe Aiken saw her as a threat and wanted to shut her up."

"Possible," I said. "Any other thoughts?"

"Money," Bowers said. "It's always about money with people like this."

The money angle intrigued me too. Especially because of the presence of Ellis – who was one of the richest men around here.

"I made a few calls about the Claymore company finances," Teena said. "Pretty much everything is as expected. Valerie Claymore is the titular CEO, the one they trot out for TV and public appearances. But it looks like she doesn't have much to do with the day-to-day Claymore operations. Ronald Claymore did all that when he was around. Now Aiken seems to be the one pulling the strings."

"What does the company's financial health look like?" I asked.

"Hard to say. I mean the company earns hundreds of millions of dollars a year. But there have been a lot of setbacks because of the economy and recent protests over animal rights. So, there could be some kind of short-term cash flow problem for them. But, at least on paper, there's a lot of money in Claymore Cosmetics. It's just hard to figure out where it's all going. But that's probably true for any big corporation. As for Aiken, he doesn't have the best reputation in certain financial circles – but then no one ever said Wall Street was made up of choir boys."

"How about the girl? How much is Samantha worth?"

"Nothing right now. But there's a trust fund – set up by her father before his death – of thirty-five million dollars. She starts getting annual withdrawals from that on her eighteenth birthday."

If she lives to get it, I thought.

"Assuming the worst, that she's dead, who gets that money?" I asked.

"Well, it would stay with Mrs. Claymore and her husband."

Hollister, Bowers, Teena and I agreed this was interesting. But still all speculation. We'd need hard evidence to determine that Samantha Claymore's trust fund had something to do with her disappearance.

So what next?

"Follow the money," Bowers said. "Isn't that how the saying goes?"

"Pretty hard to do when you can't find any kind of money trail," Hollister pointed out.

"And what in the hell is Melvin Ellis doing in the middle of it all? Talking to Bruce Aiken in Edgartown the day Samantha disappeared?" Teena asked.

"Let's ask him," I said.

"Aiken?"

"No, Ellis. I need to question Melvin Ellis about this case."

"Damn, that's not going to be an easy job for you to do."

If she only knew…

I'd been to Melvin Ellis' house before.

But it had been years since I'd gone inside the house, rather than just stare at it from the outside. Or seen the house only in my nightmares.

And going back inside it all these years later was going to be a really traumatic experience for me.

But I knew I had to do it.

To get answers about Samantha Claymore.

And maybe to get some answers about myself too.

CHAPTER 23

Lincoln Connor was standing outside the Cedar Cliffs police station smoking a cigarette when I came out that evening. He gave me a wave.

"Detective Pearce," he said. "Want to join me for a few minutes?"

"I don't smoke."

"How about we walk somewhere for a drink then?"

"I don't drink."

"We could grab a bite to eat? I know you eat. I saw you scarfing down a pizza the other night."

I smiled.

"Look, I saw this place around the corner," he said. "It's upstairs on a balcony overlooking the marina. Beautiful scene on an August night. What do you say? I'd really like to talk to you some more."

"Why?"

"I'm interested."

"Interested in me or Samantha Claymore?"

"Both."

"Well, at least you're honest about it."

"I'm an honest guy. Just like my namesake, Honest Abe Lincoln."

I had to admit he was damn charming. Not just the obvious flirting. It was the way he looked at me. The way he made me feel. It had been a long time since I'd felt that way. I'd originally planned to stop off at the Black Dog again on my way home. But sitting on a balcony overlooking the Cedar Cliffs Harbor with a good-looking guy somehow seemed more appealing in the moment.

What the hell, I said to myself... why not?

It was only a few minutes' walk to the place, and we got a table next to the water. A waitress came out to take our order.

"I'll have a beer," he said. "Michelob Light."

The waitress turned to me.

"Beer for you too, ma'am?"

"No!" I said, practically shouting.

Both she and Lincoln Connor gave me a funny look.

"I'll have a club soda," I said.

When the waitress brought our drinks to the table, Connor took a big sip of his beer and then looked across the table at me.

"So, you're an alcoholic, huh?" he said.

"What makes you say that?"

"The way you reacted when she offered you a beer."

"I said no, didn't I?"

"Yeah, but you seemed like you really wanted to say yes. Besides, you told me before that you don't drink. And most people I know who don't drink are recovering alcoholics. Unless they're all about being healthy and pure of body. But you don't come across as all that wholesome to me so..."

I shook my head in amazement.

"You figured that out about me in just a few minutes?"

"I'm a reporter. That's what I do. I figure stuff out."

"Sounds like you're a pretty good reporter."

"I'm the best."

"The best? That's a strong statement."

"Okay, maybe I'm not the best yet. But I will be. All I need is one big story to put me in the national spotlight."

"And you think the disappearance of Samantha Claymore is that story?"

"It could be."

"I'm not talking to you about the case."

"Fine."

"Really? You're okay with that?"

"Sure, we can talk about something else."

"Like what?"

"You. Now that's a good story."

"What's so interesting about me?"

"Are you kidding? You're a helluva story. Decorated homicide cop who solved a bunch of big murder cases. The darling of the New York City media for a while. I looked you up. The tough cop who looked super-hot too. You were the poster girl for female detectives in New York. That is, until you left the NYPD and came back to Martha's Vineyard. Why did you walk away from being a big city cop for this?"

"I had my reasons."

Connor nodded. I was pretty sure at this point that he knew one of the reasons. And I was right.

"Did it have anything to do with your partner Tommy Ferraro being shot and killed?"

"I don't want to talk about Tommy."

Connor didn't push it. I suppose he was afraid I might get up from the table and walk out if he did.

"So why did you come back to Martha's Vineyard?"

"It's where I grew up. I decided I needed a change from all the pressures of New York. Professional, personal – I thought coming back to someplace quiet like Martha's Vineyard would be healthy for me. At least for a while until I figured everything out. Of course, I didn't figure on landing such a sensational high-profile case like Samantha Claymore, a case so big it even attracted a hotshot TV reporter like you."

He smiled. It sure was a nice smile. The truth is Lincoln Connor was kinda winning me over. I enjoyed spending time with him like this, even though I still missed Zach.

"Is your family still on the island?"

"No. My father's dead and my mother lives in an assisted living facility on Cape Cod. I'm an only child. So, it's only me here now."

"Were you close to your parents?"

"Not particularly. My father and I didn't have a good relationship. I hadn't spoken to him in years and I didn't even go to his funeral."

"Did he mistreat you in some way?"

"No, not really."

"He must have done something pretty bad for you to write him out of your life the way you did."

"Sometimes it isn't what a person does that hurts you, it's what they don't do."

CHAPTER 24

Melvin Ellis lived on the most western point of Martha's Vineyard – overlooking the ocean and near the cliffs of Gay Head. Technically, it's called Aquinnah now after the Native American tribe that once lived here. The name was changed from Gay Head by the Martha's Vineyard government a number of years ago. But many longtime residents still call it Gay Head. I'm one of them.

It's the same area of the island where Jackie Onassis and her children had their summer estate.

So it's where the really big money lived.

Before the press conference, I'd only seen Melvin Ellis in person as a little girl, when he came to the restaurant my father owned in Vineyard Haven to discuss some kind of business. I never knew exactly what they talked about, I was too young then to understand. But I remember my father was always very deferential around him.

Ellis was a guy you didn't want to get on the wrong side of.

And now I was going to knock on his door and ask him what he knew about a missing teenage girl.

There was a big main residence on the Ellis property with ocean views from nearly every window; a guest house; another resident building for the staff; a swimming pool; and a tennis court over miles of prime real estate. I drove up to a locked gate with a security guard keeping watch.

"I'm sorry, ma'am, but no one is allowed past this point unless you have specific authorization," he said, with a haughty tone and a bit of a smirk. He seemed like a man who enjoyed his job. Keeping away anyone who wasn't important enough to see Melvin Ellis.

"Here's my authorization," I said.

I showed him my Cedar Cliffs police badge.

The smirk on his face disappeared then.

I always loved that.

A police badge opens a lot of doors.

"I see. Is Mr. Ellis expecting you?"

"No, he's not."

I hadn't called ahead. I wanted to just show up at his door and see what happened. I had no idea what his involvement might be – or if there was any involvement at all – in Samantha Claymore's disappearance. But I figured having the element of surprise on my side might make it easier to figure out.

"May I tell Mr. Ellis what this is about?"

"I'll do that myself."

"Very well."

He went into the guardhouse, made a call to the house and then walked back over to my car.

"Keep driving up this way and you can park by the front door. Someone will greet you there."

As I got closer to the house, I felt a shudder run down my spine. And a rush of bad memories that I tried to push out of my mind. Because – as I knew all too well – I had been inside the Ellis house once before. It was a long time ago. But not long enough to erase the nightmare of what happened to me that night.

Melvin Ellis met me at the front door. I guess he was concerned about why a detective was showing up like this unannounced.

"I'm Detective Abby Pearce with the Cedar Cliffs police," I said. "I need a few minutes of your time, Mr. Ellis."

"Of course. I remember you from Samantha Claymore's press conference. What is this about?"

"The disappearance of Samantha Claymore."

"Is there a new development?"

"Actually, this is about you."

"I'm sorry, I don't understand."

"I'll explain it all to you. Maybe you can help me with some questions that I have about Samantha and her family."

"Anything I can do to help find that poor girl…"

He led me into the living room, which had a gorgeous window view of the Gay Head Cliffs and the crashing waves below. Damn, this house made Valerie Claymore's place look like a shack. I sat down on a long couch, and he took a chair across from me.

"Would you like a drink?" he asked.

God, would I like a drink.

"I'm fine," I told him.

He waited expectantly to see what I would say. He was clearly curious about why I was there. And why not? But I liked that. It gave me the upper hand.

"I'm here because I want to find out about your relationship with the Claymore family."

"What relationship are you talking about?"

"Do you know Bruce Aiken and Valerie Claymore?"

"Yes, I do."

"How well do you know them?"

"Not well. We've had a few business discussions together. That's all."

"You were seen talking to Bruce Aiken in Edgartown recently, Mr. Ellis. On the same day and in the same place, in fact, that Samantha Claymore disappeared. So, I'm curious. Did you see Samantha Claymore that day? Did you have any indication she was in trouble?"

"Oh my God," Ellis said. "I mean sure, Bruce and I met for lunch that day in Edgartown. But I had no idea it was around the same time his stepdaughter disappeared. I'm sure there's no connection at all though, Detective. It must just be a bizarre coincidence that we were all in the same place at that time. That's the only possible explanation."

Well, yes, it could be a coincidence.

Except for one thing.

Bruce Aiken was supposed to be in New York City then. According to his wife, he didn't arrive in Martha's Vineyard until he brought the ransom money. So, what was he doing meeting with Ellis in Edgartown that day?

I asked Ellis a few more questions, but I didn't get any useful answers from him.

"I really hope you find out what happened to Samantha Claymore," he said as he walked me out of the house and back to my car. "Please don't hesitate to ask me if there's any more I can do to help, Detective Pearce."

I nodded.

"Thank you for your time."

He looked at me closer now.

"You look familiar. Not only from the press conference. Have we met before?"

"Many years ago."

"When?"

"Here on the island. I grew up here, but just came back a few months ago. I was Al Pearce's daughter."

"Of course. I heard you'd left the Vineyard. I was sorry to hear about your father's death. My condolences to you. It must have been very difficult for you to lose him to cancer."

I shrugged. "We weren't that close."

"How's your mother?"

"She's living on the Cape now. I left this place right after my high school graduation to go to college. Until recently, I hadn't come back."

"My son graduated from Martha's Vineyard High. Did you know Mark?"

Did I know Mark Ellis? I thought of all the ways I could answer that question for him. But I didn't say any of them out loud. Instead, I simply replied, "Yes, I did."

"He lives in Los Angeles now. He's a big Hollywood producer and theatre agent. I'll see if he remembers you, Abby."

I wasn't sure if he would.

Like I said, it was a long time ago that I was last in this house. And I didn't stay very long either.

But I sure remembered.

I remembered Mark Ellis all too well.

CHAPTER 25

That night I took out my senior yearbook from high school and paged through it.

There were no happy memories for me there. I wasn't even sure why I kept the damn thing. Maybe it's the same reason you touch a sore tooth with your tongue, just to see how badly it hurts. Maybe the pain serves some kind of purpose. Maybe it even makes you feel better somehow. Maybe it reassures you that you're still alive.

There weren't a lot of pictures of me in the yearbook. One in a cap and gown on graduation day. A casual shot sitting in the school cafeteria. Another for the Junior Achievers Club. I joined that because I thought it might be a good place to meet boys. I was not exactly cool in those days. But the boys I met were even more uncool than I was.

Like I'd told Bowers, I was kind of weird looking and awkward through most of my high school years. No one ever asked me out. I wasn't very attractive.

But then the summer before my senior year I got pretty. I guess I just matured physically. By the time I got back to school in the fall, I wasn't awkward anymore. I was cute. I thought that was the answer to all of my problems back then.

Looking through the yearbook now, I could see myself transforming on the pages. I looked different from picture to picture. I was going through a lot of changes then, mental and physical. I was growing up. And I was confused. I know everyone is to some degree in high school, but back then I thought I was the only one who had ever felt that way.

In one of the earlier pictures, I was sitting in the cafeteria next to Janis Fairly, a pretty blonde who every guy in school wanted to go out with. We had been friends when we were younger, but then kind of drifted apart. Probably because she was so popular, and I wasn't.

I stared at my face in that years-old picture, and all of my insecurities came flooding back. The loneliness, the desperation, the confusion. I was looking at the camera with an almost puppy-like look of eagerness. Like I couldn't wait to see what the future held for me. But I know now what was coming for me after that day in the high school cafeteria. I was so stupid then. So naive.

Sooner or later, as I knew I would, I turned to a picture of Mark Ellis. He looked as handsome as I remembered him. Curly blond hair. Big blue eyes. He was my high school crush. The guy I always wanted, but knew I could never have.

"You remember my son, Mark," Melvin Ellis had said to me at his house. "I think you were in the same class together."

How could I ever forget him?

I used to have this sixth period civics class with Mark. I always showed up early to make sure I got a seat close to him. I'd sit there and stare at him for the entire period. I don't think I learned anything at all about civics that entire year. After class, I'd follow him down the hall. Watching him talk to people, flash his smile and be cool in a way I could never hope to be.

A few times, I tried to talk to him. He was polite and answered my questions, but you could tell he wasn't interested in me. He just looked through me, as if I didn't exist. Then he'd spot some pretty girl, and he'd be gone. And I'd be left standing there alone. I used to think there was nothing worse than being alone or ignored.

As it turned out, I was wrong about that.

Especially when it came to Mark Ellis.

Because, when I got pretty, Mark Ellis started to pay attention to me. He even took me to the senior prom. And that's when everything went terribly wrong. I was still paying the price for it today. My visit back to the Ellis house had made me realize that more than ever before.

In the back of the yearbook was a picture of me with my mother and father from some family day event at the school.

I'd seen the picture many times before, of course, but it never failed to amaze me. The way I was looking up at my father, with this expression of love and admiration on my face.

I was daddy's little girl back then.

I thought he was perfect.

I was wrong about that too, of course.

That night, when I went to sleep, I had the dream again.

The one where I'm watching Samantha Claymore go into the big house that I had been in.

Melvin Ellis was in the dream this time.

And so was his son Mark, looking as handsome and charming as I remembered him.

I saw them grab Samantha, drag her into the house and then… I woke up.

I lay in bed breathing heavily and shaking, with Oscar looking at me to make sure I was all right. I patted him on the head to let him know everything was okay, got up and walked into the kitchen. I didn't want to go back to sleep right away. I opened up the refrigerator, poured myself a glass of water and carried it with me back to the bedroom.

I took out my picture of Samantha Claymore. I'd been carrying it with me ever since we started searching for her. Sometimes I just looked at her face and tried to imagine the pain she was going through at this moment. I wondered if it was like the pain I'd suffered when I was her age.

I made a vow to the girl in the picture now: "I'm going to save you, Samantha. I couldn't save myself, but I'm going to save you. I won't let them hurt you like they hurt me."

CHAPTER 26

"What do you remember about esteemed citizen Melvin Ellis?" I asked Stan Larsen.

"Melvin Ellis, the big financier?"

"That's the only Melvin Ellis on this island."

"Why are you asking me about him?"

"You lived on Martha's Vineyard for a long time. You knew a lot of people. I just wanted to find out what you could tell me about Ellis."

"Well, I know he's got a lot of money." He laughed.

"Do you recall him being implicated or involved in any kind of criminal activity back then?"

"Such as?"

"Oh, I don't know. Money laundering. Bribery. Tax evasion. Fraud. Murder. Kidnapping. Counterfeiting. Spitting on the sidewalk. Jaywalking. Whatever…"

"Not that I'm aware of. Where are you going with this, Abby?"

I'd called Stan Larsen again because I'd enjoyed talking with him the other day, and I wanted someone else – besides just the people I worked with – to discuss the case with. In the old days, he used to help me with my homework and give me life advice too. So why not run some of the things bothering me past him now like I used to?

I told him how Melvin Ellis had showed up on a security video in Edgartown meeting with Samantha Claymore's stepfather on the same afternoon she went missing.

"That doesn't necessarily mean anything," he said when I was finished.

"Probably not."

"You don't sound completely convinced of that."

I told him then about the possible connection with Ronald Claymore's death five years ago.

"And how would Melvin Ellis fit into all of this?"

"I have no idea," I said.

"Then why the questions about Ellis?"

"I just have a feeling this is somehow connected."

There was more to it, of course.

But I didn't want to tell anyone the real story about me and Melvin Ellis' family.

Not even Stan Larsen.

There was one new development on the case that I shared with him though. I'd just uncovered it that morning. It was about Samantha Claymore's trust fund. And about the ransom note.

"I learned more details about Samantha's trust fund," I said. "It was a thirty-five million dollar trust fund spread over sixty years. Do the math. How much would that be each year?"

"Uh, I guess about $500,000 or so."

"Actually, a bit more than $500,000."

"Okay."

"Do you know the amount the ransom demanded in the note after the girl disappeared? The amount her stepfather Bruce Aiken scraped together in New York and brought with him to Martha's Vineyard? $583,000. That's pretty interesting, huh? Who would know to demand the same amount Samantha Claymore was supposed to have received in her first payment? This suggests that whoever wrote that note knew a lot about the Claymore family. Or was even a member of it. Like Bruce Aiken. Maybe Aiken was having money troubles. And he figured this was a quick way to solve them. Take out Samantha's first-year trust as a ransom, but then keep it for himself."

"Except no one ever claimed the ransom."

"Yeah, it could mean a change in plans? Or maybe she was dead? But even if she was, the kidnapper would have tried to collect the ransom anyway…"

"Okay, so why didn't anyone follow up the ransom demand?"

I brought up something then that had been in the back of my mind for a while.

"What if Samantha wrote the note? What if she'd had enough of the circus that is her crazy mother and shady stepfather and all the questions over her father's death? She tries to get her first-year trust by pretending she's been kidnapped. If she can get them to pay up, she can run off somewhere and live off that."

"That's a pretty ambitious plan for a sixteen-year-old girl."

"Sixteen-year-old girls can be pretty ambitious these days."

"Same problem with that theory though: why no effort to claim the money after the ransom note?"

I had no answer for that.

I didn't have answers for a lot of things on this case.

"I wish I could help you more, Abby," Larsen said. "But I'm a long ways away from Martha's Vineyard. And I'm not a police professional. It sounds like you need a partner to work with on this case. Someone you can trust for advice."

We talked some more, about life besides the case. I told him about my vegetable garden; and even about my marriage and the breakup with Zach.

It reminded me of the conversations I used to have with him when I was growing up – about school, about boys, about life.

They were the kind of conversations I wished I could have had with my real father.

Before everything changed…

CHAPTER 27

"Why did you go to see Melvin Ellis?" Chief Wilhelm wanted to know.

"Because that's where the investigation took me."

"You know who Melvin Ellis is, right?"

"Of course, I do. I grew up on this island."

"He's one of the most powerful people around – on this island, and in the country. Not the kind of man you want to upset by badgering him at his own home."

"I didn't badger him. I simply went there and asked him about being in Edgartown with Samantha Claymore's stepfather on the day she disappeared. He said he didn't know anything about it. I thanked him for his time and left."

"You shouldn't have gone there without telling me first," he growled.

I'd told Wilhelm now about my visit to Ellis' house because I thought he should know, given who Ellis was in terms of political stature and power. I figured he might be concerned. But I never expected him to react like this. I'd never seen Wilhelm so worried about upsetting someone as he was about upsetting Melvin Ellis.

In retrospect, I guess I should have seen it coming. Barry Wilhelm wasn't a real cop. Not like the cops I'd known and worked with in New York. He'd gotten to where he was by pleasing people in power and not rocking the boat in any way.

That was the most important thing to him.

Even more important than solving a crime like the disappearance of Samantha Claymore.

But not for me.

I knew what my priorities were.

And I wasn't afraid of taking someone on – even someone like Melvin Ellis – if I thought they could help me find her.

"Let me remind you," Wilhelm said, "that there are only a handful of big towns on the Vineyard. So, the fact that Ellis was in Edgartown – one of the biggest towns – for a lunch meeting in the same place and on the same day the girl disappeared is entirely plausible."

"Even meeting with Samantha Claymore's stepfather? Bruce Aiken was supposed to be still in New York that day."

"You don't know that. Not for sure."

"His wife told me he'd been in New York, and would bring in the ransom money from there."

"Maybe he was here, and then went back to New York City before finding out the girl was missing."

"Seems strange to me."

"What does Aiken say about it?"

"I haven't asked him yet. I'm going to do that soon. But I wanted to hold off a little bit before I did that."

"Why?"

"Because I've found out a lot of strange things about Aiken and the people around him. I want to find out more before I confront him about any of it."

I told Wilhelm about how one of Aiken's people, Muzzy Malone, had been the skipper of the boat Ronald Claymore took the day he drowned. How quickly Valerie Claymore had Ronald Claymore declared dead and remarried Aiken afterward. About Eddie Haver, who said Samantha Claymore claimed her father had been murdered.

"That was an accidental drowning," Wilhelm said.

"How do you know that?"

"It was officially ruled an accident at the time."

'Well, Samantha Claymore apparently isn't so sure of that – and she was there on the boat when her father died."

Wilhelm looked upset. Even more upset than when I'd told him about going to see Melvin Ellis.

"Look, I don't know what it means," I told him. "Or if it has anything to do with Samantha Claymore. I mean there's no real evidence yet for any of it, just a lot of speculation and unsubstantiated claims. But there were a whole lot of things going on here before Samantha went on that bike ride. I want to find more out about Bruce Aiken and Valerie Claymore and the boating accident that killed her husband Ronald Claymore. I think we should talk about this at the next press conference. Just say we're taking another look into the boat accident in the wake of the girl's disappearance and—"

"No!" Wilhelm said sharply.

"Excuse me?"

"No, you're not going to talk about a boating accident from five years ago that has nothing to do with the search for Samantha Claymore. The girl is all you should be focused on right now. Find Samantha Claymore. That's your priority, Pearce. Nothing else. Do you understand?"

"Yes, sir,' I said. "I agree that she is the priority here."

Wilhelm nodded. He seemed satisfied. Even though I wasn't going to give up on the boat angle or the Melvin Ellis angle. But I wouldn't tell him any more about it until I had something solid.

"Anything else?" he asked.

"Well, there is one thing I wanted to talk to you about."

"What's that?"

"I need help."

He gave me a funny look. Like maybe he thought I was talking about needing help for my drinking. But this was about the job.

"I'm the only detective on the force. That's fine for normal, low-level Martha's Vineyard crime. But this is a sensational, high-profile case that is very complex, as you know. I need a partner. Someone to work with, someone to exchange ideas with – someone I trust who can help me find the girl."

"Okay. I can get someone from uniform to work with you. At least for the duration of this case. We've got enough summer temps to fill any holes. We'll give you a partner. Who do you want? Bowers? Hollister? I know those are the two you're the closest with. Which one do I promote to detective?"

"Teena Morelli."

That really surprised him.

"I thought you two have never got along?"

"No, we haven't."

"Teena thinks she should have your job."

"I know."

"So why do you want her as your partner?"

"Because she's the best cop on the force," I said.

CHAPTER 28

I shook my head in frustration as I walked past Meg Jarvis' desk.

"You know, everyone told me what an easy gig this job would be when I took it. After all the big crimes I covered in New York City, I'd be a detective in quiet, peaceful Martha's Vineyard. They said nothing bad ever happens here. And then, as soon as I take this job, a teenage girl goes missing for the first time in probably the island's whole history."

"Samantha Claymore is not the first girl to go missing on Martha's Vineyard," she said.

My heart stopped.

"There was someone else?"

"A few of them. Kids disappear everywhere, even on Martha's Vineyard."

"Why didn't you tell me?"

"Why should I?"

"Well, they might have some connection with Samantha Claymore."

"Nah, these cases were all closed. Different kinds of things. Runaways, suicide, that sort of ending."

"Can I see the files?"

"How far back?"

"I don't know… let's say missing girl cases in this area over the past three years."

A little while later, Meg gave me a list of all the cases of missing teenage girls over the past several years. Like she had said, there were a number of them. More than I had expected.

But none of them appeared to be very significant.

Because most of the girls had been found.

The bottom line is that most missing people – especially young ones – do return home. In fact, nearly ninety-nine percent of them come back alive. There are so many options for authorities to find missing kids now – public alerts, social media – that sooner or later you find someone who knows what happened to them.

Of course, a lot of missing kids aren't really "missing." They run away, get in an accident, stay overnight at a friend's house without telling their family, go willingly with a sexual partner.

Most cases ended with answers like that. The missing kids came home, explained where they were, apologized for any confusion and concern they'd caused – and life went on for everybody.

I read – and reread – all of the cases a number of times. Looking for something – anything – that might link them together in some way. Or, more importantly, might link any of them to the disappearance of Samantha Claymore. No matter how far-fetched the link might seem.

Most of them didn't show any sort of connection, as far as I could see.

Except for three.

I reread the first two:

LINDA ELLISON – fifteen years old. Did not return home from a school picnic near the western end of the island. Her parents filed a missing person's report, and police searched for her for two days. But, after forty-eight hours, she returned. There was no explanation provided for where she had been or how she got home. The case was closed after her return.

RUTHIE KOLTON – Seventeen years old. Disappeared on the beach at Gay Head. Ruthie had been a troubled teenager – fighting with her parents, school officials and the police. She'd been arrested on several minor charges, including intoxication and stealing. She had been undergoing psychiatric therapy, according to her parents. When she went missing – and her clothes, purse and phone were found neatly stacked on the beach near the water – it was assumed that she had walked into the ocean and killed herself. No body was ever found.

The connection I noticed was the location. Ruthie Kolton and Linda Ellison had both disappeared on the western end of the island.

Melvin Ellis' mansion was in the Gay Head area. I had no idea of the significance of this – or whether Ellis had played any part in what I was dealing with – but I wrote it down as a detail in the notes I was taking anyway.

A third case intrigued me too:

CARRIE LANG – Sixteen years old. Rode her bike to Allie's General Store in Tisbury, the central part of the island, to get ice cream one afternoon. She didn't return home that day, and the police began looking for her. She was found a week later in a motel room in Providence, Rhode Island with a boy who worked at the gas station near Allie's. The boy was initially charged with kidnapping, but the charge was later dropped when Carrie said she'd gone with him willingly because she was afraid and in danger – and he'd promised to protect her. There was no explanation of what she was afraid of. At this point, the police closed the investigation.

Allie's Store, the place where Carrie had disappeared, was also not far away from Gay Head and the locations of the other two missing girls.

And the house of Melvin Ellis.

There was one other thing I noticed in the files too. The investigating officer in all three cases had been my predecessor Norm

Garrity. Garrity had been the chief detective for years before he died. It made sense that he would have been involved in all these investigations. But I wrote his name down in my notes too.

I sat there now staring at the names on my list:

LINDA ELLISON

CARRIE LANG

RUTHIE KOLTON

Two of them happened near Gay Head and the Ellis house. One of them not that much further away.

What did any of this have to do with Samantha Claymore?

Probably nothing.

But they were all teenage girls from Martha's Vineyard who went missing.

I was once a teenage girl on Martha's Vineyard.

And something bad had also happened to me in that same area back then.

I couldn't help the nagging feeling that it could have been me in any of these three cases.

CHAPTER 29

If Teena Morelli was grateful for me getting her promoted to detective, she sure didn't show it.

"So I'm now a detective for the duration of this case?" she asked.

"Yes."

"And whenever Samantha Claymore is found, I go back to being a uniformed cop."

"That's the plan at the moment."

"Then it's not in my best interest to solve this case. I mean the longer Samantha Claymore is missing, the longer I get to be a detective. And draw detective's pay. I should milk this thing for as long as I can."

I hoped she was kidding.

We were in a car on our way to talk to Valerie Claymore and Bruce Aiken again. I wasn't sure what we'd get out of it. But we needed to go through the motions of updating them regularly with whatever information we had. Which wasn't much at the moment.

Maybe I could find out more about Aiken's movements on the day his stepdaughter disappeared. Plus, there was that whole connection with Muzzy Malone, the skipper on Ronald Claymore's doomed boat ride. I still wasn't sure if his death had anything to do with Samantha's disappearance now, but I couldn't stop thinking there had to be something there.

Teena was driving, and I was in the passenger seat. It was the first time I'd ever seen her out of uniform. She was wearing black jeans, a black blouse with a rawhide vest, sharkskin leather boots and a cowboy hat. She looked tough, but pretty cool too. I figured her to be about forty. She had dark frizzy hair and a curvy body. I had no idea about her personal life, but I'd seen her that day at the Black Dog talking with a man. Now that we were partners, at least for a while, I figured I should find out more about her.

"I like your boots," I said to her. "It's a nice look for you."

"Thanks, but I wear them as more than just a fashion statement."

"What do you mean?"

"Hides my ankle holster."

She took one hand off the steering wheel, reached down and pulled off her right boot. Underneath it was a Beretta in a small holster strapped to her ankle.

"You're full of surprises, aren't you, Teena?"

"Hey, a girl can't be too careful."

Teena was a pretty aggressive driver. Going on the Beach Road as fast as she could, passing slower cars, honking at bikers and pedestrians who wandered in her way. She was clearly a woman in a hurry, in her job and probably in the rest of her life too.

I knew working with her was going to be a handful. But I meant what I said to Wilhelm: I was convinced she was the best cop on the force. Except for me. And I was determined to use her – and every other means at my disposal – to find the Claymore girl.

"How long have you been on the force, Teena?" I asked.

"Four years," she said.

"So you weren't here when Ronald Claymore drowned on the fishing boat?"

"Well, I was here on the island. But I hadn't joined the force yet. I remember hearing about it. It was big news at the time. The media descended on the island then, like they're doing now."

"Who would have been working then?"

"Jeez, let me think. Bowers got here after me. But Hollister would have been here. Meg Jarvis too. Plus Wilhelm, of course."

I thought back to my conversation with Chief Wilhelm about Ronald Claymore's death.

"I told Wilhelm what I'd found out," I said to Teena. "About the skipper working for Bruce Aiken now and Ronald's quickie death certificate. He listened, but wouldn't consider the possibility that it was anything other than an accident. Or for us to go public with our questions about what happened to Ronald Claymore. He told me to stop wasting my time on it."

"No wonder."

"What do you mean?"

"Wilhelm was the one who investigated Ronald Claymore's death on the boat – and ruled it an accidental drowning."

Bruce Aiken was talking on the phone when we went into the living room at the Claymore house.

"What's this guy like?" Teena whispered.

"You haven't met him yet?"

"No, I'd left by the time he showed up with the money."

"Oh, you're going to love him," I said.

Aiken, preoccupied with his phone call, barely acknowledged our presence. Valerie Claymore was sitting on the couch next to him, with her feet curled up underneath her and looking over at Aiken. Like she was waiting for permission to talk to us. For a woman who was supposed to be a high-powered cosmetics executive, she sure acted more like a Stepford wife.

"Has there been anything new on Samantha?" she asked me.

"Not yet, I'm afraid."

"Oh, my God… poor Samantha!"

"We don't know yet that any harm has come to her."

"But the longer this goes on, the worse it seems. Right?"

"I'm afraid so, but there's still hope. We're doing everything we can to find your daughter, Mrs. Claymore. Rest assured of that."

Aiken hung up the phone. "Sorry for the delay," he said, "but that was a very important business call."

Funny, I figured finding out more about the disappearance of his stepdaughter would be more important than a business call – but not for Bruce Aiken.

I introduced Teena to both of them, explaining she was an additional detective now working with me on the case. Mrs. Claymore shook hands with Teena, but Aiken just looked Teena up and down – from the cowboy hat to the biker boots – before giving her a perfunctory hello. I think he was even less impressed with her than he was with me.

"Are you certain that every resource you have is being put into this investigation?" he asked me.

"What do you mean?"

"Well, it seems as if it's just you two working the case."

"Would you prefer some other detectives?" Teena asked.

Yep, she noticed the way Aiken looked at her. She didn't like this guy any more than I did.

"No, I just mean this is such a big case and all…"

"Mr. Aiken," I said. "We have every possible law enforcement resource devoted to the search for Samantha. That includes the entire Cedar Cliffs Police Department and the other police departments on the island. We're also working with the FBI. And with state troopers who have turned out in large numbers to help us look for Samantha. But this is a big island. We don't even know for sure how she disappeared. Or if she was taken against her will."

"Of course, she was taken against her will. There was a ransom note. I'm still sitting on all that ransom money. That was what my earlier call was about. All of this money had to be taken out of active accounts that we were planning to use for a major investment project. And now it's here doing nothing. Do you understand how frustrating that is for me?"

"Yeah, it was awfully inconvenient of the girl to disappear right in the middle of a business deal," Teena said.

Aiken glared at her. "I don't like your attitude."

I tried to defuse the situation as best I could.

"Please, Mr. Aiken, we're trying to do the best we can here. And we'd really like to have your cooperation in order to accomplish that. I do have a few questions to ask you. Your answers might help."

"Of course," Valerie Claymore said. "I'd be happy to answer anything you want."

Aiken didn't look happy about it, but he nodded too.

"Mr. Aiken, did you know Ronald Claymore, your wife's previous husband?" I asked.

"Yes, I knew Ronald."

"How well?"

"We had some business dealings together."

"And then, a few months after his death, you married Mrs. Claymore?"

"What does that have to do with anything?"

"In the days prior to her disappearance, Samantha was apparently talking to friends about her father's death. She even suggested there was something suspicious about it."

"Well, yes, Samantha was very close to her father," Valerie Claymore said. "And, once he was gone, she worshipped his memory even more. Especially because she was there with him the day he died. It was a traumatic experience for a little eleven-year-old girl, as I'm sure you can imagine. So, I suppose she might have had some delusions or fantasies to cover up the reality of what really happened that day. It was just a terrible tragedy. I think Samantha knows that."

"If you don't mind me asking, why did you bring her back to Martha's Vineyard this July?"

"Well, it was our summer vacation."

"Have you spent any other summer vacation here since your husband's death?"

"No, this is the first time we've been back."

"Did you ever consider it might be difficult for Samantha to be back on this island? You knew she was terrified of the water."

"I've taken Samantha to counseling since the day her father died. The counselor thought it was the best thing to do this year. To confront her fears and traumas. He really thought it would be good for her. I guess he was wrong. And now Samantha is gone. Just like her father."

"Wait a minute," Bruce Aiken said. "I really don't see how Ronald Claymore's death – or Samantha's being upset about it – has anything to do with finding her now. Let's focus on the issue at hand. Finding the girl."

I turned to him now.

"Did you know that Muzzy Malone was the skipper of the fishing boat Ronald Claymore was on when he drowned?"

"What?"

"Muzzy Malone. The guy who works for you. The one that was holding the ransom money when you showed up here. Were you aware he was running the charter boat that Ronald Claymore and Samantha were on that day?"

Valerie Claymore started to say something, but Aiken gave her a stern look. She stopped talking.

"I'm sure Mr. Malone has had a number of employment opportunities over the years," Aiken said. "So he was with Ronald Claymore that day. He has clearly held a number of different jobs at different times. I can't tell you any more than that."

"I'd like to talk to him about it," I said.

"I've already sent him back to New York City to carry out some work for me. We could call him if you want. But I'm sure he'll tell you the same thing I'm telling you now, Detective Pearce."

"I'm sure he would, Mr. Aiken. Word for word probably."

"That's because there's nothing more to it than that."

"Okay, I have a question for you then, Mr. Aiken. What were you doing in Edgartown on the same afternoon that your stepdaughter disappeared there?"

"Who told you that?"

"We have you on some security footage. Talking to Melvin Ellis."

"We were discussing business."

"But your wife told us you were in New York City that day…"

Aiken was getting angry now. "What does any of this have to do with Samantha? I think you should spend less time worrying about irrelevant things and concentrate your energy on finding the sixteen-year-old girl that is missing. Do your job, ladies."

"Yes, sir," Teena said.

"We'll be in touch the moment we hear anything new about Samantha," I said.

CHAPTER 30

"Let's go over everything we know so far about Bruce Aiken and Muzzy Malone," I said to Teena once we got back to the office.

Teena and I were at the station, along with Meg Jarvis, trying to put together some profiles of Malone, Aiken and the rest of the cast of characters here. Dave Bowers was there too, because I knew he'd be good at tracking down information we needed online. And I'd invited Vic Hollister to sit in even though I didn't think he could add much. I didn't want him to feel left out. Guess I have a soft spot in my heart for guys like Hollister.

"Okay, I'll start with what I've found out about Malone," Teena said. "It's a long list of stuff. Three convictions – for extortion, assault and promoting prostitution. He ran a massage parlor in New York for a while, then did the same in Boston – and was arrested for beating up his competitors in both places. There's also a number of charges and police complaints against him that had to be dropped because witnesses mysteriously disappeared or refused to talk."

"And he just happens to show up with Bruce Aiken carrying a half million dollars in ransom money?" I said.

"Maybe Aiken is a good citizen who believes in giving ex-cons a second chance."

"Somehow I don't see Bruce Aiken as a 'good citizen, second chances' kind of guy."

Teena agreed.

"What about the fact that Malone was also the skipper of the boat that Ronald Claymore died on five years ago?" I asked. "How did that happen? Did he even have the credentials to be operating a boat?"

"Actually, he did," Meg said. "He had an operator's license for all sorts of charters. I spoke with the FBI in Boston, and they had a file on him too. He previously spent time living in New England, and then set up a charter fishing business on the islands for the Vineyard and Nantucket. Although federal authorities believed the charter operation was some kind of cover-up for smuggling drugs and guns. But he was fully licensed to operate that fishing boat Ronald Claymore was on."

"Still, it's hard to believe he simply happened to be the captain of the boat Claymore died on – and now he works for Valerie Claymore's new husband."

"You don't believe in coincidences?" Bowers laughed.

"Do we have any idea how Claymore and his daughter wound up on that specific boat with Malone?" I asked.

"We only know that there was a specific appointment made with Malone for a fishing trip for the two of them," Teena said.

"Who made the appointment? Ronald Claymore?"

"No, his wife."

"Valerie?"

"Yes. She scheduled a six a.m. fishing trip with Malone for her husband and daughter."

Damn. Maybe that's what Eddie Haver meant when he said Samantha believed Valerie Claymore had "murdered" her father. Could she really have been in on a murder plot? But why? For the money? Why would she put her own daughter at risk too? Samantha could have drowned that day with her father.

"What about the ruling of accidental death?" I asked. "Was there any indication at the time that it might have been more than an accident?"

"I was here when that happened," Hollister said. "And no, we never discovered anything suspicious. Everyone had to dive into the water when the boat caught fire and swim to safety. Malone and the girl made it, Claymore obviously didn't. The only thing Malone might have been blamed for was shoddy maintenance on the engine. But that's all."

"The official ruling was that it was nothing more than a tragic boat accident?"

"That's right."

"And that report was signed off on by Captain Wilhelm."

"Sure. He was the chief at the time. Like he is now."

The background on Bruce Aiken was as murky and mysterious as Malone's. For a number of years he'd led a shadowy existence, holding several positions in the financial world where it was never quite clear if what he did was legal.

In any case, he didn't become really successful until he married his first wife – an heiress named LeeAnne Seaver, whose father owned oil wells in Texas, Oklahoma and other places around the world. Aiken took over company operations and suffered a series of financial reverses that left the company teetering on bankruptcy. At some point afterward, LeAnne Seaver plunged from her penthouse roof in Manhattan, dying in what was ruled a suicide. Supposedly she had been under a doctor's care and taking a lot of sedatives.

Just like Valerie Claymore, I thought to myself.

Shortly after his wife's death, Aiken met and married Valerie Claymore and took over the day-to-day operations of Claymore Cosmetics.

"Sounds like he's a lot better at wooing rich women than he is at handling money," Bowers said.

I thought about how smarmy Aiken seemed to me. But I could see that his charisma might appeal to a certain kind of woman. Women like LeeAnn Seaver and Valerie Claymore.

"One more thing," Bowers said. "From what I've been able to ascertain from a bunch of online sites, Claymore Cosmetics might not have been in as good a shape as people thought. There's speculation about a real cash flow problem."

"Same as when Bruce Aiken had financial problems when he ran the business for his last wife."

"Exactly."

"Maybe he's a bad businessman – or maybe he's been stashing away money in secret for himself."

I thought again about the strange way he'd handled the ransom money on that first night after his stepdaughter disappeared.

"What if he snatched the girl, or had her snatched by someone like Malone, and then was going to give the ransom money to himself?" Teena said.

"Except no one ever followed up on that ransom note. How do you explain that?"

Teena shrugged.

"Okay, how about this then? The girl was due to start getting her trust fund payments soon. Maybe Aiken didn't have the money. He gets rid of the girl so he doesn't have to pay her out of the trust fund, which he's already looted."

"I definitely think that all of this has something to do with Bruce Aiken," I said. "And also maybe Melvin Ellis. I just don't what or how or why."

"Something funny is going on with the Claymore family," Teena said to me afterward. "And it could be related to the girl's disappearance. It's too much to all be a coincidence. Muzzy being on the boat when Claymore died. Aiken being in Edgartown at virtually the same time Samantha was last seen there."

"We need to put public pressure on them to open up and give us some real answers to all these questions," I said.

"How about we insist to Wilhelm we want to go public with the boat stuff and Muzzy's background?" Teena suggested. "That might force them to talk."

"I tried, but Wilhelm won't do it. He insists there's no link between the father's boating death and the missing girl. He's not going to reveal any of this to the press. But I agree with you. The best way to find out more is to get these stories to the public. Get the media to splash them all over the air and the newspaper and the internet."

"But how do we do that? If Wilhelm told you to keep it under wraps, you can't just ignore him and announce it at a press conference? How do we get it to the media?"

"I have an idea…"

CHAPTER 31

Lincoln Connor had left me all his contact information. I texted him now and asked him if he wanted to meet me for lunch. It didn't take long to get a response. He called me right back.

"Lunch?" he said.

"That's right."

"You and me?"

"Uh-huh."

"Just the two of us?"

"That would be the arrangement, yes."

"You must want something from me."

"True."

"Besides my charming company, that is."

"Also true."

"What do you want?"

"Let's talk about this over lunch."

I told him to meet me at the Cedar Cliffs station. When he arrived, we walked over to the marina a block or so away. The water was filled with boats like it always is during August. There were lots of shops and food places alongside the pier. I walked over to one of them, bought two hot dogs with sauerkraut and mustard, plus a couple of sodas, and then brought them over to a bench where Connor was sitting while he waited for me to get the food.

"This was not exactly what I had in mind when you invited me to lunch," he said.

"This is lunch."

"I was thinking about a real sit-down meal."

"We're sitting down, and we're eating. Plus, these are real good hot dogs. Take my word for it."

He smiled and bit into his.

"Wow, that is good!" Connor said.

"Told you so."

"What's it going to cost me though?"

"Nothing. My treat. I bought the whole thing."

"Yes, but I figure there's still a price I'm going to have to pay for you feeding me and being so nice. What is it?"

"I need a favor," I said.

I told him everything I'd found out about Ronald Claymore's death. About the connection to Bruce Aiken and Muzzy Malone. About the way she had her husband quickly declared legally dead before marrying Aiken. About Muzzy Malone's criminal background. I also said that Samantha Claymore had been talking about her father's death – and asking new questions about it – before she disappeared.

I did not tell him about Samantha's claims to Eddie Haver that her father had been murdered. Or about Bruce Aiken's strange appearance in Edgartown on the same day his stepdaughter disappeared there. And nothing at all about Melvin Ellis. But I figured it was enough to get Lincoln Connor's interest.

I was right.

"I don't have enough substantial criminal evidence to subpoena anyone or force them to talk. And Bruce Aiken or Valerie Claymore aren't going to voluntarily tell me anything. Neither is Muzzy Malone. That's where you come in. If you could put some of this on the air – not making any allegations, simply stating the facts – it could shake something loose. What do you think?"

Connor nodded. "I can work with that."

"That's what I was hoping."

"Do you think it has anything to do with the girl's disappearance?"

"I don't know. But this might help us find out. It will be like throwing a rock in a pond to see where the ripples go. Let's you and me make some ripples here."

"Okay, but won't this be easy to trace back to you? People will figure you leaked this information to me. That could cause you problems. Aren't you afraid of that?"

"I'm telling this all to the FBI and State Police too. The FBI is based in Boston, like you. And the State Police are on the mainland. So, I'm hoping people will figure that's where you got your tip from. A source from the FBI or State Police, not some little town detective on Martha's Vineyard. Maybe you could even describe your 'source' for the story with details that make it sound like it came from somewhere else other than the Cedar Cliffs Police Department."

Connor said that worked for him. We finished off our hot dogs, and I asked him if he wanted to go for a second round. What the hell? It was a nice summer's day, the hot dogs were good and it was nice to not be eating alone for a change. He said yes, and that he'd buy this time.

When he came back with the food, he brought up something else as well.

"If I'm doing this favor for you…"

"Well, it's not completely a favor. I mean you're getting a pretty good story out of it."

"Okay, it's kind of but not totally a favor. I'm fine with that. But I'd like to ask you to do something for me in return."

"What?"

"Tell me about you."

"Why do you want to know?"

"Like I said, I'm interested in your background."

"You know all about me. Big city cop gets tired and stressed by the New York pressure, comes back to the quiet little island where she was born to be a small-town cop. That's the story."

"No, I want the real story. I want to know everything."

"So, you can put it on the air for another exclusive?"

"Not for a TV story. Totally off the record. Just you and me talking."

"I'm not sure I can trust a hotshot reporter like you to keep anything I say off the record."

"I give you my word. Nothing public. I'd really like to know more about Abby Pearce. About the death of your partner. About your drinking. About your move back here. I'd like to hear that story."

I put my hot dog down on the bench where we were sitting. Suddenly it didn't taste so good. I took a sip of the root beer I was drinking and looked out at a cruiser that was pulling out of the marina and headed for the open sea. Sometimes I sat there and watched the boats go out and wished I was on one of them.

So, I could make my way up past the Cape, along the shoreline of New Hampshire and Maine, maybe all the way to Nova Scotia. Or head south to Florida and the Keys or the Caribbean while all my cares and worries melted away in the hot sun. But, of course, that was all a fantasy. Just like it had been a fantasy when I thought I could run away from my problems by coming back here from New York City.

I still carried all my emotional baggage with me, wherever I was.

"Talk to me about Tommy Ferraro," Lincoln Connor said to me.

I hadn't spoken to anyone about Tommy Ferraro in months.

Maybe it was time.

And so that's what I did…

CHAPTER 32

"I was assigned to the Chelsea stationhouse on West 19th Street as a homicide detective. Tommy was my partner. A good cop. A good guy. About forty, had a wife and two kids, lived out on Long Island – Hicksville, I think the town was. I went out there for dinner a couple of times with him and his wife. A real nice family.

"One night, Tommy and I are in the car and we hear this call for a burglary at a sporting goods store on West 22nd Street. The store owner has been shot and killed – and the gunman fled with money he took from the cash register. Nothing too unusual there for us on the homicide beat. We answered plenty of calls like that all the time. And it all seemed very routine at first.

"The uniformed cops at the scene had already interviewed witnesses who said the gunman had fled west and appeared to have ducked into a building near Eighth Avenue. Tommy and I went down there to check it out. Well, when we get there everything's all dark. No sign of anyone inside or out. We couldn't tell if it was an apartment building or office building or warehouse or what. But we knew the killer was probably in there.

"I radioed back to the scene requesting backup for us to go in. But Tommy didn't want to wait until they got there. He said he wouldn't actually go inside until the backup arrived, but wanted to check out the outside perimeter to figure out the best way to handle it. He told me to wait next to our car, and cover him from there in case anything went wrong.

"Tommy's about halfway from the car to the front of the building when I spot something coming out of a window. I thought I saw the glint of gun metal, but I wasn't sure. I had a split-second decision to make. Did I assume it was a gunman and open fire to protect Tommy, who was standing in the open? But what if it was just someone sticking their head out to see what was happening? That's every cop's nightmare. You've got less than a second to make a life-and-death decision."

"And you…?"

"I didn't shoot. I held my fire."

"The guy in the window did have a gun," Connor said softly.

I nodded.

"He opened up and cut Tommy down before he knew what was happening. Tommy never had a chance. Then the guy pegged some rounds toward the car where I was. I fired back, but it was too late. He managed to get on the fire escape, climb up to the roof and get away. They caught him about a week later."

"And your partner?"

"He died. Right there in the street."

"They shouldn't have blamed you for that. You had a decision to make. Other cops probably would have held their fire too until they were sure. No one wants to take a chance on shooting an innocent civilian."

"True. But in my case it was something more. First, I'm a woman. And no matter how many strides women have taken in recent years, there's still a lot of men on the police force who don't feel comfortable working with women. They're always ready to show we can't be counted on in a crisis. But, even more than that, there was my drinking. A lot of people knew about it by then."

"Had you been drinking that night?"

I shook my head.

"But the NYPD decided to hold a departmental hearing into my actions. There was a lot of testimony about my drinking. Were my reflexes slowed down in any way by it? Was my judgement impaired? In short, would Tommy still be alive today if I weren't an alcoholic?"

"What did they decide?"

"That there was no wrongdoing on my part. That there was no connection between my drinking and what happened that night. That I had done the best I could under difficult circumstances – and that Tommy Ferraro's death was unavoidable. The panel of judges said they were certain of that beyond a doubt."

"They exonerated you. Then what's the problem? If they say they're sure…"

"I wasn't sure," I said quietly. "Can you understand that?"

He didn't say anything.

"I had to ask myself the same questions the members of that panel did, and I wasn't so certain about the answers. Had all the alcohol dulled my reflexes? Would I have responded a second faster if I had been in top physical condition? Would Tommy still be alive today?" I paused for a second. "I honestly don't know. And that's something I have to live with forever."

"And that's why you decided to leave the NYPD and come back to Martha's Vineyard?" he asked.

Should I tell him the rest?

About how bad my drinking got. How it was the kind of drinking where from the minute you got up to the minute you went to bed, you thought about nothing else. The kind of drinking where there were mornings you didn't remember the night before. The mornings where I woke up with my hands trembling, my body aching, and feeling like I wanted to die. But I'd still want another drink.

About the pleading and the fights and finally the end of my marriage to Zach because he couldn't live with me anymore.

About my father dying and my mother selling the house where I grew up to move to an assisted living facility – which resurrected so many demons from my past.

"There were a lot of reasons," I finally said. "I just thought it was a good thing for me to do, to get away from everything that happened in New York City."

"Well, I'm glad you told me the whole story." Lincoln Connor smiled.

It wasn't the whole story.

Not by a long shot.

But Lincoln Connor didn't need to know any more about me.

CHAPTER 33

He broke the Ronald Claymore story that night on Channel 6's eleven o'clock news.

I watched it at home. Lincoln Connor had tipped me off after our lunch that he was going to do it on the eleven p.m. broadcast. I worked at the station until ten, putting in another long day searching for Samantha Claymore. But I left work before Connor went on the air. I figured if this blew up in my face, I was better off somewhere else when it happened.

I was lying in bed, eating some pizza I'd picked up before driving home, watching him on TV. Oscar was with me, but I think he was more interested in the pizza I was eating than Lincoln Connor.

"Fascinating new details have emerged in the search for cosmetics heiress Samantha Claymore on Martha's Vineyard," Connor was saying. "Not about the location of the sixteen-year-old herself, but about some of the tragic and mysterious Claymore family history leading up to the girl's disappearance a week ago.

"Five years ago, Ronald Claymore – founder and owner of Claymore Cosmetics and father of Samantha – died in a boating accident in the waters off of Cedar Cliffs. Eleven-year-old Samantha Claymore was also on that boat but she survived the tragedy.

"Soon afterward, Claymore's wife Valerie had him declared dead and remarried. Her new husband, Bruce Aiken, now has the man who piloted Ronald Claymore's doomed boat working for him, even though this man, Muzzy Malone, has a long criminal record. Samantha Claymore, according to friends, had been asking questions about her father's death – and the subsequent investigation – in the days before she disappeared.

"What does all this have to do with the search for Samantha Claymore? Maybe nothing. But it is an intriguing series of circumstances that I'm told law enforcement are looking into closely for potential leads on Samantha herself.

"Stay tuned for more on Ronald Claymore's fatal boat trip…"

By the time the broadcast was over, my phone was blowing up with calls.

The first came from Peter Randall, Cedar Cliffs mayor.

"What's going on?" he asked. "Is this the same stuff you were telling me about pursuing the other day? The stuff Wilhelm wasn't interested in? How did this reporter get ahold of this information?"

"Oh, you know the media," I said. "They always find a source. I have no idea who that might be though…"

"Yeah, right," he grunted. "Do me a favor and drop the 'I have no idea how this could have happened' shtick. You're smart, Pearce. You had a reason for what you did. You leaked some potentially explosive information on purpose. Right? I figure you're hoping it might shake something loose about Samantha."

"That sure would be nice," I told him.

"Well, let me know if you find out something about the girl."

Valerie Claymore called too. She was very upset. Wanted to know how information about her ex-husband's death got in the hands of a TV reporter. She said it made it seem like she had done something wrong getting remarried so quickly. And that law enforcement – maybe even me – thought she might have something to do with her daughter's disappearance.

I assured her that was not the case, even though I wasn't totally sure. Mostly, I let her talk. I'd discovered that was the best way to deal with Valerie Claymore and her various moods.

At one point, she told me that her husband Bruce Aiken was so upset by the broadcast that he had stormed out of the house and was flying back to New York City tonight. Which was interesting. Of course, we could always track him down in New York if we needed to. But it would make it more difficult to question him.

And then, of course, there was the call I was really expecting: one from Chief Wilhelm.

"Ronald Claymore's death was an accident, pure and simple," he said. "I worked that case myself. Why would the media suddenly start asking questions? What are they trying to do to me? Do you have any idea how this reporter could have found out about Ronald Claymore's case? We agreed this wasn't something we wanted to go public with at the moment. But now we have to. Because it's out there, dammit!"

He didn't seem to suspect me, and I pushed the idea further by suggesting the leak came from the state troopers or FBI workers we'd consulted on the case.

"They probably talked to a lot of the same people I did. So, they got the same information. They must have decided for whatever reason to tell the press about it."

I wasn't completely sure he believed me.

But he had no proof that I had anything to do with the leak.

We talked about what was going to happen next.

"We're going to get a lot of questions about this," he said. "We'll have to hold another press conference tomorrow. I want you there. Got it?"

I said that was fine with me.

Because I knew there weren't many answers I could give to the press. I wasn't on the force five years ago when Ronald Claymore died. Wilhelm was though. And he was the man who'd handled the investigation and ruled it an accident. So, he was the one the media was going to be demanding answers from.

"I love it when a plan comes together," I said to Oscar after I hung up the phone.

Oscar was still eying my pizza intensely. So, after I took a big bite of the slice in my hand, I gave him a small piece. He wolfed it down quickly. I'm never sure if it's good to feed your dog rich foods like pizza. But then again I'm never sure if it's good for people like me to eat rich foods either. But, what the hell, it was good pizza – and I was enjoying it. No reason Oscar shouldn't too.

The two of us sat there eating pizza until it was gone.

Then I fell asleep.

Yep, it had been a good night.

I'd thrown a rock into the pond, just like I wanted, to make some ripples in the water.

Hoping something would break very soon.

And it did.

CHAPTER 34

On the ninth day after Samantha Claymore's disappearance, one of the search teams found something: a pink plastic sandal half-buried in a sand dune on Island State Beach off of Beach Road.

It was the same road Samantha had been riding her bike on to Edgartown when she was last seen.

I called Mrs. Claymore to ask if her daughter had been wearing pink plastic sandals that day. She didn't remember. I asked if Samantha owned a pair of pink plastic sandals. She thought she might, but she wasn't sure.

Yep, they really had a close mother-daughter relationship.

I took the sandal from the search team, put it into an evidence container and drove with it to Mrs. Claymore's house. When she saw the sandal, she did remember it. Samantha had a pair like this, she told me. When I asked her to check and see if they were in Samantha's closet, she came back and told me they weren't. So, Samantha must have been wearing them when she left on the bike trip.

"What does this mean, Detective Pearce?"

"We can't be sure."

"But if she lost the sandal, something bad could have happened to her at that spot."

"There's no sign of anything besides the sandal, Mrs. Claymore. No blood, no sign of violence. Nothing but the sandal."

I didn't say it out loud, but I thought about how there was also no sign of a body there.

That was a good thing.

As long as we didn't find Samantha Claymore's body, there was hope that she was still alive.

But the missing sandal was a bad sign, no question about it, even if I didn't want to convey that to Mrs. Claymore.

And it raised a lot of questions.

The biggest question was why Samantha's sandal was left in this location and her bike left in Edgartown. The location of the beach with the sandal was midway between Cedar Cliffs and Edgartown – at least two miles from the bike rack in Edgartown.

That didn't make sense.

I said this to Mrs. Claymore.

"Maybe the sandal fell off while she was riding," she said hopefully.

"That's possible, I suppose."

"It got buried in the sand, and she couldn't find it. So she slipped out of the other sandal, and walked around barefoot when she got to Edgartown. Samantha loved to walk barefoot. She did it all the time. It could have happened that way."

"Then what happened to the other sandal?" I asked.

"I guess she would have put it in the basket of her bike."

"Except it wasn't there when we found the bike."

"Maybe she put it in her bag and took it with her after she parked the bike. What do you think about that?"

"I guess we won't know for sure until we find Samantha and can ask her about it," I said, trying to put this latest development in the most positive light that I could.

But even Valerie Claymore wasn't buying that.

She knew, like I did, that there were a lot of reasons Samantha's sandal could have wound up in that sand dune.

All of them bad.

Mrs. Claymore started to cry. I wasn't sure if these were real tears or another performance like she put on at the press conference.

But I didn't stay around to find out. I took Samantha's pink sandal, put it back into the evidence container, carried it out to my car and drove to the Island State Beach site again. Valerie Claymore was still crying when I left.

Back at the site, the search teams were going over every inch of the area, looking for anything at all. Digging up sand, looking through the long grass and bushes, interviewing beachgoers and motorists passing by in the hopes one of them might have been here that day and seen something that could help us. But the team turned up nothing.

Samantha Claymore's pink sandal was the only clue we found about whatever happened to her.

It wasn't much of a clue.

But it was the only one we had.

Except for the video.

And that's when it hit me. The video. I knew there was something about the video of Samantha Claymore window-shopping in Edgartown that bothered me. Now I knew why.

I called Dave Bowers and asked him to set up the video for me to watch again. I said I was driving back to the station and would be there in ten minutes.

"You want to watch the video again?"

"I need to check something on it."

"C'mon, Abby, we must have watched that video a hundred times already," Bowers pointed out.

"So, let's go for a hundred and one."

"What are you looking for?"

"I'll know when I see the video."

"Is this about the sandal the search team found in the dune on the road to Edgartown?"

"I think it might be."

"What's the connection? I don't see it."

"If Samantha Claymore lost her sandal on the way to Edgartown, what was she wearing on her feet in that video after she got here?"

CHAPTER 35

Yes, like Dave Bowers had said, I'd watched the video – the last glimpse we had of Samantha Claymore before she disappeared – maybe a hundred times already.

But watching it now I saw things I hadn't seen before.

It started the same way. An image on screen of a small mini-mall hallway off of Main Street in Edgartown.

The video showed a few random people walking by, and then Samantha came onto the screen. I could see clearly now – she was wearing a pair of white flip-flop beach sandals.

Not pink sandals.

This time, I also noticed that she had very specifically – almost intentionally – held up her left hand with the ring from her father on it to the camera. Making it so conspicuous on screen that you couldn't help but notice it.

Then there was the T-shirt which said "Hi, I'm Sam" on the back. She had seemingly kept that pointed in the direction of the security camera for the entire time she was on screen.

I realized too that we never got a clear view of her face on camera. Only glimpses of it from the side. It sure looked like Samantha Claymore, especially with the strawberry blonde hair. But then I noticed something dark at the bottom of her hair.

"Look at the hair," I said to Bowers.

"Strawberry blonde. Same as we saw in the picture."

"Can you get any closer in on the hair?"

"Why?"

"Look at that patch of hair near her neck. There's something blackish there."

When he got it closer, it was what I thought I'd seen. Dark hair. Protruding out from all the blonde.

"You think she dyed her hair?"

"Or maybe it's a blonde wig."

"Why would a sixteen-year-old girl wear a wig?"

Then there was the issue of the sandals. She was wearing a pair of white flip-flop sandals in the video. Not pink. They weren't even the same style as the pink sandal we'd just found in the dune.

So how did Samantha Claymore lose a pink sandal on her bike ride to Edgartown – and then show up on this video an hour or two later wearing white sandals?

There were three possibilities I could think of.

One, she had two pairs of sandals with her. She lost the pink sandal on the bike ride to Edgartown somehow, and then put on her second pair – the white sandals – when she got there.

Two, she went barefoot when she got to Edgartown, like her mother had suggested. Then she went into a store and bought the white sandals, the ones in the video. Of course, there was no evidence anywhere that she had made a purchase, but it could have happened that way.

Three, she lost the pink sandal on a previous bike ride along Beach Road. She simply never told her mother about it. The pink sandal we found wasn't from the day she disappeared, but from some earlier time.

All three were possible explanations for the white sandals she was wearing in the video.

But all of them seemed unlikely to me.

Because I had come up with another explanation.

"Do you realize we never get a full look at her face?" I said to Bowers. "That's always bothered me about this video. I mean it sort of looks like her from the side. The facial features are basically the same. And the blonde hair looks like hers. Plus, there's the T-shirt and the ring. It's easy to jump to the conclusion this is Samantha Claymore."

Bowers realized what I was saying.

"Do you think it isn't her we're looking at on this video?"

"I think it's someone who tried to look like Samantha Claymore. But they didn't count on the switch in sandals after she lost one on the bike ride to Edgartown."

Bowers stared at the picture on the screen again.

"It looks like Samantha Claymore to me," he said. "Even from the facial features."

"It does. But it could also be someone else who looked similar to Samantha. Especially if that person was wearing a blonde wig and Samantha's T-shirt and ring."

"Do you know who she is then?"

"I think I do."

I had noticed it the first time I met her.

I'd told her she looked a lot like Samantha. She laughed and said sometimes people even thought they were sisters.

The day she'd served me an ice cream cone.

"Who is she?" Bowers asked.

"Samantha Claymore's best friend," I said. "Bridget Feckanin."

CHAPTER 36

Bridget Feckanin was not at her job in the Ice Cream Emporium in Cedar Cliffs.

The girl on duty told us she'd been called in as a replacement for Bridget who hadn't shown up for her shift that day. Her manager said she'd missed her last shift too.

Bridget's manager gave us her home address – and Teena and I drove out there to see her.

I wasn't happy with Bridget Feckanin. I'd suspected she was holding something back from me when I interviewed her about Samantha Claymore, but now I saw just how big the secrets she'd been hiding really were.

"I don't get it," I said to Teena in the car. "Why would she do something like this? Posing as Samantha? Why pull off this kind of a stunt?"

"Seems pretty obvious. The two of them – Samantha and Bridget – did this together. Deliberately made that video so we'd think we knew what happened to Samantha in Edgartown that afternoon, even though she wasn't there. Which means maybe Samantha wasn't snatched by someone at all. This is all simply some hoax the two of them put together. All of it. Samantha's disappearance, the ransom note, the security video. Just two kids playing a sick joke."

"I think it's more than that," I said. "Maybe that's how it started out. As a prank. But I think things are out of control now. And they are in danger. Both of them. We need to find them, and quickly."

"You don't think she'll be at home?"

"Do you?"

"Probably not."

"The missing shifts at work this week aren't a good sign."

"But why would she disappear?"

"To avoid answering our questions."

"Except she had no way of knowing we found out about the video. As far as she knew, we still thought it was Samantha Claymore on the video. And that's only if we'd even found the video. So why stop showing up for her job at the ice cream parlor?"

"That's something we'll have to find out from Bridget Feckanin."

"If we can find her."

"Well, there is that…"

Teena shook her head in frustration.

"You're right, Pearce," she said. "I don't get it either."

Bridget Feckanin was not home when we got to the quiet street between Cedar Cliffs and Vineyard Haven where she lived.

Which was not surprising.

But her mother's reaction was.

"Thank God you're here," she said. "I was just about to call the police. My daughter is missing. I have no idea where she is."

"How long has Bridget been gone?" I asked.

"I haven't seen her for two days."

"And you're just thinking about calling us now?" Teena asked, echoing my own thoughts.

I wasn't a mother, and so I didn't have a handle on what parenting was like in today's world. But it did seem to me that a sixteen-year-old girl gone for at least forty-eight hours should sound an alarm that something might be wrong.

"She was supposed to be staying at a friend's house. I asked her to text and call me, but Bridget's a very independent girl. It didn't surprise me that I hadn't heard from her."

"What made you so concerned just now?"

"Her boss called from the ice cream parlor. Said she hadn't been there in two days. That didn't make sense to me. She loved that job, it was her first summer employment – and she talked about it all the time. Then her boss said that the police had been there looking to ask her some questions. I called her friend's house. But Bridget wasn't there. Not only that, she'd never even been there. Or made any plans to spend the past two with them. So where could she be?"

Teena and I tried to reassure Mrs. Feckanin that everything was going to be all right, but I don't think she believed us. We didn't believe us either. Two teenage girls – best friends, no less – both missing on Martha's Vineyard within days of each other. Something was going on here. And, whatever it turned out to be, it wasn't good.

We called in a missing person's report on Bridget Feckanin, and also alerted Samantha Claymore's search teams to the fact we were now looking for two missing teenage girls. Mrs. Feckanin provided us with a headshot of Bridget – taken for her high school yearbook – and we sent copies out to everyone.

She looked young and happy in the picture, just like she'd been that day we met at the ice cream place. But she'd been hiding secrets from me then, and she was still hiding those secrets now. What the hell were they? And what did they have to do with Samantha Claymore?

There were two other children in the house, Mrs. Feckanin told me. A boy eleven, and a girl nine. We interviewed both of them in hopes their sister had told them something about where she was going. But neither of them knew anything. They were so much younger that Bridget never shared much personal stuff with them, Mrs. Feckanin explained.

Mr. Feckanin was in Boston for a business meeting, so we spoke to him on the phone. He couldn't tell us anything more, but said he was on his way back and would be home in a few hours. He asked us to call him if there was any news at all about Bridget. I promised I would. But I hoped that if there was any news, it wouldn't be the kind of news he didn't want to hear.

Before we left, we searched Bridget's room.

On Bridget's computer, I discovered that she had downloaded a series of files. All about a news item that had happened several years ago. That of the death of Ronald Claymore and the rescue of the then eleven-year-old Samantha from the shore.

There was also an email to Eddie Haver. Samantha's boyfriend. The email was dated two days earlier. Right before Bridget disappeared. It said: "I'll call you later and tell you everything. About Samantha, about me… all of it."

CHAPTER 37

"Where is Bridget Feckanin?" Teena demanded to know from Eddie Haver.

"I don't know!"

"What about Samantha Claymore?"

"I don't know that either."

We were in an interview room at the Cedar Cliffs police station. We'd picked Haver up from his house earlier, and drove him to the station for questioning.

The idea was to scare him into talking. And so far, Teena was doing her best to achieve that.

Eddie Haver sure looked scared. There was an attorney in the room with him, but it was someone local who didn't seem to know much about criminal law. The attorney looked scared too. Teena – all six foot of her, dressed in her customary leather vest and cowboy boots – towered over the diminutive Eddie Haver as she grilled him. Hell, I even found her a bit scary.

"When is the last time you were in touch with Bridget?"

"Bridget? I don't know… I haven't heard from her in a while."

"Wrong answer!"

Teena slammed down a printout of the email exchange she'd taken off Bridget Feckanin's computer. The one that said she was going to tell Eddie Haver everything that was going on.

"Do you want to answer my question again?"

The kid stared at the printout in front of him.

"Let me explain the situation you're in right now, Eddie," Teena told him. "We can hold you indefinitely in custody as a material witness. We can also hit you with a number of criminal charges, including obstruction of justice. Maybe even being an accomplice to a kidnapping. And, if Samantha or Bridget turn up dead, you'll be a suspect in that too. Am I getting through to you, Eddie? Do you want to go to jail?"

I intervened at this point and asked Teena if I could talk to her outside. I made it sound as if I was concerned she was out of control.

"Nice job in there," I said to her once we were outside the interrogation room and had closed the door behind us.

"Thank you. I thought I was pretty good too."

"Let me take it from here."

"Good cop, bad cop, right?"

"Right."

It was a plan we'd worked out beforehand to see if we could get Haver to spill everything he knew.

"And now you're going to be the good cop," Teena said.

"I'll do my best to calm him down."

"You know, I could have played the good cop too."

"Yes, but you do bad cop so well."

"Okay, smartass, now it's up to you. You go in there and get that kid to tell us what he knows. You're supposed to be the hotshot detective. Let's see what they taught you down in New York City."

When I went back into the interrogation room, Haver and the attorney looked relieved to see it was only me, not Teena.

"Look," I said, "I'm the lead detective on this case. And I don't want to put you in jail. If you cooperate and tell me everything you know – I think I can get you out of here and back home in time for dinner. What do you say?"

Eddie Haver looked at his attorney. The attorney nodded. First to Haver, then to me. There was a quick conference between the two of them, and then the attorney said, "My client will assist you in any way that he can."

I called out to Meg that we needed someone to take his official statement. And then Haver started talking:

"I don't know anything about what happened to Sam or Bridget. I really don't. I did know, because Bridget told me after she sent that email, about her dressing up as Sam that day in Edgartown. But she made me promise not to tell anyone. She said it would be dangerous for Sam if I did. And for her too. I was only trying to protect them both.

"I've known Bridget for a long time, from growing up here. First in grade school, then middle school and now high school. We're good friends, Bridget and I. Nothing romantic though. More like brother and sister. We talk a lot. She was the one who introduced me and Sam to each other, and we all spent time together. Until this thing happened."

I didn't interrupt. I let him tell his story. I learned a long time ago that was the best way to get information from people. Let them tell their story at their own pace. Then go back and ask questions to fill in the missing pieces later on.

"All I know is that Sam was obsessed in those last few days with the death of her father – her real father, she called him – five years ago. I think she'd repressed a lot of what happened that day on the water. But coming back to Martha's Vineyard for the first time since it happened seemed to jog some memories loose. Anyway, she said she knew that everything on the boat didn't happen the way everyone always said it did."

"Do you know what it was that she found out about her father's death?"

"Not really."

"Last time we talked, you said she believed he'd been murdered."

"That's what I thought at the time."

"And now?"

"That's what Bridget talked about when she called me two days ago, right before she disappeared. She didn't say anything about going anywhere. But she did say she had the thing about Sam's father all wrong. That Sam didn't think he was murdered anymore."

"So she accepted that he died in the accident?"

"No."

"Well, if it wasn't murder and it wasn't an accident, what did she think happened to him?"

"Sam thought that her father was still alive."

CHAPTER 38

In the midst of all this, there was still something else nagging at me. I couldn't forget about those three missing girl cases I'd had Meg look up for me.

There was no reason to think there could be a connection between them and whatever happened to Samantha Claymore. I mean, one appeared to be a suicide – and the other two girls returned home safely, according to the information in the files. But I still had this uneasy feeling in my stomach.

Call it a detective's instinct – I wanted to know more about these three girls.

I looked at the three files again:

RUTHIE KOLTON

CARRIE LANG

LINDA ELLISON

Ruthie Kolton had been a troubled seventeen-year-old with run-ins with the law and school officials. Her clothes, purse and phone were found stacked on the beach near Gay Head – authorities decided she simply walked out into the ocean to commit suicide.

Ruthie Kolton's parents didn't have much to say about their departed daughter when I went to see them. Like everyone else, they talked about her troubles and all the rest of the problems they'd had with her. They said her death – which they had no reason to think was anything besides a suicide – seemed inevitable to them.

They said there was nothing they could have done to save her, she was a really messed-up kid.

Ruthie's younger sister, Becky, was there while we talked. I wondered if her parents felt the same way about her. She didn't say much, just listened until I left. The bottom line for me was that Ruthie Kolton was pretty much a dead end.

Unfortunately, Carrie Lang and her family had left the island years ago, and I couldn't find a forwarding address.

But Linda Ellison and her parents were still around.

"Ms. Ellison, this is Detective Abby Pearce with the Cedar Cliffs Police Department," I said when I got her on the phone. "I'm investigating the disappearance of a teenage girl on the island. I wondered if I could talk to you and your daughter about her experience a few years ago."

"What does my daughter have to do with this girl?"

"It might help the ongoing case if I heard about what happened to your daughter and determined whether there are any similarities that could—"

"You want to know more about what happened to my daughter? Okay, how's this? A week after she got home, she took an overdose of sleeping pills."

"Is she…?"

"Dead? No, she survived."

"Was it an accidental overdose?"

"Hardly. After that, she tried to slit her wrists. She's hospitalized now and getting treatment. We're just trying to help her forget the nightmares of what she went through. I am not going to allow you to bring up those horrible memories for her all over again."

"Could you tell me any more about what these horrible experiences were?"

"Do you have a subpoena or warrant forcing me to talk to you?"

"No," I said slowly.

"Well, you'll need to get one if you want to talk to me or my daughter. And I'll fight you every step of the way."

"Ms. Ellison…"

"Goodbye."

She hung up.

CHAPTER 39

I was at home trying to figure out what to make myself for dinner when my cell phone rang. I looked down at the number. It was Lincoln Connor.

The Samantha Claymore story had exploded all over the media again with the disappearance of her best friend Bridget – and I wondered if there'd been a break in the case I didn't know about yet.

"Hi," I said. "Is something happening on the missing girls?"

"Nah, nothing like that. I stopped by the station to see if you were there. They said you'd gone home for the night. You live out near Chilmark, right? I'm driving out that way now to pick up something from a source. It shouldn't take long. I thought maybe we could get together for a meal afterward? A real meal this time."

I thought about another night of eating alone and falling asleep in front of the TV with only Oscar for company. Don't get me wrong, Oscar is great company. But a man might be even better entertainment. Even if it was a man like Lincoln Connor that I didn't totally trust. On the other hand, he was damn good looking. Not to mention charming.

"Sure, stop by – we can find some place to eat around here," I said, and gave him directions to get to my house.

Oscar raced to the door when the doorbell rang. The minute I opened it, he jumped onto Lincoln Connor, happily wagging his tail and licking his face. Lincoln reached down and petted him.

"He likes you," I said.

"Dogs have good instincts."

"Actually, Oscar likes everyone."

"He's always this happy?"

"It's because I just told him a joke."

"You tell jokes to your dog?"

"Sure. Watch this."

I leaned down and looked Oscar in the eye.

"Guy goes into a doctor's office and complains he can't hear. The doctor tells him to get a hearing aid. 'They work great – I wear one myself,' the doctor says. 'What kind is it?' the guy asks. The doctor looks at his watch. 'Ten minutes after four.'"

I laughed uproariously.

And Oscar licked me frantically.

"If you tell a joke to a dog, it makes him happy," I explained. "He has no idea what you're saying. But the way you tell it makes him react the way he does."

"You tell your dog a lot of jokes?"

"I talk to him all the time."

"You talk to your dog?"

"Sure, I have a lot of conversations with Oscar."

"Except you're the only one doing the talking – he can't answer back."

"Those are the best kind of conversations to have."

A short time later, we were at a nearby restaurant called Menemsha Galley, eating hamburgers and fries by the water. He was drinking a beer. I had Diet Coke. Normally I would have really wanted a drink in this kind of situation. But I was too focused on Samantha Claymore – and now Bridget Feckanin – to think about much else. Even drinking.

We talked about our careers, our personal lives. I told him about my divorce, he said he'd never been married but had come close a few times. He told me about some of the big stories he'd covered as a Boston TV reporter. Murders. Terrorist attacks. Political scandals.

He also asked me more about my career with the NYPD. "You closed a lot of high-profile cases there, didn't you? Once, you stopped a bank robbery on your own and saved everyone inside. Another time you talked a suicidal woman down from jumping off the observational deck of the Empire State Building."

"A lot of it was simply being in the right place at the right time. And then getting lucky. Like that bank robbery. I had just walked in there to cash a check when I saw what was going on. I was in plain clothes. There were three guys in there with guns – they assumed I was another customer. I had a big advantage there. They'd already shot the security guard, who was wounded on the floor. I couldn't take a chance they'd hurt more people. So, I pulled out my gun and shot the leader. The other two were so stunned I was able to get the drop on them too. It became a media sensation. 'Cop single-handedly stops robbery.' But any officer would have done the same thing I did that day. I didn't have a lot of choice."

"It was still courageous."

"As for the woman on the Empire State Building, there was a lot of luck with that too. It turned out she was an alcoholic. She'd lost her job, her husband and her family because of it. She felt there was no way she could go on. When I told her I was an alcoholic too, well... I guess we formed a kind of bond. I was able to get her down off that ledge, into a rehab and help her try to put her life together again. Last time I talked with her – yes, I still keep in touch – she was doing pretty well."

I took a sip of my Diet Coke.

"The case that I'm proudest of though was Daisy Carmichael. Do you remember her?"

"The little girl who got kidnapped?"

I nodded.

"She was six years old. Lived in Soho, Manhattan with her mother and father. One day they walked her to the bus stop to catch the school bus. But she never made it to school. She disappeared. For days, there was a big search for her – but no one turned up anything.

"The only lead we had was someone seeing a man in a black van sitting near the bus stop that morning. So, we tried to track him down. But do you know how many black vans are registered to people in New York City? My captain eventually told me to give up on it and move on to other cases. But I didn't, I couldn't. I kept looking for the driver of that black van."

"How many people did you talk to?"

"A lot. I knocked on so many doors, checked out so many black vans. It seemed hopeless."

"But you found the right one?"

"The break in the case came when I talked to a guy who didn't even own his van anymore, he'd sold it a few months before. I was about to cross him off the list when I asked who he'd sold it to. He said he'd sold it to his brother-in-law. Weird guy, he told me. Always talking about little girls."

"Jesus!"

"Yeah. When I talked to the brother-in-law, I could tell by his responses he was the one. I got him to give up the information on the girl's location. She was in an abandoned warehouse. That's where he'd been keeping her. It turned out he was a real psycho. Kept saying how pretty she was, and how he wasn't going to hurt her – he just wanted to wait until she was old enough to marry him. Anyway, we got her home safely. There were a lot of emotional scars, of course, but she's alive. That's the main thing."

Connor let out a low whistle of admiration. "That's amazing."

Eventually we came back to talking about Samantha Claymore and her best friend. The interview with Eddie Haver had complicated things, giving us more questions instead of answers about both Samantha and Bridget. When I'd pressed him on why Samantha thought her father was still alive, he brought up the roses someone had sent her for her sixteenth birthday. Earlier, he'd said he didn't know anything about the roses. But now – under pressure (and the threat that I'd bring Teena back in to question him) – he said Samantha had told Bridget her father knew how much she loved roses, and that this must have been some kind of message to her that he was alive. Still, it wasn't much to go on. And it didn't help explain what might have happened to Samantha and then Bridget.

I talked for a long time about everything we were doing to find the two girls.

"You take this really seriously, don't you?" Lincoln asked.

"Of course. It's the biggest missing person case – probably the biggest crime – in the history of this island."

"No, I don't mean just the part of it that's your job. You've taken this case really personally from the start. Almost like you knew the missing Claymore girl."

I sighed. He was right. I told him about how Samantha Claymore had been coming out of her "socially awkward" phase this summer. And how I identified with that because I'd gone through the same kind of experience growing up.

"I took out my high school yearbook the other night. I saw myself the way I was back then. It wasn't a pretty picture. I always felt so awkward, so different, so left out. I hated that feeling. Anyway, all those fears and insecurities came back again when I looked at that yearbook."

"You didn't feel you were attractive?"

"I wasn't."

"And now?"

"Now I think I look pretty good."

"Me too." He smiled. "So, you don't have this insecurity anymore?"

"The problem with feeling unattractive," I said, finishing off the rest of my soda, "is that it never goes away completely. Even if you become pretty, you still don't always feel pretty."

"Do you think those are the same kinds of emotions Samantha Claymore was feeling this summer?"

"I don't know, but I'd love to have the chance to ask her."

"Me too." He smiled again.

We'd taken his car, so he drove me home afterward. As he was walking me to the door, he stopped and kissed me. "That was fun," he said. "Can I come in for some coffee?"

"I don't think that's a good idea."

"Why not?"

"Because 'coming in for a coffee' is really just code for having sex, Lincoln. I've been around. I know how this works. And I'm not having sex with you."

"Okay. Good to know. But do you not find me attractive?"

"I'm a cop working on a case, and you're a journalist covering the case. There are standards for a law enforcement officer in this type of situation."

"Believe it or not, I have standards too. And a journalist is not supposed to have sex with a source. So – no sex until we find Samantha Claymore."

"That's a deal," I said.

He kissed me again.

I kissed him back.

I'm not sure what would have happened after that under normal circumstances.

But these weren't normal circumstances.

CHAPTER 40

Early next morning my phone began to ring.

I looked at the screen and saw the call was from Dave Bowers.

When I answered it, he gave me the news I'd been waiting for – and dreading at the same time.

"We've found a body out near Gay Head," Bowers said. "It's a young girl."

The body was at the bottom of one of the massive cliffs overlooking the ocean at Gay Head.

The breathtaking red clay cliffs had been formed millions of years ago and drew thousands of tourists each summer because of the spectacular ocean views from the top. There were walking trails along the beach and others that led all the way up to the top of the cliffs.

Every once in a while, there was an accident when someone fell or slipped on the sand at the cliff edge. Was that what had happened here? It was possible, I suppose, but I doubted it. Besides, what would a teenage girl be doing at the top of the cliffs by herself out in Gay Head?

Damn.

Gay Head again, I thought to myself as I drove out there. Lots of bad stuff sure had happened around Gay Head, not least those missing girl cases I'd read about in the files.

Just like something bad had happened to me out near Gay Head a long time ago.

The time I'd gone to the big house – the one owned by Melvin Ellis – when I was a teenage girl.

But I tried to put it all out of my mind and focus on what I'd been told by the people on the scene so far.

The body was spotted by a jogger on the beach lying on a ledge extending out from the cliff, about twenty-five feet above the ground. A helicopter was dispatched and from above the ledge was able to determine it was the body of a young girl. You couldn't see her face – it was covered with sand and rock from the fall – but the clothes and body shape identified her as female.

The position of the ledge meant that the only way she could have gotten there was from above. From the top of the cliffs. Instead of landing on the beach though, the body apparently hit the ledge first – and that's where the girl died.

Rescue crews were now attempting to hoist themselves up with ropes and other climbing equipment to retrieve the body.

As I drove up the road leading to the beach area, I saw a police car sitting at the entrance. Vic Hollister was inside.

"Do they know yet?" I asked him.

"Know what?"

"If it's Samantha Claymore or Bridget Feckanin?"

He looked baffled for a minute, until he realized what I was saying.

"Jesus, I don't know, Abby. They told me to maintain security out here. That's all I'm doing. I'm just doing my job. You'll have to ask Bowers. He's there with the rescue people now."

I liked Hollister, but he drove me crazy sometimes with his lack of initiative, curiosity or just plain energy as a police officer. All he wanted to do was work his shift and go home. I guess that's why he'd never advanced to a higher position even after all those years with the Cedar Cliffs Police Department.

Bowers filled me in on what he knew when I got to the scene. "We still don't know if it's Samantha Claymore or Bridget Feckanin. The rescue team is almost at the body now, then they'll bring it down. Probably in a few minutes."

I looked up at the cliffs high above us.

"Whoever she is, that's where she had to come from, huh?" I said to Bowers. "Way up there on top."

"Only way she could have wound up on that ledge."

"What do you think happened?"

"Offhand, I'd say there are three possibilities: One, she committed suicide by jumping; two, she accidentally fell; or three, someone pushed her."

I nodded.

"But which one was it?"

"Hey, you're the detective."

Yeah, I'm the detective.

I called Teena and she said she was going to jump in her car and head here too. They were getting ready to bring the body down now.

"Any idea who it is yet?" she asked. "Samantha or Bridget?"

"Or maybe some other teenage girl," I said, telling her about all of the similar cases I'd recently been through in the files.

"My God, that is scary."

"Yeah, I know."

I called Wilhelm too, of course. He said I should keep him updated and let him know as soon as there was an ID on the dead girl. But he didn't suggest coming to the scene, like Teena had done. Wilhelm was a lot like Hollister. Both of them had been on the force for a long time, but neither really handled big cases or went that extra mile to solve them.

Except Wilhelm also wasn't like Hollister.

He had handled a few major cases here.

In fact, he'd signed off on all three of the missing girl cases I'd researched.

Plus, he investigated – and ruled accidental – the death of Ronald Claymore.

What did that mean? I had no idea. But there was a part of me that didn't trust Wilhelm.

The rescue team was bringing the body down on a stretcher. I ran over to the spot where it would arrive just as Teena got on the scene. We waited there together until we could get a good look at the victim.

It was a teenage girl, all right.

A teenage girl we were looking for.

No question about it, the girl looked a lot like the picture of Samantha Claymore I'd been carrying around with me.

Except for the hair.

It wasn't strawberry blonde, like we'd seen on the security video from Edgartown. It was dark, curly hair. Just like the dark, curly hair I'd first seen at the ice cream parlor.

"It's Bridget Feckanin," I said.

CHAPTER 41

We were awaiting the results of the autopsy on Bridget Feckanin. Teena and I were sitting with Wilhelm in his office. Autopsy results can take anywhere from a few hours to a few weeks, depending on the circumstances of the death. In this case, I didn't expect it would take long. Everything seemed pretty cut and dried. But you never know with autopsies. Sometimes there are surprises.

"I hope this autopsy gives us some clue about what happened to her," I said.

"We know what happened to her," Wilhelm said. "She plunged off a cliff and landed five hundred feet below."

"But why?"

"Maybe she was depressed about her friend being gone. Or maybe she had something to do with it. We still don't know why she pretended to be Samantha Claymore on that security video from Edgartown. Maybe she felt guilty about whatever happened to her, and decided to kill herself."

"Or maybe someone pushed her off that cliff," Teena said.

"Who would do that?" Wilhelm asked.

"Maybe the same person who took Samantha Claymore," I said.

"That's all speculation. We need hard facts. What do we know so far from the scene?"

Teena took out her notebook and started reading from it.

"The body was badly bruised, presumably from the fall. No signs of any other injuries – like bullet wounds, stab marks or anything. All that points to a simple fall from a great height, which killed her. And she must have come from the top of that cliff. It's the only way she could have landed where she did on that ledge. We're actually lucky that happened. If she'd fallen only a short distance in a different direction, she could have landed in the ocean instead. Then we'd never have found the body.

"We located the spot where she went off the cliff. She left behind her purse and a phone and hat she was wearing. They were piled on the ground next to the edge where she must have put them before whatever happened to her happened. The ground was a bit messed up, with a lot of footprints nearby – presumably hers. Sure, that might mean someone else was there with her. But it could also be the result of her walking over to the edge back and forth several times before she jumped. Lots of suicidal people have second thoughts before they finally do it.

"There's also the possibility it could have been an accident. But that seems unlikely, given the fact she placed her phone and handbag and hat on the ground so neatly together. Also, what was she even doing up there? Gay Head is a long way from where she lived."

But not a long way from the Melvin Ellis' house, I thought to myself.

I remembered that the way Bridget had left her belongings on the ground was similar to what one of the other missing girls had done at Gay Head several years ago.

But I didn't say anything about that to Teena or Wilhelm.

Because they would want to know what the significance was.

And I had no idea what it all meant.

"Let's talk about Ronald Claymore," Teena said now. "Because we still haven't figured out how – or if – it has anything to do with what's going on now here."

"The Claymore boat accident has nothing to do with this," Wilhelm said. "It was a drowning, pure and simple. You're wasting everyone's time talking about this, both of you. We need to focus on the things happening now. How did Bridget Feckanin die? And where is Samantha Claymore?"

"Except that the Ronald Claymore controversy is out there – people are already talking about it because of that TV reporter," Teena pointed out. "I don't think we can ignore it."

"Well, let's make sure there are no more leaks to the press," Wilhelm said. "I don't know who tipped him off but we need to make sure it doesn't happen again. He's looking for a story, and he doesn't care how much trouble he causes for us to get it. You saw what he did to you at that press conference, Pearce – he tried to embarrass you. I don't have to tell you how careful we need to be. He cannot get any more information from our investigation. Right?"

"Absolutely," I said.

Teena gave me a look and – I thought – a quick smile.

I'd never told her that I leaked the Ronald Claymore story to Lincoln Connor.

But I'm sure she figured it out.

"What about the search parties out looking for Samantha Claymore?" Wilhelm asked.

"They're still out there," I said. "State troopers. Volunteers. Everyone on the island police forces that we can spare. We're going through beaches, woods, ponds and anywhere else you can think of looking for her. But this is a big island. There are a lot of places she could be. Dead or alive. Unless she left the island. Then it's a different ball game. But we have to assume she's here somewhere. So, we'll keep looking."

"How long can we do that?"

"As long as it takes."

My cell phone suddenly vibrated in my pocket. I took it out, looked down and saw I had a text from the medical examiner's office. *Call me, I have the autopsy results* it read.

I punched in the number, then listened as the medical examiner went through the details of what they knew about Bridget

Feckanin's death. Massive trauma injuries from the fall, bruises and numerous broken bones. But no sign of any injuries – gunshot or otherwise – that might have led to her death beforehand. Nothing from the autopsy that would help us understand why she went off that cliff.

"Pretty much as we expected," I said to the examiner when she was finished.

"Yeah, well I've got something else you weren't expecting."

"On the cause of death?"

"No, but we ran some further tests on the girl after we did the basic autopsy. In case we missed something. And damned if we didn't find something really interesting…"

"Okay," I said slowly.

"Bridget Feckanin was pregnant."

CHAPTER 42

It was nearly two weeks since Samantha Claymore had disappeared, and we were no closer to finding her than we were at the start.

And now the one lead we had in the case – her best friend, who had apparently posed as her in the last security video – was dead.

The fact that Bridget Feckanin was pregnant when she died – although intriguing – didn't tell us anything either. The medical examiner said she had been in the beginning stages of the pregnancy. She might not even have been aware of it yet. Or maybe she was, told the father – and he killed her to keep it a secret. Of course, if we ever did find a suspect in Bridget's murder we might be able to compare his DNA with the DNA of her unborn child. Still, that was all speculation, and I didn't have any idea where to go next on the case.

But, behind every dark cloud, they say there's a silver lining. Of course, someone also said – I'm not sure if it was the same person – that when it rains, it pours. I've never been sure which one was supposed to be the operative theory. I thought about that as I walked back to my desk after hearing the autopsy results.

I saw there was a voice mail from Zach on my phone. Zach. My ex-husband. "We need to talk," he said in his message. "Let's Zoom. It's been a long time since we've seen each other. I'll call you in an hour."

Things were looking up, I decided. It had been almost six months since I'd last seen Zach. Now we were going to talk again. And even see each other again. Even if it was only on Zoom. I fixed myself up a bit – then sat at my desk waiting for him to call. I didn't want to take a chance on anything going wrong. I rehearsed in my head what I was going to say to him.

First, I was going to quit being coy about my feelings. I'd tell him everything. How I'd quit drinking. How I was dealing with my problems. I'd tell him I wasn't the same person as back then in New York. This was the new, improved Abby Pearce. I'd tell him how much I missed him. It would be easy for me to say all these things, because they were true.

It was a little after 12:30 when I clicked on the Zoom link. Suddenly, there was Zach on the screen in front of me. I almost didn't recognize him at first. His hair was shorter. He was wearing a sports jacket and shirt I'd never seen before. And, most startling of all, he had no mustache. Zach always had a shaggy mustache when I was with him. But now it was gone. He was clean-shaven.

It's always strange talking to someone you used to be very close to, but aren't anymore. Things that seemed so casual before turn into a much bigger deal. I mean I knew this guy, but I also didn't know him. I didn't know what was happening with the state troopers, I didn't know what was happening in his life outside the job and – most of all – I didn't know what the hell happened to his mustache.

We sat there making small talk for a few minutes.

"I haven't had a drink in nearly six weeks," I said finally. "I know that probably doesn't sound like much, but it's kind of a big deal."

"That's great," Zach said.

"Yeah."

"Do you think…?"

"I can keep it up?"

"Sorry, it's none of my business."

"Sure, it is."

"Okay, do you think you can stay off the drink?"

"I can't easily answer that," I said. "Every day is a challenge. But I know I have to stop. And I'm not sure I ever understood that before. Everybody else always wanted me to stop. You, my friends, people at work. But it doesn't happen like that. The only person that matters is me. I have to do it for myself, not for anyone else. I know what's at stake for me right now, and that's why I'm not drinking."

I took a deep breath.

"Zach, I think I was very unfair to you. I created a situation in our relationship that made it impossible for you to continue. You were the innocent victim of my drinking. I'm sorry."

He shrugged. "I always thought I should have been able to stop you. God knows, I tried."

"I know you did. But the more you tried to stop me from drinking, the more you became the enemy. At least in my mind. It was a no-win situation. I'm sorry I put you through all of it."

Zach smiled. "We were really great together for a while, weren't we?"

"Yes, we were. But I always knew it wouldn't last."

"What?"

"Because of my drinking. We were so happy together, and I was sure I'd mess it up eventually with my drinking. Which is what I did."

"That's kind of fatalistic thinking," he said.

"I'm a pretty fatalistic person," I said. "I'm always prepared for the worst. Or at least I used to be."

"And now?"

"Now things are looking better."

"Why?"

"Hey, you and I are talking again together, aren't we? That's a step in the right direction. Who knows what this could lead to?"

He smiled, but it was a sad smile. That's when it suddenly dawned on me what was coming.

"I'm getting married," he said.

And not to me, I thought.

"Her name is Jill," Zach said. "She's a trooper with me. We've been going out for the past few months, and it's gotten serious. Anyway, we got engaged last week, and I thought I should tell you. And, since we can't meet up in person, I wanted to do it face to face over Zoom. I know this isn't easy, but we've always been honest with each other. I wanted to be honest with you about me and Jill."

I've had my heart broken a few times in my life. But it never gets any easier.

"Does Jill know that you're talking to me about this right now?"

"Of course."

"You told her?"

"I tell Jill everything."

Somehow I made it through the rest of the conversation, sitting there with a stupid smile pasted on my face as he told me about his new life. Most of the words were a blur. Zach did all the talking, I hardly said anything. But there was one question I had to ask him. One thing I needed to know.

"What happened to your mustache?" I asked.

"I got tired of it."

"After how long?"

"Sixteen years."

"And one morning you just wake up and shave it off?"

"Jill didn't like it. She said it was itchy."

"I always liked your mustache."

"I know, but…"

He didn't finish the thought. He didn't have to. It didn't matter what I thought anymore.

CHAPTER 43

"Did you really think you were going to get back together with him?" Teena asked me.

"No."

"Are you being completely honest?"

"Okay, yes."

"Yes, you are being honest? Or yes, you thought you and Zach would get back together?"

"Maybe," I said.

"Which one is it?"

"I'm not sure."

"What do you remember feeling?"

"I wanted us to try."

I needed to talk to someone about all this. I'd tried to reach Stan Larsen in California, but he didn't pick up the call. I just left a message asking him to call back.

Then I'd thought about Teena. A cop's best friend is supposed to be their partner. Tommy Ferraro had been my best friend back in New York, until I let him get killed on the street. Teena Morelli, for better or worse, was my partner now. So, I'd told her about Zach's engagement. I also told her about my dinner with Lincoln Connor.

"What are you looking for, Abby?" she asked when I was finished.

"I just want to be desired by someone."

"We all do."

"Well, it's been a long time since anyone desired me. I haven't intimately been with a man in a long time. But I'm actually not the kind of person who hates to be alone. I like being alone a lot of the time. When I was with Zach, I sometimes wished I could go to sleep without having to deal with someone else in my bed. But then, in the morning, there was always something comforting about Zach being there. I just like waking up next to someone. Does that make any sense at all?"

Teena nodded.

"You want to be wanted," she said.

"Something like that."

"Are you looking for something long-term with Lincoln Connor?"

I shrugged.

"From what I can tell, Lincoln's probably not the best choice for that."

"I know."

"But?"

"I think I want to see him again."

"Because of Zach?"

"I just want to wake up one morning with someone again."

We were sitting in a car outside Valerie Claymore's house. The car was unmarked and we'd pulled into a secluded spot so no one from inside the house could see us. We had another car, with Hollister and Bowers inside, at Bridget Feckanin's house. I wasn't sure what I hoped to accomplish here. But, even though we still had search parties out looking for any sign of Samantha, I still had the feeling that Valerie Claymore and her new husband were hiding secrets.

"What about you?" I asked Teena. "You never talk about your personal life. Did you ever find the right man to spend your life with?"

"Sure did. Married him too."

"Great."

"Yeah, it was a good marriage."

"Was?"

"Right. Nick was my lover, my best friend in the world, my soulmate. He was the perfect husband. Except for one thing. Nick only ever did one thing wrong. He died."

She said it casually, as if she was talking about someone she didn't know. But I could tell it was an act. Teena played the part of a tough woman well, but there was a lot of vulnerability hidden under that exterior. And that vulnerability was apparent now when she talked about her husband.

"I'm sorry. When did he die?"

"A few years ago. Right before I joined the Cedar Cliffs police force. In fact, that's why I joined the force. Nick and I had this business – an art and antiques place in Edgartown – where we sold paintings and trinkets and the like to tourists. We ran it together. It was fun then. But, after he was gone, it wasn't fun for me anymore. At that point, I wanted to do something more substantial, more important with my life. Something that helped make up for the emptiness I felt without Nick. So, I became a cop."

"How did your husband die?"

"Heart attack. It was all very sudden. He went out jogging on the beach one morning, I was organizing some stuff in the store. And he never came back again. They found him dead on the beach about a mile away."

Teena shook her head.

"You know what the worst part is? Maybe even worse than him being gone? It's that I never got to say goodbye. I was working in the store and he was just going out for a quick run. And the last conversation I remember having with him that day was about our storage closet. I'd been pestering him for weeks to clean it up, and he kept promising he would – but never had. That was what our last exchange was about. You know, you have hundreds of conversations with your spouse about all sorts of things. Most of them aren't about telling each other how much you love them. I wish I could have told him that at the end."

I nodded. Listening to Teena made me realize my problems with Zach and Lincoln were pretty insignificant.

I wasn't sure what to say.

So, I decided it was a good time to tell her something I'd been thinking about for a while.

"I want to thank you, Teena," I said. "You've been really great, really helpful to me on this case. I know we got off on the wrong foot. But you're a good police officer. And a good person. I'm glad we're working together."

"Listen, I want to solve this case as badly as you do. Know why? Because then you'll be a hero, and maybe leave here for some big city job like the one you had back in New York. And then I'll get your job. The job I should have had in the first place. Let's be clear on that, Pearce."

"Crystal clear." I smiled.

She was trying to be tough Teena again.

Except she'd opened up the door enough for me to see the real person inside.

And now it was too late for her to close that door again.

After an hour and a half of sitting outside the Claymores' house, something finally happened. A garage door opened, and a car with two men inside pulled out. Bruce Aiken was sitting in the passenger seat of the car. I got a glimpse of the driver's face as he drove past where we were parked. It was Muzzy Malone.

Neither were in New York City.

Malone and Aiken were both on Martha's Vineyard.

What were they up to?

Teena was driving our car. We waited until Aiken and Muzzy Malone were ahead of us, and then followed as carefully as we could. They drove down Beach Road as if they might be heading for Edgartown. But instead turned off at Katuna Drive which extended west across the island. They drove all the way west to Gay Head. We kept following them, right until they went through an iron security gate and the gate closed behind them.

It was a place I knew well.

I'd recently been inside it myself.

Melvin Ellis' house.

CHAPTER 44

The house in Gay Head again – the mansion owned by Melvin Ellis.

The same house I'd gone to a long time ago with Ellis' son Mark when I was a teenager – about the same age as Samantha Claymore.

The same house that had haunted me ever since because of what happened that night.

And the same house that now seemed to play some kind of a role in Samantha Claymore's disappearance – and maybe the death of Bridget Feckanin too.

I mean Melvin Ellis was with Bruce Aiken in the same place – and apparently at almost the same time – as Aiken's stepdaughter Samantha went missing. Now Aiken goes to Ellis' house, along with Muzzy Malone – the captain of the fishing boat Samantha's father was on when he died. And the Feckanin girl's body was found not far from the Ellis house. There were simply too many connections for me to believe it was all a coincidence.

Not only that, but two of the island's other missing girls had disappeared on Gay Head, near Ellis' house. And the third case happened only a short drive away.

Was Samantha Claymore inside that house now?

Had other teenage girls been there in the past?

I decided to go back and delve deeper into the cases of those three missing girls from the past.

*

I started with Ruthie Kolton's parents. She was the troubled seventeen-year-old girl who'd never been found – but her clothes, purse and phone had been stacked neatly on the beach in Gay Head. This was similar to the crime scene where Bridget Feckanin either jumped or fell or was pushed to her death. The assumption back then was that the Kolton girl had gone into the ocean to commit suicide. But I wasn't so sure about that.

Unfortunately, Ruthie Kolton's parents weren't much more help than they had been the first time I interviewed them. But this time, they did tell me that their daughter had been acting strangely in the days before she disappeared.

"She was upset about something," Mrs. Kolton said. "I tried to find out what it was, but she wouldn't tell me. Ruthie didn't share much with us. I told all this to the police, but I think they just figured that whatever had been upsetting her was the thing that led to her suicide."

She and her husband wanted to know if there was anything new about their daughter's death. I said there wasn't, I was just doing a routine follow-up. I felt bad opening up the wounds of the families by revisiting these horrible memories, but the Koltons seemed more curious than concerned.

Just like the last time, I got the feeling that they had moved on from their daughter. She was a messed-up kid, she killed herself. Tragic, but life must go on. I didn't see the other daughter there this time. I wondered what her life was like. I hoped she didn't wind up like her sister. The bottom line was that I didn't get anything useful out of Ruthie Kolton's family.

But I hit pay dirt with one of the other girls. I was able to track down a friend of Carrie Lang, who told me Lang was living now in the Boston area and gave me her phone number. Lang was the sixteen-year-old who disappeared after riding her bike to get ice cream at Allie's General Store in Tisbury – then was found a week later at a motel in Providence, Rhode Island with a boy who worked at a gas station nearby.

It seemed on the face of it that the two had simply run off together. But I remembered from the file that Carrie Lang said she had gone voluntarily because he'd promised to protect her from something – or someone – she was afraid of. There was no explanation in the file of what she was afraid of back then, and I assumed she was simply lying to cover up her relationship from her parents.

Except I learned differently when I got her on the phone. She was working as a hostess in a restaurant in Cambridge and was taking college courses part-time to one day become a teacher.

"My parents were originally going to send me to college," she explained. "I was supposed to go to Cornell. That was where my father had gone. But, after everything happened, I didn't want to take their money anymore. So, I left and am here making it on my own. I don't want anything from them."

I was confused. "Why are you mad at your parents?"

"Because they weren't there for me when I needed them, they didn't believe me when I told them the truth – so to hell with them."

I asked her to tell me more and, to my amazement, she did.

"A lot of it is very fuzzy in my memory. I remember going to Allie's General Store in Tisbury that day. But I never got inside the store. When I parked my bike, someone grabbed me and then everything went dark. I felt a prick in my arm. I'm pretty sure I was injected with some kind of drug.

"The next thing I knew I was in a moving car. I was tied up and blindfolded, but whoever did it must have been in a hurry because the blindfold kept slipping down. So, I could see a few things. I remember seeing a sign that said we were heading west on State Road – and then I remember a house. A big house. That's where they took me."

A big house.

"Could this house have been near Gay Head?" I asked.

"Yes, that makes sense. Why?"

"Just a guess. Any idea who owned the house?"

"No, the rest of it is a blur. I guess because of the drugs I'd been injected with. All I remember is that it was a huge house. I was carried up a long flight of steps and laid down on a bed. I felt another prick, and knew I'd been injected with more drugs. I know there was a man there – maybe more than one man – who did things to me. You know, sexual things. I was sixteen years old. I didn't understand what was happening. And then, after a day or two – I lost track of time – a man put me back in the car, untied me and dumped me on a road. He said if I told anyone about what had happened, he would come back and kill me. But I did. I told my parents. And that's when it started getting really crazy."

"Because they didn't believe you?"

"I think they did at first, but then something changed. They told me – ordered me – not to tell anyone about it. They said I should forget it ever happened. That we would never talk about it again. I was home now, and that was all that mattered. There was nothing to be gained by telling sordid stories. Do you have any idea what that felt like for me? Going to my parents for help? And they made me feel dirty? I realized I couldn't count on them."

I sure did know what it felt like.

But I didn't tell Carrie Lang that.

I let her keep talking.

"That's when I called Jimmy at the gas station and told him everything. I was afraid whoever did this to me would come again. Jimmy believed me. He picked me up, we drove to Providence and that's where we were when the police found us. They made it sound like I had been missing up to that point. But I had been home for days. Jimmy didn't kidnap me or anything like they said. He was the only one there for me, the only one I had to protect me."

"Just out of curiosity," I asked, "what happened to Jimmy after the police released him on the kidnapping charge?"

"He's here with me in Cambridge. I married him. When you find a person who does for you what Jimmy did for me, well… you hold onto them. Those kind of people are hard to find."

Linda Ellison, the last girl on the list, was the toughest for me to approach. She was the one who went missing for forty-eight hours after a party on the west side of the island, but then returned home safely. I needed to find out what happened to her during those forty-eight hours. And I was intrigued that this yet again happened near Gay Head, where Melvin Ellis lived.

But she was also the girl whose mother had warned me against contacting her. She had tried to kill herself. Twice. By pills and by slitting her wrists. The thing that made it even more important for me was to find out what might have driven her into that suicidal state of mind.

I was able to determine that she was in a small hospital facility in Falmouth. I took the forty-five-minute ferry ride to Woods Hole and then drove the rest of the way to the facility. I wasn't sure if my Cedar Cliffs police credentials would get me in to see her, especially if her mother had said something to the hospital about me, so I snuck past the reception desk. Then I walked around the halls until I found her room. It was a small facility, so it didn't take me long.

Linda Ellison was a pretty girl. Or at least she was pretty in the pictures I'd seen of her. Blonde, beautiful, tanned – a typical teenage girl with a big grin on her face enjoying life on an island paradise. But not anymore. Now she was rail-thin, her cheeks looked sallow and she stared straight ahead without any expression or emotion on her face. There was a TV playing in her room – a game show of some kind – but she seemed oblivious to it. Oblivious to me too even after I pulled up a chair next to the bed, and introduced myself.

"Hello, Linda," I said. "My name is Detective Abby Pearce. I'm with the Cedar Cliffs Police Department. I would like to talk to you for a few minutes."

She stared at the TV screen and said nothing.

"It's about what happened to you two years ago. I'd like to find out where you went after your school picnic and if someone did something to you on that day. You're not in any trouble. I'm only looking for information. Can we talk about it?"

On the screen, a woman was bidding for a TV set. Some of the people in the audience were yelling "higher" for the price – and the host was telling her she had ten seconds to give her answer. It sure seemed like everyone on the show was having a lot of fun.

But I don't think Linda Ellison was paying any more attention to them than she was to me.

"I simply want to find out what happened to you during those forty-eight hours," I said again. "I know it must have been something pretty bad. But it will help if you discuss it with me, Linda. It really will. I'm here to help you. Will you help me?"

Still nothing. I wondered if she even knew I was there. Or if she had any idea who I was. Figuring a visual might work better to get her attention, I took out my detective's badge and held it in front of her. "Once again, Linda, I'm Detective Abby Pearce with the Cedar Cliffs Police Department and—"

That's when she began to scream. A scream so loud and terrifying and panic-stricken that it set off a furor within the facility. Nurses and doctors and security personnel came bursting into the room, trying to calm Linda down and demanding to know what I was doing there.

Later, when it was all over, I remembered one thing the most.

It wasn't me that Linda Ellison was terrified of.

It was my badge.

She was afraid of the police.

CHAPTER 45

My phone rang as I was driving back to the station. I saw it was from a number I didn't recognize. I answered it anyway.

"Meet me in one hour on the bench overlooking the Cedar Cliffs town beach – behind the lifeguard station," a female voice said.

"Who is this?"

"You'll find out when you get there."

"I have to know more than that…"

"Believe me, you're going to want to hear what I have to say."

"About what?"

"Ruthie Kolton."

She was already waiting on the bench when I got there. A teenage girl. She could have been any girl, and maybe I wouldn't have recognized her so quickly. Except I'd seen her recently. When I went to visit the Kolton family the first time. She was Ruthie Kolton's sister. Becky.

"I couldn't talk about my sister at the house," she said to me after I sat down. "Not in front of my parents anyway. That's why I stayed in another room. They never want to talk about Ruthie. They try to act like she never existed. But not me. She was my sister. And I want to know whatever happened to her."

She asked me why I was so interested in Ruthie after all this time. I explained I was new to the Cedar Cliffs force, and was just looking into some old cases to see if I could uncover any new evidence. Which was sort of the truth. I didn't say anything about my suspicions that whatever happened to her sister might be linked to the disappearance of other women, then and now.

I went through everything I knew about the case. Ruthie's clothes, purse and phone stacked on the beach. Her run-ins with the law and school officials before that. The police conclusion that she'd gone into the water and committed suicide.

Mostly though, I let Becky Kolton talk about Ruthie:

"Growing up, Ruthie and I weren't that close. Probably because of the age difference. I mean she was seventeen at the end, running around with boys and going to parties, and I was still riding my bicycle. We didn't have much in common.

"I knew my parents had a lot of problems with her – the drinking and staying out late. They were very upset about what she was doing. And I didn't want them to be mad at me too. So I did my best to keep my distance from her. She was the bad girl in the family, I wanted to be the good girl. There'd be days, sometimes weeks, when we barely talked to each other.

"But at the end, right before she disappeared, she did talk to me. I think she wanted to talk to someone she could trust. And, even though I was younger, I was still her sister. I knew something had been bothering her. She seemed upset, nervous, almost paranoid that she was in danger."

Just like the other girls, I thought to myself.

"Before that, she'd been strange in other ways too. She suddenly had money. More money than we'd ever received from our parents in an allowance. She was buying clothes, jewelry and, yes, drugs all the time. When I asked her where the money came from, she said something about how she'd found a 'sugar daddy.'

"Right before she disappeared, she told me about this wealthy man on the island who gave her hundreds of dollars if she came to his place and gave him massages. She told me that he liked teenage girls, and was willing to pay for them.

"She said this was fine for a while. That she even recruited other girls she knew to spend time with him and his friends. He took videos of all this, which didn't bother her – but she suspected some of his male visitors would be upset if they knew about the cameras.

"Then one day one of the girls Ruthie recruited – she said it was a friend of hers from school named Linda – didn't want to do it anymore. Linda tried to quit, but he drugged her and made her perform favors for him anyway. He said girls never said 'no' to him. If they did, and if they ever told anyone about what he was doing, he said he would destroy them. Not just their reputations, but their lives. Ruthie said she and the other girls lived in fear of this man."

Ruthie's friend Linda.

Was this Linda Ellison, the girl in a catatonic state in the hospital now?

Becky Kolton said she didn't know Linda's last name, but it sure seemed likely.

I asked Becky the obvious question:

"Who was the man?"

"I never found out."

"But you must have asked her?"

"Yes, but she was afraid. I think she regretted telling me as much as she did. And she didn't want to get into more trouble with this man if he ever found out. I wasn't sure if I believed her. Not then anyway. I thought maybe she was making it up. Or hallucinating from all the drinking and drugs she'd been doing.

"But then, after she disappeared, I told my parents what she had said. I thought they would go to the police. But they never did. They told me that Ruthie was gone, it was a tragedy – but there was nothing to be gained by airing all of this dirty laundry. They said I should just forget about it, so that's what I did.

"I'm telling you now because you weren't here then. And because you really do seem to want to find out the truth. So do I. I'm now the same age Ruthie was when this all happened. I want to find out the truth about my sister, Detective."

"So no one ever told the police about what she said this man was doing to young girls?" I asked.

"Not that I know of."

"And why wouldn't your parents say something? Why wouldn't the police want to find out this was going on right here on Martha's Vineyard?"

"I remember something else Ruthie said in that last conversation. She said she told the man that all she had to do was go to the police and he would be arrested. For trafficking, rape – and maybe kidnapping. But he just laughed. And then he told her something that really scared her."

"What?"

"He said the police were in on the whole thing."

CHAPTER 46

"He said the police were in on the whole thing."

Those words raced through my mind as I walked back to the station after meeting with Becky Kolton. The police were in on it? Of course, it wasn't me she was talking about. I wasn't here when Ruthie Kolton disappeared and supposedly killed herself.

But Chief Wilhelm was. A lot of the rest of the force too. Plus, Norm Garrity, my predecessor. As Detective he would have been involved back then.

Garrity was actually the lead investigator on all three cases. And Wilhelm was already Chief. By the time I got back to the station, my paranoia was running wild. Maybe there were other people on the force involved too. I thought I could trust Teena. And probably Meg Jarvis. But I wasn't sure about anybody else.

I waited until Meg was in the coffee break room until I approached her. I didn't want anyone interrupting us at her desk. I wasn't sure what she could tell me about Garrity. But she'd worked here for a long time – even longer than Wilhelm – and I liked her. She seemed like the best choice to try to find out more.

"What did you think of Norm Garrity?" I asked her.

"Why are you bringing him up?"

"I'm just curious. Did you like him?"

"Norm was a nice guy. Hard worker. He was here a long time. And then he died. Not much else to say."

"That's a helluva epitaph for the guy."

"Look, he was never a fireball like you. Or even like Teena. But he was a good cop. Just like Wilhelm is a good cop. They're the kind of people you find on a small-town police force like this. They're fine for the kinds of crimes we have to deal with."

I nodded.

"What did Norm die of?" I asked.

"What do you mean?"

"Well, his obituary in the *Vineyard Gazette* never gave the cause of death. Just said natural causes."

"I'm not sure that was ever specifically determined."

"Was there an autopsy?"

"You know how it works. If there's evidence of a crime or something suspicious, we do an autopsy. If there's not, it's listed as natural causes. There's a lot of people around here where the cause of death is simply natural causes. Could be old age."

"Except Garrity was fifty-four. That's not old. And I find it difficult to believe that the Cedar Cliffs Police Department wouldn't want to determine the cause of death of its own detective."

Meg shrugged. "What do you want me to tell you, Abby?"

"The truth."

She looked down at the coffee she was drinking. Trying to decide what to say, I guessed. Then she looked back at me.

"This is just between us," she said.

"Okay."

"You didn't hear what I'm about to tell you from me."

I agreed.

"Norm ate his pistol."

"He killed himself?"

"Yes. He apparently went into the bedroom of his house, closed the door, put a gun in his mouth and pulled the trigger."

"So why was it ruled natural causes?"

"No one wanted to bring that kind of shame and embarrassment on his family or on the department. Like I said, he was a good guy with a good record. Why ruin that by saying he committed suicide? They felt it was better to be vague about the cause of death on the official record. No one got hurt that way. He got an honor funeral from the department, and everyone was satisfied."

Except it was a lie, I thought to myself.

"Any idea why Garrity would kill himself?"

"Norm didn't talk much to me. Or to anyone. He was a bit of a loner. But I did sense that something was bothering him at the end. He seemed nervous, upset – almost paranoid. I asked him about it, but he wouldn't tell me anything. Said that it was his problem, and he'd have to deal with it."

"Did he give you any more details?"

"Not really. But he did ask me to check on a contact with the FBI in Boston. He said he wanted to talk to some federal authorities about a big case they might be interested in. I had the feeling that might have been what was on his mind at the end, but I never found out for sure."

"And you don't know what happened with the FBI?"

"He made an appointment to meet someone there, but never had the meeting."

"Why not?"

"Because he died first."

So just before he unexpectedly died, Norm Garrity had reached out to the FBI to set up a meeting about a case he was working on. Was that a coincidence? Or something more sinister?

There was one other thing that still didn't make sense to me.

"How could a police suicide like that be covered up? And on an island? Wouldn't someone ask questions about his death?"

"Not after the official report was filed and said he died of natural causes. End of story."

"Who signed that report?"

"Chief Wilhelm," Meg said.

*

I finally heard back from Stan Larsen, and I told him about me and Zach. Or, more precisely, how there was no me and Zach anymore.

"Damn, that sounds like a brutal conversation," he said. "How are you doing now, Abby?"

"Oh, I've been better."

"Are you… drinking again?"

Uncle Stan and I never talked about my drinking, even though he was aware of it. But it was an obvious question at this moment. Alcoholic woman gets her heart broken, alcoholic woman turns to the bottle for solace. Except I didn't do that. Not this time.

I'd thought about it. Even came up with a scenario where I'd take the ferry over to a bar in Cape Cod where I could drink without anyone recognizing me – and telling Chief Wilhelm. I'd have a vodka or two – just enough to calm me down – and then take the ferry back to Martha's Vineyard. I'd walk Oscar and get a good night's sleep and then be back at work in the morning without anyone finding out.

But I didn't do that.

Because I knew what would happen if I went to a bar. I would not stop after one drink. Or two drinks. Or maybe even ten. I would keep on drinking. I would not get home in time to feed and walk Oscar. Or get a good night's sleep. I would not be in good enough shape to go to work in the morning. I would be royally screwed, like I was that night I drove my car into a ditch in East Chop.

And I would very likely jeopardize my chances of staying on the Samantha Claymore case and finding her.

That was the most important thing to me right now.

"I'm not drinking," I told Uncle Stan.

"Do you think you will?"

"I haven't had a drink today."

"What about tomorrow?"

"I haven't had a drink today," I repeated.

He understood. "The mantra, huh? That's good, Abby."

"Yep, one day at a time," I said.

He asked me about the case and I filled him in on everything. The other missing girls.

My fear that police on the Cedar Cliffs force – particularly Chief Wilhelm and the late Norm Garrity – might be involved.

And my focus on Melvin Ellis as a key player in the disappearance of Samantha Claymore and the death of Bridget Feckanin.

"Do you have any hard evidence against Wilhelm and Garrity?" he asked me when I was finished.

"Not yet."

"But you do think they're a part of this?"

"Yes. And that scares the hell out of me, Uncle Stan. I need to know who I can trust on my own police force."

CHAPTER 47

"Let me see if I've got this straight, Abby," Teena said to me. "You believe this is about more than just Samantha Claymore and Bridget Feckanin. You think this case might also involve other teenage girls who went missing here over the past few years.

"You also suspect that the police are involved in some way. Particularly, Norm Garrity, your predecessor who would have been the lead investigator on these other cases. And even Chief Wilhelm. And you wonder if Garrity's suicide is suspicious because he had scheduled an appointment with the FBI before he died. Uh, did I leave anything out?"

"Melvin Ellis," I said.

"Oh, right. And you also think that Melvin Ellis, who happens to be the most powerful person on this island, is somehow a part of all this. This conclusion is based on the fact that several of the other girls went missing around Gay Head, where Ellis lives; he showed up on that security video with Bruce Aiken in Edgartown; and we followed Aiken and Muzzy Malone to Ellis' house. And… why else do you suspect Ellis?"

"I know a lot about the Ellis family."

"How?"

"From personal experience."

"Not a good experience, I assume."

"No."

"And this involved Melvin Ellis?"

"His son."

Teena sighed.

"Do you have any idea how crazy this all sounds, Abby?"

"I do."

"But you're telling me anyway. Why?"

"Because you're the only person I can trust right now."

We were sitting together in a car in the parking lot behind the police station. I didn't want to talk about this with her inside the station. I had thought about going to the Black Dog, but someone might overhear us there. And if we sat on a park bench in town, people might notice us there too. Meeting in the car seemed like the best plan. I suppose I was being paranoid, but at this point I felt I had good reason to be.

I'd been thinking about this ever since I left Becky Kolton and she told me about her sister.

I had a theory now about what had happened to those other missing girls.

"It's the oldest story in the world – wealthy older man uses money to lure young impressionable girls to him," I said. "For himself and maybe for some of his friends. And a lot of these friends are people in powerful places. So, this wealthy man is able to get away with what he's doing because of his money and his powerful connections. I think that's what is happening on Martha's Vineyard now. And I think I know who is responsible."

"Melvin Ellis?" Teena asked.

I nodded. "Melvin Ellis."

"What do all these people protecting him get out of it?"

"Money, of course. For instance, I checked Garrity out. His house here was way more expensive than you'd expect. He also had a condo in Florida and drove a Ferrari. Pretty good for a guy like Norm Garrity, who was working on detective's pay for a small-town police force in Cedar Cliffs.

"Same's true for the girls. Ellis probably lures underage girls to his place by offering them money to perform sexual favors for

DANA PERRY

him and his friends. Some of the girls then recruit their friends to join them at his mansion. They think it's fun and an easy way to make money. At least that's how they feel in the beginning.

"And don't forget about the power of blackmail. It's likely Ellis made videos of the people that came to his place, and that meant he had a hold on them. They couldn't take the chance that he'd make those videos public and ruin them. Maybe Ellis did that with some of the girls too. Threaten to release the videos he had of them. These girls were fourteen or fifteen. It wouldn't take much to scare them into doing what he wanted them to do."

"What about the deaths? How does that fit in?"

"My theory is they were killed if they threatened to go public with what they knew. That could have been what happened with Ruthie Kolton – maybe she was murdered, and someone made it look like a suicide. Becky Feckanin was pregnant. They might have thought they needed to shut her up so no one found out what was happening with girls like her. The other deaths we know about could be the same."

"And you figure that's what happened to Norm Garrity too?"

"Why not? Maybe he suddenly got a fit of conscience about what he was doing – or not doing – to allow this to happen. They find out he's planning to meet with the FBI. So they kill him and make it look like suicide. Then the Cedar Cliffs Police Department, led by Wilhelm, covers it up even more by ruling it a death by natural causes. I mean, Wilhelm signed off on all the missing girl cases Garrity investigated. Wilhelm agreed with his conclusions that they were suicides or accidents or runaways."

"You think Wilhelm is part of it?"

"That certainly seems logical."

"Who else in our department?"

"It could be anyone on the force. Hell, I can't even be sure about you, Teena. But I have to talk to someone about all this."

"What about Samantha Claymore? How does she fit in?"

"I don't know. But it has to be connected to this. And with the death of her father five years ago. I really believe that. That's the only way this makes sense. Samantha's stepfather, Muzzy Malone, and maybe her mother are somehow involved in this. And we don't know how many other girls besides Samantha and Bridget might have been victims."

I wasn't sure what Teena would do at this point. Tell me I was out of my mind. Get out of the car and leave me sitting here alone. Maybe even go into the station and tell Wilhelm and everyone else everything I'd said about them. But Teena did not do any of these things.

"You really have this thing about Melvin Ellis?" Teena said. "Why?"

"I have my reasons."

"Do you want to tell me what they are?"

"Like I said, I had a bad experience with his son. I went to high school with him."

"What happened?"

"It was a long time ago."

"But obviously you haven't forgotten."

"It's not the kind of thing you can ever forget."

"So talk to me about it…"

CHAPTER 48

From the window of the car where we were parked near the police station, you could see the Cedar Cliffs beaches, the boats in the harbor and the waves breaking on the shore. The sun glistened off the waves and I thought about how much I loved the beauty of this island. That's why I had come back to Martha's Vineyard. Hoping to find peace and contentment in all this beauty, and escape my bad memories of New York City. But there were bad memories for me here too. No matter how far you run, you can't escape your memories.

"It was the night of my high school prom," I said. "I went with his son, Mark Ellis. I had a big crush on him in high school. Lots of girls did. He was the cute, popular, rich guy we all wanted. And here he was inviting me to the prom. Out of all the girls in school, he invited me to be his prom date. I was so excited that night. I had a new white dress. A new hairdo. An expensive corsage. It was supposed to be a magical evening,"

The memories of that long-ago night were as vivid to me as if they'd happened yesterday.

"After the dance, we went back to his house – the mansion on the beach near Gay Head – with some of his friends. That's when Mark opened up the liquor cabinet. Now you have to understand something. I had never had a drink before that night. I didn't tell anyone though. I wanted to be cool. I wanted to fit in. I wanted Mark and his friends to like me.

'Someone made vodka martinis. I can still remember the taste of that first drink. The feeling of the vodka going through my body, making me feel warm and comfortable and good all over. And then Mark kissed me. It was so perfect. I remember having a second drink, and then a third. Then I blacked out.

"The next thing I knew I was staggering into my own house back in Vineyard Haven. My prom dress was ripped, there was alcohol all over it and there... was blood too. I was a virgin before that night."

"Mark Ellis had sex with you while you were in that condition?" Teena asked.

"He raped me."

"My God!"

"My parents called a doctor. Then my father stormed out of the house to confront Ellis. I figured he might hit him. Or get him sent to jail. One way or another, I figured Mark Ellis was going to pay for what he did to me. But he never did. When my father came back, he told me to forget about what happened. He said he knew I'd been through a terrible ordeal, but what was done was done. He said nothing could be gained by prolonging it. He told me never to talk about it again."

"Why would he say that?"

"I never knew."

"What did you do?"

"I freaked out. I ran out of the house screaming. My parents had a friend, this man named Stan Larsen. He was like a second father to me. I told him the whole story. He was very understanding, like my own father should have been. I said I wanted to stay with him and not go back to my house. But eventually my father showed up and took me home."

"And that was it?"

"Yes."

"Your parents never talked about it with you again?"

I shook my head. "As far as they were concerned, it never happened. I was so humiliated. I was convinced everyone in town knew what happened to me. I didn't want to leave the house. I kept waiting for my father to say something. To help me through it. To explain why no one was paying the price for this terrible thing.

"But he never did. Day after day, he'd come home from the restaurant he owned and read his paper and watch TV without saying a word to me. It was almost like I didn't exist. I felt like I was damaged goods.

"That's when I really started to drink. It was an escape for me. When I was drinking, I felt better. Nothing else made me feel that good. So I kept drinking. It made a lot of sense to me at the time.

"After I graduated from high school, I moved away. First to college and then to New York. I never came back here – even for holidays or during the summer. My only connection with my parents was a handful of phone calls on holidays or birthdays – all of them completely superficial and excruciatingly uncomfortable.

"Then my father died. It was very sudden and unexpected so I wasn't prepared for it. I didn't go to the funeral. I know that sounds terrible, but I couldn't deal with it. Instead, I started drinking again. And then I kept on drinking. Drinking was all I wanted to do. Nothing else seemed to matter anymore. Not my job. Not my friends. Not even Zach, the man I loved so much. Sometimes at night, I'd lie there in bed looking at Zach sleep and wonder how long it would be before he abandoned me the way my father had."

"What is it you wanted from your father before he died?" Teena asked.

"Answers."

"For what he did? Or, more precisely, what he didn't do?"

I nodded.

"I wanted him to talk to me. I wanted him to hold me. I wanted him to tell me how much he loved me, that he'd protect me and never let anything bad happen to me. But now he's gone. That's why I was able to come back to Martha's Vineyard after all his time. He's not here, my mother's not here anymore – I thought it could be a fresh start. I could finally put the past behind me."

"Except now Melvin Ellis is our prime suspect and potentially a deadly sexual predator."

"That can't be a coincidence," I said. "I mean I was raped at that house years ago."

"Do you think Melvin Ellis could have had anything to do with your attack back then?"

"I'm not sure… like I said, I don't remember most of what happened that night."

"But you believe he is luring teenage girls to his house for sex?"

"Like father, like son," I said.

CHAPTER 49

There were still regular press conferences being held with the media on the island about the search for Samantha Claymore. I handled most of them, not Wilhelm. He liked it that way, and I knew Mayor Randall did too.

Not that I had much to say.

Mostly, I repeated the details about the search teams: where they'd been that day and what they had uncovered. Which was nothing. I answered many questions about Samantha – and also Bridget Feckanin – with "no comment" or "that is still under investigation." I had other things I could talk about, of course – but I wasn't ready to reveal any of them yet.

The media contingent had thinned out, no longer as big as it was during the early days of Samantha Claymore's disappearance. There wasn't much for them to put on the air. Even after Bridget Feckanin's death, many of them were at home waiting for a big development to happen. Once that happened – if that happened – I knew they would be back in full force.

One reporter who was still around though was Lincoln Connor.

I liked that for multiple reasons – professional and personal.

But right now it was the professional part I cared about the most.

Oh, Lincoln had contacted me a number of times asking me out again. I kept saying no. Not that I didn't want to see him again. I did. I liked him. I was attracted to him too, I had to admit. But this was not the time for me to get involved in a romance.

Especially with a reporter looking for a big scoop on the Samantha Claymore story.

But I did want to talk to him. I needed to talk to people I could trust. And, believe it or not, I trusted Lincoln Connor.

"Want to take a walk with me later tonight?" I asked him as the media began leaving the latest press conference.

"A walk where?"

"Along the beach."

"Sounds romantic."

"Just business."

"Okay, I can live with that."

I figured a walk along the beach – the part that was deserted as you left town – would avoid attracting any attention. Especially if we waited until it got dark. So that night we met up near the Cedar Cliffs ferry terminal, then walked along the water away from the public beach and down a deserted stretch to the east.

"Okay, we can talk now," I said once we got there.

"What's the topic?"

"Melvin Ellis."

"The big money guy who lives here?"

"Yes, him."

"What does Ellis have to do with anything?"

I stopped walking, and looked out at the water of Nantucket Bay. There were white-capped waves breaking peacefully on the shore at our feet. It seemed incongruous that we could be standing in such a beautiful place talking about an evil man like Melvin Ellis.

"I need you to promise me that what I'm about to tell you is completely off the record."

"Sure. You got it."

"No, I mean you have to absolutely promise me on this. I gave information to you last time for you to put on the air. But not this. You can't do anything with what I'm about to tell you. If anything comes out of it, you'll be the first person to know. You'll get the exclusive. You have my word on that. Do I have your word on absolute secrecy until then?"

"Yes, I promise that I won't do anything – you can trust me, Abby."

He said it like he meant it. So I took a deep breath, and then I started to talk:

"I think there might be something really bad going on here on Martha's Vineyard. Someone preying on teenage girls. More than just Samantha Claymore or Bridget Feckanin. There's been a series of other missing girl cases here in recent years. They were all closed with explanations, but... well, there could be more to it."

I didn't give specific names of the victims. I didn't mention anything about the police possibly being involved. But I did talk about Melvin Ellis.

"Wow!" he said. "How close are you to going after him?"

"I'm not sure. I need evidence to bring down someone as powerful as that. You've covered a lot of big stories – some of them involving rich powerful people like Melvin Ellis. Any idea on how to get what I need to nail Ellis?"

"The best evidence would be found in his home on Gay Head," he said. "You know the house I'm talking about, right?"

I nodded. I sure knew that house.

"What kind of evidence do you figure might be inside?"

He shrugged. "Who knows? Maybe pictures of young girls, evidence of videotaping, or even articles of clothing left behind by some of the teenagers that had been there. Then, you would be able to go after some of the girls and get their testimony. If you did that, then the dominoes might start to fall and you could build a case again him."

"Which means I have to figure out how to search Melvin Ellis' mansion. I need to find out what he has in there. I need to go through everything inside until I find the evidence that I'm looking for."

"Have you told anyone else about this?" he asked.

"My partner Teena Morelli and a family friend. Just people I can trust."

"And you trust me?"

"When I met you, Lincoln, I thought you were an asshole. You tried to embarrass me at that first press conference."

He smiled.

"And now?"

"I don't think you're an asshole anymore."

"Good to hear."

We walked back along the beach toward the ferry terminal and the Cedar Cliffs police station.

"So what is going on between you and me?" he said before we got there. "When can I see you again?"

"You're seeing me right now."

"You know what I mean, Abby. Something started that night outside your house. I'd like to finish it."

"We can't do that, Lincoln. Not now."

"Not until we find Samantha Claymore, huh?"

"That's the deal."

Lincoln leaned over and kissed me.

Like he did that night outside my house, only longer.

I kissed him back.

It was nice.

"Let's find her in a hurry," he said.

CHAPTER 50

Peter Randall said I should come to him if I ever needed help on the Samantha Claymore case. Of course, like the others, I wasn't sure I could trust Randall, but I decided it was time to take him up on his offer anyway.

Randall was happy to see me. I imagine he thought I was bringing him some news about Samantha Claymore. Some answers to the mystery of her disappearance. But I didn't have any answers. Only more questions. And, as he would soon find out, I was bringing him even more problems.

"Have you found anymore out about Samantha Claymore?" he asked hopefully.

"Yes and no. I don't have any new information on her whereabouts. But I have uncovered a lot of things that I believe are related to this case."

I ran through it all with him. The other missing girls. The details of Norm Garrity's death – and the fact that he'd scheduled a secret meeting with the FBI before he supposedly committed suicide. The reasons I believed Melvin Ellis could be involved – possibly as the central figure – in a criminal operation that provided sex to the rich and powerful. How the death of Ronald Claymore here five years ago might be connected too. And, last but not least, how Ruthie Kolton had told her sister that "the police were in on this too."

Randall sat there in stunned silence. This was certainly not what he had expected to hear from me when I walked into his office. I wasn't sure how he would react.

"Have you talked to anyone else on the force about this?" he asked finally.

"Just my partner, Teena Morelli."

"No one else?"

"I can't. Some of them might be involved."

"What about Chief Wilhelm?"

"Wilhelm's the one who signed off on all those missing girl cases Garrity investigated. Wilhelm signed off on Garrity's death being from 'natural causes'. And, he also investigated the death of Ronald Claymore – which was declared an accident. No, Wilhelm is the chief suspect in terms of police involvement in all this. That's why I came here to see you. I don't have anywhere else to turn."

"How about the FBI?"

I shook my head.

"I'm not sure about them either. But if someone found out Garrity was going to see the FBI right before he died, that means there's a leak in the Boston bureau offices. I can't take the chance that the same thing won't happen again if I try to bring them into this."

Randall sighed. His office was right next to the beach at Cedar Cliffs, and there was a big window overlooking Nantucket Sound.

No question about it, Martha's Vineyard was a beautiful place to live. Randall must have looked through that window many times before and marveled at how lucky he was to be mayor of such a beautiful place. Except now things weren't so beautiful. Dark secrets from the past were emerging and turning Martha's Vineyard into a nightmare.

And he – and I – had to deal with it in the best way we could.

"What do we do?" Randall asked me.

"We need to search Ellis' mansion."

"Search Ellis' mansion," he repeated slowly.

"Yes. That's where evidence of his involvement most likely is. Videos. Photos. Articles of clothing. Maybe even DNA from victims. I mean he could have girls in there too."

"Do you think Samantha Claymore is there?"

"It makes sense, doesn't it? We can't find her anywhere else on the island. And who would suspect she was even there? To throw us off the track, Ellis shows up at the press conference to put up big money as a reward. It's the perfect cover for him. We've just got to search his house."

"You realize, of course, that Melvin Ellis is the richest and most powerful person on this island. And one of the richest and most powerful in the country."

"As everyone keeps telling me. Yes, I am aware."

"And you don't have anything to go on other than suspicion, speculation and circumstantial evidence. What if you're wrong? What if Ellis has nothing to do with this? What are you proposing we do here?"

"We need to get a search warrant for Ellis' house. And go through the place from top to bottom. That's the only way to nail him. I can't go to Wilhelm and ask him for a warrant. I mean the guy freaked out when I went to visit Ellis the first time. And I'm not comfortable trying to get one from a local judge, he could be bought and paid for by Ellis too. But maybe you could approach the U.S. attorney's office. Say some of these girls might have been taken across state lines, and get a federal warrant. We'll turn the Ellis mansion upside down."

"My God!" Randall said.

"I know, we're taking a big chance. But, if we're right, the lives of several teenage girls are at stake here. Samantha Claymore may even be one of them."

Neither of us said anything for about thirty seconds, until finally I spoke again.

"There's something else you should know," I said.

I told him about my own ordeal at the Ellis house. How I'd been raped there as a teenager. And how nothing was ever done about it.

"I'm sure that would come up again if we do go after Ellis. He'd claim this was a personal grudge on my part. Maybe it is. But it's also my job. Whatever happened to me at that house, well... it's happened to other girls since then. And we need to stop it."

Randall sighed. "I don't think we have enough evidence from what you've told me to authorize a federal search warrant," he said.

"The evidence is inside the house."

"But you need other evidence in order to get in there."

"What will it take for you to get that search warrant?"

"Get me some more evidence against Melvin Ellis," he said.

CHAPTER 51

Could I trust Peter Randall? I wasn't sure. Could I trust Lincoln? I wasn't a hundred percent sure about that either, despite the attraction between us. In fact, there was only one living thing in the world that I knew with absolute certainty that I could trust, no matter what happened.

"I'm sure Melvin Ellis is involved in this," I said to Oscar, when I got back home that night. "But how? And what about the police – potentially members of my own Cedar Cliffs force? Then there's Bridget Feckanin. Who was the father of her baby? And how did she die? I think there's a connection between all of these things. And that it somehow involves Melvin Ellis. The evidence against him is inside his house. But, in order to get to that evidence, we need other evidence to justify a search of the damn place. In other words, we need evidence to get the evidence. Quite a conundrum, huh?"

Oscar was finished with his bone. He came over to me now, jumped up on my lap and licked my face. That's the good thing about a dog. Endless devotion. No matter what you do or say. It made me think about Lincoln Connor, and wonder if a relationship there was possible. But it also made me think again about Zach.

I knew I shouldn't but I pulled out the scrapbook again, the one I'd brought with me from New York. The pages held memories of happy times. Some not so happy times too.

There were lots of pictures of me and Zach together. Also, a number of articles I'd kept about my arrests and awards and honors in the NYPD. One of the headlines, along with a picture of me standing in front of a police precinct, read: "Murder is Her Business: Meet New York City's Toughest Homicide Cop." Those were heady days for me, all right.

But then there were the other articles. The ones about the death of Tommy Ferraro, my partner. For the zillionth time, I read those headlines: "NYPD Detective Slain in Front of Partner"; "Honor Funeral for Detective Tommy Ferraro"; and finally: "Slain Detective's Partner Cleared in NYPD Probe of His Death."

There was a picture of Tommy there that I loved. He was standing by his car, a gun on his side, looking every inch like the tough, professional cop that he was. It was taken a few weeks before he died. Looking at it now, it was still hard for me to believe that he was really gone.

I'd been close to his family – his wife and children – when we were partners, and I'd tried to keep in touch with them after he died. I would call his wife and pour out my grief. But I stopped calling her after a while. I always felt she blamed me for her husband's death. And why not? I blamed myself too.

I closed the scrapbook, put it away in a drawer and vowed once again to not look at the damn thing.

"There's nothing I can do to bring Tommy back to life," I said to Oscar. "And there's nothing I can do to change what happened to me the night of my high school prom. But it's not too late for me to save Samantha Claymore. And that's what I'm going to do. I'm going to save that girl. And maybe I can get justice for those other missing girls too. What do you think?"

Oscar didn't disagree with me.

He never did.

It was nice to have someone I could trust on my side.

CHAPTER 52

Vic Hollister, of all people, was the one who got me the evidence I needed to go after Melvin Ellis. Or at least enough evidence to confirm that I was on the right track.

"We found Samantha Claymore's ring," he called to tell me. "The black onyx ring from her father. And the one that Bridget Feckanin was wearing on that video in Edgartown when she pretended to be Samantha."

"Where was the ring?"

"You're not gonna believe this."

"Somewhere near Melvin Ellis' house?"

"That's right."

I'd sent one of the search teams to the area around Gay Head, hoping they might find something – anything – that would help me build a case against Ellis.

But this was better than I ever expected.

When I got to the scene, I saw that the ring had been found in some tall grass alongside the road that led right to the main gate of the Ellis property. That put Bridget Feckanin – assuming she was still wearing the ring – right here before she died on the cliff overlooking Gay Head beach.

Why would Bridget be outside the Ellis' house? She might have been inside before she died. That was a pretty plausible scenario right now.

I realized now that the ring had not been on Bridget's finger when we found her body. How did it wind up here?

"Maybe there was a struggle and it fell off," Teena speculated when she got to the scene. "I mean it wasn't her ring, it probably didn't fit right on her finger. Maybe it was too big. And it slipped off during whatever happened to her here."

"We should be able to find that out easy enough," Hollister said.

"What do you mean?"

"There's blood on the ring."

Sure enough, there were traces of blood on the band and also the top of the ring itself. Suggesting it had been ripped off during a struggle.

An exact match of the blood to Bridget Feckanin would take a while to determine. But it was quickly learned that the blood on the ring was Type 0. Bridget Feckanin's blood type.

"Abby told me she wanted us to do another search around Gay Head since that was where Feckanin's body was found," Hollister said. "She also talked about Melvin Ellis being in that video at Edgartown. So she told me to search around his place too. Anyway, this was the result."

"Nice job, Vic," I said. "You did good."

"Yeah, every once in a while even an old police hack like me can do something right, huh?"

I realized I might have sounded condescending in my praise.

"Hey, I didn't mean it like that, Vic."

"I know." He shrugged. "I realize I'm not always a lot of help to you or the rest of the department. But I'm still a good cop. Sometimes my experience can come in handy."

He was right. Maybe I'd misjudged Vic Hollister.

I took out my phone and called Wilhelm to bring him up to date on what we'd found. He was happy to hear about the ring, but not so happy when he found out where it was located. I didn't make any direct link between Ellis, the ring and Bridget Feckanin. I simply gave him the basic details.

But I did a lot more when I called Randall afterward.

"This is the evidence we were looking for," I said. "Evidence that puts Bridget Feckanin outside Melvin Ellis' house. We've got to search inside and see what other evidence might be in there."

I looked up the road toward the house and wondered what we might find inside. Evidence of the girls who had been brought there. Videos Ellis might have used to blackmail them. What had Bridget Feckanin been doing here? And what about Samantha Claymore? Could she be inside that house right now?

"You realize what the repercussions will be if we go into Melvin Ellis' house like he's a suspect, and don't find anything?"

"Do you realize what the repercussions will be if we don't? Samantha Claymore's life – and maybe the lives of other girls too – is at stake if we don't act here."

"I don't know…"

"I'll take full responsibility for this. If it goes badly, you can blame me. But we have to see what's inside that house, no matter what."

There was a long silence on the other end of the phone.

I thought for a second Randall might have hung up on me.

But he was just taking in everything I said.

"Will you get that search warrant for Melvin Ellis' house?" I asked.

"Let me see what I can do," Randall said.

CHAPTER 53

My morning wake-up routine usually goes like this: Alarm clock goes off, Oscar jumps on to the bed and licks my face, I drag myself out of bed to walk him, feed him and get ready for work.

But this morning was different. A ringing sound woke me up, but it wasn't from my alarm clock. It took me a few seconds to figure it out, but I finally realized it was my phone. I looked down at the screen. It was Chief Wilhelm. Then I glanced over at my alarm clock. Six a.m. Something must have happened.

"What's going on?" I started to ask him. But I never got any more out. He was screaming so loudly at me that he drowned me out. I had to hold the phone away from my ear to make out what he was saying. There was no question he was really mad at someone. As it turned out, it was at me.

"What in the hell were you thinking, Pearce? Were you drinking again? You must have been to do something so stupid and damaging. You've screwed yourself, the department and the whole damn town with this."

"What are you talking about?"

"Did you tell a reporter that we are looking at Melvin Ellis as a potential suspect in the Samantha Claymore disappearance? And for the murder of Bridget Feckanin? And possibly for the kidnapping of other girls who went missing here in the past few years?"

Jesus!

"Well, did you, Pearce?"

"Yes, but…"

"Why would you do something like that?"

"It was supposed to be off the record."

"Well, it's sure 'on the record' now. Turn on your TV."

I did. There was a newscaster talking about the breaking news out of Martha's Vineyard on the Samantha Claymore case. The newscaster wasn't Lincoln Connor. But it was all the same information I'd told him during our supposedly confidential conversation the other day on the beach.

"Sources say that the Cedar Cliffs Police Department is trying to get a warrant to search the mansion of Melvin Ellis for evidence on any of these missing girl cases. The lead investigator on this is Detective Abby Pearce, who recently moved back to Martha's Vineyard after a controversial stint in the NYPD. Pearce apparently told a source that she was 'determined to get Ellis, no matter what.' Stay tuned for more on this breaking story. We'll bring you updates as they come in throughout the day…"

I sat there stunned, staring at a picture of Ellis on the screen. Then I realized Wilhelm was still on the other end of the line.

"Chief, I'm sorry. I never meant for this to go public."

"Then you shouldn't have talked about it with a goddamned reporter."

Wilhelm was right, of course. I'd screwed up big time.

"What do you want me to do?"

"Get the hell in here to the station. We need to figure out some kind of damage control. There's going to need to be a press conference today. You'll have to publicly apologize. You'll say Melvin Ellis is not a suspect in the disappearance of Samantha Claymore and that we are not looking at Melvin Ellis for any other kind of criminal activity. That this is all a big mistake. Understand?"

"I'm not sure I can say that. I still—'

"You'll do it if you want to keep your job on my goddamn police force!"

Then he slammed down the phone.

I punched in the number I had for Lincoln Connor. I hoped he was still asleep so I could wake him up and scream at him the way Wilhelm just did with me. But he was awake. I had the feeling he was waiting for my call. Or had been about to call me to gloat about how he'd played me.

"You son of a bitch!" I said. "You promised me, as a journalist, as someone who wanted to be in a relationship with me, that this was off the record – and then you stabbed me in the back!"

"Abby, it wasn't me."

"What are you talking about?"

"I didn't break the story."

"You're the only reporter I talked to about it."

"Maybe so. But the *Boston Globe* broke the story overnight. Everyone on TV – including my station – is picking it up from them. My producer is pissed at me for getting scooped on it."

"I don't believe you."

'Honestly, Abby…"

"How dare you use the word 'honest' with me after the lies you've just told?"

"Let's talk about this rationally…"

"I don't ever want to talk to you again!"

It was my turn to slam down the phone. My next call was to Teena. She was awake too and had seen the TV reports. I filled her in on everything, interspersing my explanation with profanity and anger at Lincoln Connor for betraying me.

"Maybe he's telling the truth," Teena said when I was finished.

"What?"

"I read the *Globe* story. And I've watched the TV newscasts. None of them mention anything about Channel 6, his station. Why would he betray you if he wasn't going to break the story himself? Why would he give that information to the *Boston Globe*? That doesn't make sense."

She was right. None of it made sense. I was so mad at Lincoln Connor that I hadn't thought the whole thing through. I'd needed someone to blame for this. And Lincoln Connor seemed like the obvious choice. But what if it wasn't him? How did the information I gave him get out there?

"Did you tell anyone else all this besides Lincoln Connor?" Teena asked.

"No, he was the only one."

"You're sure?"

And that's when it hit me.

I had told someone else.

My friend.

My champion.

The man who had helped me get my job with the Cedar Cliffs police force.

The man who'd said he was going to help me bring down Melvin Ellis.

Mayor Peter Randall.

CHAPTER 54

The house that Valerie Claymore had rented for the summer in Cedar Cliffs was as beautiful and impressive as it was the first time I'd been there. At least on the outside. There was the swimming pool. The wraparound porch. The magnificent living room window overlooking the ocean.

But I didn't see it as a beautiful house anymore. I saw it as a house that hid dark secrets, like the secrets I believed other houses on the island – especially the mansion of Melvin Ellis – hid too.

One of the secrets Valerie Claymore's place held the key to was the whereabouts of her sixteen-year-old daughter Samantha.

I had to come back here again to find out the truth.

The Ellis leak had turned into a media debacle. First, Wilhelm held a press conference and disavowed any suggestion that we were investigating Melvin Ellis. He said there would be no effort to get a search warrant to search Ellis' house and described any such suggestion on my part as rogue and irresponsible.

Then Mayor Randall told the press he was shocked that the police would smear the name of an esteemed citizen like Melvin Ellis, questioning my judgement and ability to lead the Samantha Claymore investigation. I knew I'd told Randall I'd take responsibility if this all went wrong, but this went far beyond that.

I realized now that Randall – not Lincoln Connor – must have been the one who leaked the information to the press. He was the only other person that I told.

Why would Randall do this?

Well, the obvious answer was he was involved with Ellis. And, by discrediting me in public, I was prevented from going through with any efforts to search the Ellis mansion for evidence about Samantha Claymore and Bridget Feckanin.

The icing on the cake came when Melvin Ellis also met with the media and invited everyone – reporters, police and civilians – into his house to search it for anything they thought might be there. Ellis said he wanted to show that he had nothing to hide. Of course, any evidence of his wrongdoing would have been gone as soon as he found out, presumably from Randall, about what I'd planned. But a public stunt like this made it impossible for me to move against him, no matter how convinced I was of his guilt and involvement with Samantha and Bridget.

And so I was doing the only thing I could think of to find Samantha Claymore and get the answers I was looking for.

By going back to the beginning of this case.

The beginning was Valerie Claymore reporting her daughter missing.

It was another sunny, gorgeous August day. A beach day. Even though it was still morning when I got there – barely ten a.m. – Beach Road was packed with vacationers headed for the State Beach which ran down the east side of the Vineyard, all the way to South Beach.

I got out of my car, walked to the front door and rang the bell. I hoped Bruce Aiken wasn't there. Or Muzzy Malone. I wanted to talk to Valerie Claymore alone.

She answered the door still dressed in her bathrobe. Apparently not an early riser. On the other hand, maybe she hadn't even been to bed yet.

"Is there news about Samantha?" she asked.

It was the question everyone asked me.

Maybe someday I'd have an answer for them.

"No, nothing," I told her.

"Then why are you here?"

"I need some information."

"I've already told you everything I know. What else do you want from me?"

"The truth."

She led me into the living room and sat down awkwardly on the couch. Her eyes looked bloodshot and tired, and I remembered the concoction of pills I'd seen her taking the last time I was here. I had a feeling she pretty much lived on them. But then who was I to criticize someone for substance abuse? We all pick our own poisons. Her condition probably wasn't ideal for further questioning, but I didn't really have a choice.

"A number of things have come up in the investigation," I told her. "Things that on the face of it don't seem to directly involve your daughter's disappearance. But I believe there is a connection. I don't think you've been completely forthcoming with me about your daughter's disappearance. And at this point I'm not even sure if she was kidnapped or left voluntarily because of another incident in your family's past."

"What are you talking about?"

"The death of your husband."

"That's ridiculous."

"Is it?"

"Of course. Ronald died five years ago. What does that have to do with Samantha being gone now?"

"Because this summer you brought your daughter back to the place where it happened – and I think that's what started everything. Did you know that before she disappeared, your daughter was telling people that you were responsible for your husband's death? In fact, she blamed you for 'murdering' him."

"It was an accident. I had nothing to do with what happened to Ronald."

"I didn't say you did."

"Then why…?"

"But I'm also not sure anymore that it was an accident."

"Who would have wanted to kill Ronald?"

"Maybe your current husband, Bruce Aiken. How do you explain the fact that the man who works with him now, Muzzy Malone, was running the boat your husband was on when he died? Did you know that Aiken's first wife died under mysterious circumstances shortly before he met and married you? And do you know what he's doing with all the money he makes from your company? Do you know where the intended ransom money is right now? Do you—"

"That's enough. Of course, I know everything about Bruce. I'm not stupid. But you've put it together in a way that sounds terrible. You're trying to upset me, to confuse me. You should be out looking for my daughter. Why aren't you doing that instead of sitting here asking me ridiculous questions?"

"Like I said, I think getting the answers to these things is the best way to get answers about Samantha."

Valerie Claymore looked at me as if she wanted to say something, but then stopped. She was reluctant to tell me whatever she knew. Or maybe afraid. Afraid of Bruce Aiken and Muzzy Malone and probably Melvin Ellis too.

"Are you scared about what your husband might do if you talk to me?"

She didn't say anything.

"Muzzy Malone?"

Still nothing.

"What about Melvin Ellis?"

"Why are you asking me about Melvin Ellis?"

"I think he's involved."

"With my daughter's disappearance?"

"With a lot of bad things."

"I don't understand. I heard that you suspected him of something. But then I saw the police chief and mayor deny any interest in his involvement. Why are you still talking about him?"

"Because I still think he is involved. With the disappearance of your daughter and other girls. Maybe with your husband and Muzzy Malone too. I need your help to find Samantha, Mrs. Claymore. I need you to tell me everything that you know about your husband and Muzzy Malone and Melvin Ellis."

I sat there for quite a while with her, talking like this and hoping I'd get something useful from her. But I didn't. She kept telling me she didn't know what I was talking about and that none of it had anything to do with her daughter. I didn't believe her. And I think she knew I didn't believe her. But there wasn't much I could do about the situation. I finally decided to leave.

As she walked me to the door, I handed her my card with all my contact information on it. She already had one, of course. But I wanted to make sure she'd use it. "Call me anytime," I said. "Whenever you're ready to tell me more."

She nodded. And then she suddenly blurted out: "My daughter hates me. Why does she hate me so much?" She looked distressed now. Maybe the pills she'd been taking to calm her down had begun to wear off.

"Lots of teenage girls hate their mothers," I said. "But you still have to be a good mother to her. You need to do the right thing for Samantha. Help me get her back by being completely honest with me about everything you know."

For a second or two, I thought this might be a breakthrough. But then she shook her head. "I told you before… I don't know what you're talking about. Go find Samantha, Detective. Do your job."

"That's the same thing your husband told me," I said. "Keep that card with my number close, and call me whenever you're ready."

Valerie Claymore looked down at the card in her hand and – I thought later – almost nodded, like it was something she was considering.

She was still staring at the card when I left.

Standing there in the doorway as I walked back to my car.

It was the last time I'd ever see her alive.

CHAPTER 55

Valerie Claymore was found dead in bed by her housekeeper the next morning.

There was no sign of violence or foul play. She was simply lying in bed, the television on and with some Claymore Cosmetics business papers scattered around her. It was as if she had read them, closed her eyes, gone to sleep and just died.

The housekeeper screamed when she discovered Mrs. Claymore, called 911 for the paramedics – who arrived and pronounced her dead at the scene. The Cedar Cliffs police were notified, and Teena and I showed up shortly afterward.

There were pill bottles scattered around the bedroom, for various prescriptions Valerie had been taking. Valium and other medications. But the most obvious thing was an open bottle of sleeping pills on the bed stand next to Valerie. It was almost empty. The obvious conclusion was that she had overdosed – either intentionally or accidentally – and that caused her death.

Except I didn't believe that.

"I pushed her Teena. I pushed her really hard yesterday when I was here. I could tell she was close to reaching some kind of emotional breakthrough – making a decision about what to do next. But I had no idea this was the way things would turn out. I only wanted the truth from her."

"Maybe it was all too much for her," Teena said. "Her daughter, her marriage, the money problems in the business. She turns to pills, which she seemed to do a lot, and takes so many of them that she kills herself. Maybe on purpose, maybe not. But it all winds up the same: The woman committed suicide."

I shook my head.

"I don't think that's what happened. I think she wanted to finally confront her problems, not run away from them. That was the feeling I got from her. She knew things – about her daughter. Maybe she went to her husband and demanded answers from him."

"And you figure he killed her?"

"Him or Muzzy Malone. Who seems to do the dirty work for him."

"They forced her to take the pills? Enough to kill her?"

"It wouldn't be hard to do, given the emotional state she was in. Keep feeding her the sleeping pills, forcing them down if she resisted – and her death would look like a suicide. Why not? She's depressed about her daughter missing. It has a certain logic to it."

"Why would they kill her?"

"To keep her quiet."

"But she's Aiken's golden goose – the only way he has access to the money."

"We don't know those details. Maybe everything in her will goes to him if she dies. Or maybe, even if she doesn't, what she knew about him was so dangerous that he had to make sure she didn't talk to us."

"Seems hard to believe."

"Hey, that's the pattern here. Bridget Feckanin was possibly killed because she was pregnant. Maybe other missing girls over the years have been killed to keep them quiet, like Ruthie Kolton. Don't forget Aiken's first wife – another wealthy woman – supposedly died in a suicide. And we're still not sure what happened with Ronald Claymore and Muzzy Malone on that boat five years ago."

Neither Aiken or Malone were anywhere to be seen at the house. The housekeeper said they'd been there the previous evening. So where were they now?

"Let's put out an APB alert to pick them both up," I said to Teena. "Assuming they're still on the island. We don't want them to leave."

"There's not enough evidence – no evidence really – to say they killed her."

"So, we'll pick them up as material witnesses."

"Material witnesses," she repeated.

"Sure. They were the last people to see Valerie Claymore alive. The housekeeper told us that. And they're meant to be in New York. We need to question them to determine if there was a crime committed here. Which I'm sure will turn out to be the case."

"An autopsy might help answer some of our questions too," Teena said. "Not only about how many pills Valerie took. But there might be evidence of physical force or assault used to make her swallow them."

"All the more reason we need to get Aiken and Malone to the station where we can question them."

The medical examiner's team was finishing up their work. Valerie Claymore's body was gently lifted into a black body bag. Then it was carried out to a waiting ambulance, taken to a funeral home and left on a metal table until funeral arrangements were made.

This part of the job always got to me. The death part. Even after all these years I'd spent as a homicide detective. Here was this woman that had been alive less than twenty-four hours earlier, and now she was a corpse. All of her money and the beautiful things she owned didn't matter anymore.

She was just another body in a bag that I needed to investigate.

"You know what's really terrible," I said to Teena. "She was alone. No daughter, no one here for her. That's sad."

Except, as it turned out, she did have someone who showed up after her death.

Teena and I were at the station a few days later when a girl walked in and came over to us. She was in her teens. Pretty, with strawberry blonde hair. I'd never met her before. Not in person anyway. But I sure knew who she was.

Samantha Claymore.

"I think you've been looking for me," she said.

CHAPTER 56

"I really messed up, didn't I?" Samantha Claymore said.

"You had a lot of people worried about you."

"I was worried about me too."

"Where have you been?"

"Traveling."

"Traveling where?"

"Lots of places. Philadelphia. Nashville. New Orleans. I kept running because I was scared. I didn't know what else to do."

"What were you afraid of?"

"That man…"

"Your stepfather, Bruce Aiken?"

"Him too. But I'm talking about the man who works for him."

"Muzzy Malone?"

She nodded.

"He was the one who killed my father. I know that now. And he wanted to kill me next."

We were sitting in an office at the Cedar Cliffs police station. Teena, Samantha Claymore and me. Samantha was drinking a Coke and eating a roast beef sandwich I'd ordered for her from a store nearby. I'm not sure if she was nervous or hungry, but she was really wolfing it down. I wondered when she'd last eaten. But I didn't ask her about that. I just sat there and let Samantha tell her story.

"I don't know how this summer turned so quickly into a nightmare for me. I hadn't been here since that trip with my father five years ago. At first it was fun. I met Bridget and Eddie. I felt more comfortable than I had in a long time, certainly more than I did back in New York.

"But then everything changed. I started thinking more and more about what happened to me and my father that day on the water. The counselor I'd been seeing in New York told me I'd suppressed a lot of those memories. But now – being in this place again – they were beginning to return.

"I remembered things I hadn't before. Little by little at first, and then a lot more when I saw Muzzy Malone up here with my stepfather. I couldn't understand why they were together. The man who was there when my father died now here working for my stepfather.

"The memories came back. Including something very disturbing I hadn't thought about since that day on the boat. Right before the engine exploded, Muzzy Malone put on a life jacket and moved to the far side of the boat away from the engine. It was as if he knew what was going to happen, and was getting ready to save himself."

"Is that why you ran away?" Teena asked.

Samantha shook her head.

"No, I mean I still wasn't sure. I had a lot of questions, a lot of suspicions. That's when I started talking to Bridget and Eddie about it. Did Muzzy Malone kill my father so Bruce Aiken could marry my mother and get all of our money? Was my mother involved too? Or at least aware of what was going to happen to my father?

"I was on that boat with my father. Could my mother have had my father murdered and left me to die that day too? All of these questions were swirling around in my mind. But it was later, when Bridget and I went out to the house… that's when it all happened. It was after that when I started running."

"Then what—" Teena started to say but I shook my head at her. I wanted to let Samantha keep talking on her own. A lot of it didn't make much sense so far, but I was hoping it would as she went on. In any case, I wanted to hear the story in Samantha Claymore's own words.

"Bridget said there was this man who had a big house near Gay Head and that she and some of her girlfriends would sometimes go out there. That the man – and some of his friends – would pay a few hundred dollars each time for massages or other stuff.

"She said it was harmless and that they just wanted to be around young girls. She said I should come along the next time she went. She said the other girls – at least the pretty ones – loved the money they could get from these men.

"Well, I sure didn't need the money. But I wanted to be Bridget's friend. I'd never really had any friends like her in New York. Certainly not a best friend. I wanted to fit in. I wanted Bridget to keep on liking me. So I agreed to go with her.

"I wasn't exactly sure what was going to happen when I got there. I wasn't planning on massaging anyone. Or maybe I was. Maybe it would be fun to be like Bridget, I thought to myself. I'm not sure. I only know that in the end I went out there to the big house in Gay Head with Bridget.

"Except when I got there, it wasn't fun at all. The man who opened the door wasn't wearing any clothes. He just had a towel wrapped around him. Then another man came into the room where we were. He was glad at first to see Bridget, but then he recognized me. I knew him too. It was Muzzy Malone."

I thought about how Teena and I had followed Malone and Bruce Aiken to Ellis' house that day. It all made sense now. They were hooked up in this whole business with Melvin Ellis.

"Malone got upset when he saw us. He was mad at Bridget, saying she shouldn't have brought me there. Then the owner of the house came into the room to see what was going on. He was upset too. There was another man, a police officer. I didn't know who he was, but he was wearing a badge. Everyone was mad at Bridget for bringing me. At one point, Bridget and I started to leave. But, before we did, I turned around and blurted out: 'You killed my father, I know that now. Seeing you again has brought it all back to me. You won't get away with it.' I know that was stupid, but I couldn't help myself. Seeing him again brought back such terrible memories. Before Bridget and I got outside, I could hear Malone saying: 'I should have killed her on that damn boat with her father. We need to get rid of her now before she tells anyone.'

"Bridget and I ran out of the house and went back to Cedar Cliffs, but we didn't know what to do next. I couldn't tell the story to my stepfather because he worked with Malone. I couldn't tell my mother because she might be in on it. And I was afraid to go to the police since I saw a policeman at the house.

"The next day I saw Muzzy Malone in a car following me when I left my house. That's when Bridget and I came up with the plan. She would pretend she was me to throw everyone off. I rode my bike to Edgartown, left it in the bike rack and Bridget dressed like me for the security cameras in the stores. I even dropped a sandal off along the road to Edgartown to convince people I had ridden down there. Then Bridget took a shuttle bus back. That night I got on a ferry in Cedar Cliffs. I've been running ever since."

"What about the ransom note?"

"I sent that. Well, we wrote that together, and then Bridget delivered it. I told her where the video cameras were at the house so she could stay away from them. The idea was if people thought I was kidnapped, maybe Malone wouldn't be looking for me. We put a bunch of stuff into it. Anything we could think of to make it seem like the note really came from a deranged kidnapper. I did the political protest part about my family's cosmetics business. I'd been involved in demonstrations about that, and felt strongly against what they were doing to test animals. Bridget had been reading some stuff about satanic cults, so she added the '777' on the envelope and in the letter. We did whatever we could to keep everyone – the police, my family and, most of all, Malone – guessing while I got away."

I thought about the amount of the ransom, $583,000, the exact amount of her first yearly trust fund payment when she turned eighteen. I asked her about that.

"It was the first thing that popped into my head. I was in a hurry. That's why I wrote the letter in my own handwriting, not using newspaper letters or anything like that. I knew I wanted to get on that ferry and get out of there as soon as possible. Before anyone realized I was missing and started looking for me on the island.

"When I got off the ferry at Woods Hole, I took a bus to Boston. Then I had enough cash – I didn't use any credit cards because I knew how easy they were to track – to take a train to Philadelphia. I had my phone with me, but I made sure not to make any calls with it and I turned off the locations setting – so no one could track me that way. After that I made my way first to Nashville, then on to New Orleans. That's where I've been for the last few weeks."

It was a crazy story. So crazy that it must be true. Or at least most of it. But I still had questions.

I asked her then about her father, Ronald Claymore. I still wasn't sure how that fit into everything that had happened.

"Eddie Haver said that before you left you thought your father might still be alive. That he didn't die that day on the ocean. Do you still believe that? Is that what you were doing? Looking for your father?"

She shook her head.

"My father is dead," she said. "I had this fantasy for a while that maybe he was alive. Hiding like I was doing. But that's all it was. A fantasy."

She drank the rest of her Coke, then asked if she could have another. Teena went to the vending machine and brought a can back to her.

"I wanted to come back after Bridget died, but I was afraid. Then I heard about my mother. My mother and I had our troubles, but I loved her. I really did. I was devastated when I found out about her death. I knew I had to go to the police, even if I wasn't sure who I could trust. I watched you at some of the press conferences you did. You seemed sincere and honest. So here I am."

"How did you get back here from New Orleans so fast?"

"I flew."

"How did you pay for it?"

"What do you mean?"

"Well, you haven't been using your credit cards. We've monitored those. And you haven't withdrawn any money from the bank accounts in your name. How did you pay for the ticket?"

"What does it matter how I got here?" she said. "I'm back now. Isn't that what you wanted?"

I had a feeling that she still wasn't telling me everything about where she had been. But I wanted to keep her talking. So I went to a different line of questioning.

"Did you know Bridget was pregnant?" I asked her.

"Yes, she told me. But not until the last day. Right before I left."

"Did she tell you who the father was?"

"Yes."

"And who was it?"

"The man who owned the house."

Melvin Ellis. Bridget Feckanin was pregnant with Melvin Ellis' child when she died. We could do a DNA check on that now that we had Samantha's testimony. That could help us nail Ellis.

"And you know the man who owned the house, don't you, Sam?"

"Yes, you do too. He was at the first press conference with you at the beginning. I thought that was strange. Him offering money for my safe return, when I knew him and Malone wanted me dead."

I nodded.

"Melvin Ellis," I said.

"No, the other one."

"What do you mean?"

"He was the other guy with you at that press conference."

"Chief Wilhelm?"

"No, the mayor. Peter Randall. Randall was the man who owned the house we went to that day."

CHAPTER 57

It suddenly all made sense. I'd been on the trail of the wrong man all along. And the man I should have been after was the one who helped steer me in that direction.

Peter Randall fit the same description as Melvin Ellis. A rich, powerful man with a big house in Gay Head. The difference was Randall was my friend, my benefactor – or so I thought. I hated Ellis because of what his son did to me after my high school prom. I'd gotten caught up in my emotions about the case, rather than following the evidence. Which is the worst thing a police officer can do. Now I had to make it right.

"Randall played me," I said to Teena as soon as we'd left the room where Samantha was still sipping on a Coke and finishing up her sandwich. "I see that now. He played me right from the very beginning. Acting like he was my big supporter. Telling me to report directly to him because I was the only one he trusted. I'll bet he even planted the ring Bridget Feckanin had been wearing near Ellis' house to make him look guilty. And then he was the one who leaked the stuff about us planning a raid on Ellis' house to the media."

"Why would he do that?"

"To discredit me. In case I figured out it was him. The uproar over the raid in the media made me look foolish. Like I was some sort of alcoholic looking for any way to get attention on a case I couldn't solve. But, even if we had gone ahead with the search at the time, there would have been nothing at Ellis' house. Randall knew that. And that would have made me look even more foolish. No one would have ever believed me if I'd suddenly started talking about Randall as a suspect. Maybe that's why he pushed so hard for me to get my job, instead of you. He knew about my drinking, my other problems in New York – he figured he could control me. When he couldn't do that, he decided to discredit me instead. Randall's the guy we're after, Teena, not Melvin Ellis."

"So what do we do now?"

"We arrest him."

"We arrest the mayor?"

"Yes. We've got an eyewitness, Teena. Samantha Claymore. She can talk about all the things Bridget Feckanin told her about the stuff happening with teenage girls he procured for himself and his friends. It's hearsay evidence, sure. But it is compelling. Hopefully, we can use that to get other girls to come forward to testify against him and even link him to some of the missing girls."

"Do we tell Wilhelm what we're doing?"

"No, we can't tell anyone. We don't know how deep this thing goes in the department. Garrity was involved in the cover-ups. That means there's a good chance Wilhelm was. She said there was a police officer at Randall's house. We can't be sure who that was."

"So we're going to march in on our own and arrest Mayor Randall?"

"Yes."

"Please tell me you have a plan on exactly how to do that."

The first thing we needed to do was get Samantha Claymore to a safe place. If cops here were really involved, then she was in danger at the station. To do that, I was going to have to trust one other person here. Meg Jarvis. Meg had been the only other person there when Samantha Claymore walked in. So she already knew. Teena and I walked over to her now.

"We have to find someplace to put the girl for a while," I said to Meg. "A safe place."

"She's not safe in a police station?"

"Not this police station."

I went through an abbreviated version of what I knew and said that the police – people in our department – were involved. I said I couldn't trust anyone. I wasn't sure I could trust her either, but I didn't say that. I had no choice but to use her for this.

Meg was stunned, and reluctant at first to go along with what I wanted.

"You need to talk to Chief Wilhelm," she said.

"I can't do that."

"He'll know what to do."

"Wilhelm might be one of the bad guys, Meg."

"I don't believe that. I've known Barry for a long time. He might not be perfect, but he would never do something like this."

"Meg, I hope you're right about that. But I can't take the chance. We need to find a place to stash Samantha until I can get Randall and the rest of them into custody."

We finally came up with a plan. Taking her home didn't work because Aiken might be there. Meg suggested putting her up at her house, but that would be the first place someone would look if they knew Meg was helping us. We finally decided to use a hotel across the street from the station. I reserved a room there, took Samantha over and told her not to leave the room until we came to get her. Meg could take a break from time to time to check in on her without anyone noticing.

"So now the two of us go see Randall at the Town Hall?" Teena asked.

"Me, not us."

"What do you mean?"

"I'm going to talk to him first. Try to find out more before I make my move. I have a personal relationship with him. Maybe he won't suspect anything if I'm talking to him about the case. About the way he left me hanging with the media on Ellis. I'll act like I'm confused, like I'm looking for some answers – one-on-one. If you're with me... that might set off all sorts of warning bells before I can get him talking."

"What am I supposed to do?"

"Check out his mansion near Gay Head. He could be out there. See if you can tell. But don't do anything, Teena. Don't approach him, don't try to get him to talk. I simply want to know if he's there. If so, then we'll come up with the best plan for taking him in. Maybe we'll call in the state police and the FBI for help. Yeah, I know, we can't be sure about them either. But we'll figure that out once we find out where Randall is."

"Okay," Teena said, "but let me give you this before you go to his office."

She reached down and unhooked the holster and gun she carried around her ankle.

"Just in case."

"Don't you need it?"

"I have another one," she said.

I nodded and strapped the holster and gun around my ankle. As Teena said, just in case.

A short time later, I walked into the Town Hall and asked to see Mayor Randall. I thought about the times I'd been here in the past, when I thought Randall was someone I could count on to be on my side. I had to convince him I still felt the same way until I was ready to make my move.

But Randall wasn't at the Town Hall. His assistant said she wasn't sure when he'd be there, or if he was even coming into the office at all today. She said he'd been talking about going out on his boat.

I remembered Randall's boat – a big one, with all sorts of decks and staterooms – that he kept docked at the marina across the street. I went over there, found the slip where he moored it – but it was empty. Maybe he was already out on the water.

I was debating going back to the station or stopping off at the hotel to check on Samantha when I got a text.

It was from Teena.

He's here! At the house in Gay Head!

What's he doing? I texted back.

Get out here right away. It's important. And don't tell anyone. I'll explain everything when you get here. Hurry!

It normally takes forty-five minutes to drive the length of Martha's Vineyard from Cedar Cliffs to Gay Head, but I made it in less than thirty. During the drive, I kept wondering about what I was going to find. Teena sounded desperate. Maybe I should've brought in the state police or someone else for backup. But I wasn't sure who to trust.

When I got to Randall's house, I saw Teena's car parked on a road leading up to the mansion, but it was empty. I didn't see her around anywhere else either. I texted her, but didn't get an answer. I didn't want to call, because I was afraid someone might hear her phone ring.

I made my way onto the estate, past a guest house, pool and tennis court. Unlike Ellis' place, there was no security man or gate. But it was still a damn impressive place. I remembered seeing pictures of powerful and wealthy and famous people at events here.

I knocked on the front door. It seemed like an awfully obvious thing to do, but I couldn't think of anything else. No one answered. I peered in through the front window. It was a huge place, I could see that. There must be a lot of help to keep a place like this going. But where was everybody? And, most importantly, where was Randall?

That's when I noticed the boat. Randall's boat that was usually kept at the Cedar Cliffs Marina but was hooked up to a dock on the beach below. Why was it here instead of in Cedar Cliffs? Did he know we were after him? Was he planning to flee somewhere?

I approached the boat carefully, my hand on the gun on my hip. When I got to it and started to board, I took out the gun and went into a shooter's stance.

But there was nothing.

I made my way forward until I got to a door leading to a series of cabins inside.

I pushed the door open and saw a living room area.

I walked through it, found another door and made my way into the next room – and the one after that.

It was when I went through the final door on the boat that I found Teena.

She was tied to a chair and gagged.

Randall was standing next to her.

She motioned frantically at me with her eyes to the door behind me, but it was too late.

I felt the cold metal of a gun barrel against the side of my head.

"We've been waiting for you, Detective Pearce," Peter Randall said.

CHAPTER 58

"Drop the gun," I heard another voice say.

I quickly took in the situation. Teena tied up and unable to help. Randall standing in front of me. And someone else with a gun to the side of my head. I didn't really have much choice. I dropped my gun to the floor.

The man with the gun pushed me toward the center of the room, then kicked my gun away toward Randall. I slowly turned around to get a look at him. It was Muzzy Malone.

Randall reached down, picked up my gun and laid it on a table next to where Teena was tied up. It didn't make any difference though, no way she could get loose to grab it. I noticed that Teena's phone was on the table too.

"Those texts came from you, didn't they?" I said.

Randall nodded. "Of course. Muzzy here saw her roaming around outside. Muzzy is very vigilant. He grabbed her, brought her in here and we went looking for you. When we couldn't find you, we decided to make you come to us. So here you are."

"Muzzy works for you," I said. It was all beginning to fit together now. "Not Aiken."

"Of course. Muzzy watches Aiken for me. Aiken does what I tell him to do. I'm responsible for everything he has."

"You were the one who got rid of Ronald Claymore?"

"Claymore came to this house. He partook in the massages I – and the young girls – offered him. But then – when he found out the full extent of what I was doing here – he got all righteous and said he was going to the authorities. I had a video of him being massaged. I figured the threat of it would change his mind. But he said that didn't matter. He was going to do the right thing. He had thought about his own young daughter and how he didn't want her to be lured to a place like this."

"So that's when you decided to put Muzzy on that boat to kill him? You got rid of Claymore and put your friend Bruce Aiken in charge of the Claymore money – which I assume you've been siphoning off for yourself since then."

"You are pretty smart. It was a win-win for me. No Claymore, but lots of Claymore's money."

"But why does it matter? You're already one of the richest men around."

"You can never be too rich. I want to be richer than Melvin Ellis. That's my goal."

"So this is all about money?"

"Not all. I like young girls. I always have. Yes, I have a wife and family. But I need more. I like everything about them. Well, except for one thing. They grow up. And they cause me trouble. Like you are right now. But there are always more girls around. When you have money like me, you can get anything you want. And I want to keep doing what I'm doing here."

I shook my head.

"It's all over, Randall," I said. "No matter what you do to us. You've been identified as the man who has been grooming and abusing underage girls. Including Bridget Feckanin who wound up dead. I'm sure there will turn out to be links between you and some of those other missing girls."

"I'm way ahead of you, Pearce. I know that Samantha Claymore identified me. I also know there are only two officers aware of what she said. And those officers happen to be the same two that I have here with me. So once I get rid of you, and keep Samantha Claymore from telling her story, no one will ever know."

My God, he knows about Samantha. Does he know about Meg being there too? Unless she was part of it…

"How did you find out?" I asked.

"Let's just say I have friends in your department."

"Was it Meg Jarvis?"

He smiled and shook his head no.

"Chief Wilhelm?"

"Wilhelm? He couldn't figure out how to tie his shoelaces without help. No, my friend in the department is much smarter and useful than Wilhelm. He's on the boat now – let me introduce you."

He called out to someone outside – presumably who'd gone onto the deck after I came inside the cabin – to join us in the room.

I still suspected it would be Wilhelm to walk through the door, no matter what Randall had said. Or maybe Bowers, who was ambitious and presumably could be lured by Randall's money. But it wasn't either one. Instead, Vic Hollister walked into the room.

"Yes, I know what you thought of me. Not very smart, not very ambitious, not very good," Hollister said. "That was the way I wanted people to see me. I let Garrity and Wilhelm put their names to all the stuff I fed them. They couldn't believe I was capable of being devious – and so they were happy to take credit for my work. It was a perfect setup."

"Did you kill Norm Garrity and make it look like a suicide?"

"Nah. Norm started to feel guilty about everything he'd done. Or not done."

"Did you know Garrity was planning on going to the FBI?"

Hollister laughed. "We found out about that. We warned him that if he confessed to the FBI he'd go to jail for a long time. Told him it was his name on that phony paperwork, not ours. And that we had video of him with those girls too. Scared Garrity silly. The guy was a wreck. So he ate that pistol on his own. That's the trouble with having a conscience, it messes you up."

"I'm sure you don't have that problem," I said. "You deliberately planted Samantha Claymore's ring outside Ellis' house too, right?"

"Sure. We knew you were looking at Ellis for all this, so it was an easy way to point the finger at him. It kept you going in the wrong direction. That way we were able to control your investigation, at least until now."

"With Vic here," Randall interrupted, "we had a perfect pipeline into the police department. And those other two – Wilhelm and Garrity – were so weak and gullible we could steer them any way we wanted in an investigation. I pay Vic very well for that service. He has quite a bit stashed away in overseas accounts. I find that paying people guarantees their loyalty. You, on the other hand, well… you've turned out to be a problem. I didn't expect that."

"Is that why you leaked information about me wanting to search Melvin Ellis' house to the media?"

"Yes. I pretended that I was reluctant to go after Ellis, I made it seem like it was all your idea. Because I knew there was no evidence inside that house. But it pointed the finger at someone else. And it compromised you as a credible law enforcement officer. So even if you did find out the truth, no one would believe you."

"Why did you push to bring me here anyway?"

"Why do you think I did?"

"I think you figured I was damaged goods. You could use that to control me. And, if that failed, you could use it to discredit me. Like you did with the story about the raid on Ellis' house. You'd drop some more hints about me drinking or whatever… Am I right?"

"That's pretty close. But now there's a new plan for you. And your drinking is going to help. You're going to shoot your partner here. Everyone knows you don't get along because she thinks she should have your job. We'll drop the bodies off on the beach – everyone will assume you went off on a drunken shooting spree, and then killed yourself when you realized what you had done. At least that's the way we'll spin it, right, Vic?"

Hollister nodded. "Sounds good to me." My God, how could I have been so wrong about this guy?

"There are only two police officers who know the truth about me. You and Morelli here. Vic was there at the station too. But you didn't see him – he keeps a very low profile, as I'm sure you're now aware. Anyway, Vic knows you didn't take any of this to Wilhelm. So you two are the only ones who can bring me down."

They didn't know about Meg. Hollister had missed that part. Or about what Becky Kolton had told me. It was something…

"What about Samantha Claymore?" I asked.

"Don't worry, she won't get a chance to tell anyone her story either."

I looked over at Teena. I could tell she was quietly trying to break free from her restraints. But she wasn't making any progress. I was on my own here. With everything at stake. My life. Teena's life. And Samantha Claymore's life too.

"Can I have a drink?" I said to Randall.

"What?"

"If I'm going to die, I want to have one last drink. Please, I need it. A glass of vodka if you've got it, if not – anything else. Don't let me die sober. Just give me a drink…"

Randall laughed. So did Hollister and Malone.

"Damn, she really is screwed-up," Malone said. "She's about to die and all she cares about is having a damn drink. Pathetic."

They were the first words Muzzy Malone had said since he ordered me to drop the gun. Malone was all business. He was the one I had to worry about the most when I made my move. Which I was about to do.

"Please give me a drink… just one more drink!"

I fell to my knees like I was pleading with them.

But instead, I reached down and grabbed the gun from my hidden ankle holster.

The one Teena had given to me.

"Hey, what the…?" Malone yelled.

But I'd caught him by surprise. All of them. I shot Malone first, right in the forehead. He fell down dead. Hollister tried to go for his gun, but he was too slow. For all his bravado a few minutes earlier, he really wasn't a very good cop. I shot him before he could get the gun completely out of his holster. It dropped to the ground. I kicked it away from him into a corner, while he lay there moaning and bleeding.

Randall was smarter though. He lunged for my gun on the table, picked it up and grabbed Teena to hide behind for cover. He had the gun pointed at her head. "Do you want to be responsible for getting your partner killed? Like you were back in New York?"

He was playing mind games with me.

I realized that.

But I couldn't ignore them either.

Those memories – the ones of me standing there and letting Tommy Ferraro die – were burned into my mind and too bad to ever forget.

"We can all walk out of here alive, Pearce. You can live, your partner can live and I'll be able to get away. If you pull that trigger, you'll be killing Morelli here. Do you really want that on your conscience for the rest of your life?"

It was all happening very quickly now. Just like the night Tommy Ferraro died in Chelsea, I had only a few seconds to make a decision on what to do. The suspect with a gun, my partner in danger and me standing there wondering whether or not to fire my weapon.

It was all happening again.

I was pretty sure I had a shot at the side of Randall's head, but it would have to be a perfect shot.

Otherwise, I'd hit Teena.

Did I take that chance?

Or did I take the chance that Teena could wind up dead like Tommy because I hesitated?

I squeezed the trigger.

The shot hit Randall in his left ear, which exploded with blood. He screamed and dropped his gun. I quickly picked it up, and stuck it in my belt. Then, while keeping an eye on both of the wounded men – Hollister and Randall – I picked up my phone and called into the station. "Emergency backup needed. Gun battle with police officers on Mayor Randall's boat at Gay Head. One person dead, two wounded. Send everyone you can as fast as you can."

Then I started untying Teena.

"What took you so long to pull the trigger, Pearce?" she asked when I pulled her gag off.

"You might at least thank me for saving your life."

"Have we met?"

"You're welcome," I said.

CHAPTER 59

It was finally over. Samantha Claymore was home, Muzzy Malone was dead, Randall and Hollister were in jail, and Bruce Aiken was under indictment for a slew of financial corruption charges in New York and Boston. I'd accomplished everything I set out to do. And I'd conquered many of my own demons along the way.

So why did I still want a drink?

It was late afternoon, and I was basking in the glow of it all. I was front-page news in the papers. Had been interviewed for *The Today Show* and the cable news channels. There was even talk of a movie based on this case. It was the perfect tabloid story about money and power – and I was right at the center of it.

"Can I get your autograph?" Meg said to me after I hung up from another complimentary phone call.

"This is all pretty amazing, isn't it?"

"Hey, even Chief Wilhelm likes you now."

"Likes me? He's my new best friend."

Wilhelm had gathered the whole Cedar Cliffs force together in the station to congratulate me – and Teena too, of course – for cracking this case.

"We never gave up," Wilhelm said that day. "We never quit. We kept fighting until we got all the answers and justice for everyone."

When he was done, I smiled and whispered in his ear.

"What did you say to Wilhelm then?" Meg asked me.

"I told the chief that we couldn't have done it without him."

Randall was on suicide watch at a federal prison in Boston. There was a lot of worry that he could cheat justice by killing himself. He refused to talk about any of the girls he brought to his mansion, or the murders Muzzy Malone committed for him. But Hollister was talking up a storm. He knew how the legal system worked, and was trying to make a deal for himself. I guess Hollister turned out to be a lot smarter than I ever gave him credit for.

Parts of the case were not clear yet, and might never be. We knew that Randall had Bridget Feckanin killed because she was pregnant with his baby. And Valerie Claymore too because she was going to tell us everything she knew. We weren't sure if Ruthie Kolton or any other missing girls from the past were murdered like Bridget or killed themselves out of shame. Hollister insisted Ruthie Kolton was really a suicide, which is why he stacked Bridget Feckanin's clothes neatly at the site to convince people Bridget was a suicide too. "That Kolton girl was really screwed up," Hollister said during his interrogation. Of course, Hollister and Randall had played a big role in driving her to kill herself by walking into the ocean.

And there were more details about the things I'd learned on the boat with Randall, Malone and Hollister.

Muzzy Malone worked for Randall, and kept an eye on Aiken. Randall had been blackmailing Aiken for years, after secretly taking videos of him with a number of underage girls. They'd met during a business deal, and Randall invited Aiken to the island to meet his harem of teenage girls. Then he used the videos to drain much of Aiken's money, first with the heiress in New York and later with Valerie Claymore.

When Aiken's first wife starting asking questions about the missing money, they killed her and made it look like suicide. Randall had also arranged for Muzzy Malone to be the skipper of Ronald Claymore's boat the day of the "boating accident." It ensured Claymore didn't go to the authorities with what he knew was going on at Randall's mansion in Gay Head. And, after the death of his first wife, it paved the way for Aiken to marry Valerie Claymore, giving Randall another source of income. Why did Randall do it? I guess there's never too much money for people like that. Or maybe he simply liked controlling people.

Valerie Claymore must have suspected some of what was going on – with Randall and Aiken and maybe even about her first husband. Maybe that's why she used so many drugs and sedatives. But it wasn't until the very end – when she feared her own daughter's life was at stake – that she confronted Aiken about everything. Which turned out to be a death warrant. Aiken told Randall, and she was eliminated.

Claymore Cosmetics was in disarray with Valerie Claymore dead and Bruce Aiken indicted. The assumption was that Samantha would eventually take over control of the company. But she was only sixteen, so it would operate under a temporary arrangement until then. Assuming Samantha even wanted to run the company, given her opposition to some of its policies. I hoped she did. I think she could do some good things there.

And Lincoln Connor? I didn't have any further contact with him after my tirade on the phone. I said I never wanted to talk to him again, and he took me at my word. Why not? I told him I didn't believe him, even though he was telling the truth about not leaking information to the press. I should have apologized, but I never did. I'm not sure why. He covered the rest of the story like the other outlets, and then went back to Boston. I wondered if I'd ever seen him again.

It was a little after six when I left the station and headed home to Chilmark. On my way, I passed by the Black Dog. I thought about going in for a Diet Coke, seeing who I knew there and hanging out for a while. But instead I kept driving until I got to another bar in a more remote part of the island. A bar I'd gone to in the past when I was drinking. It sure looked inviting. I stopped the car out front, and sat there staring at the place for a long time. Then I went inside and took a seat.

The bartender recognized me from my past visits and came over.

"Haven't seen you in a while," he said.

"I've been busy."

"I've seen you on the news."

"I'm back now."

"You want the usual, right? Vodka on the rocks?"

I didn't hesitate.

"The usual would be great!"

He put down a coaster in front of me and slid over a bowl of peanuts. I loved all the little rituals in a bar. Then he brought me my drink. The ice cubes clinked against the sides of the glass. I picked up the drink and took a sip. The alcohol coursed through my body, warm and comforting and reassuring – like an old friend who'd been away for too long. I'd been fifty-one days without a drink, and now here I was again.

Maybe it was the alcohol that did it. People say you lose brain cells from drinking, but I always thought it made me think clearer. Or maybe it was something that had always been there, percolating in my subconscious – waiting for the right moment to click into place.

The flowers. The dozen roses Samantha Claymore had gotten on her birthday from an unknown admirer. There was no name with the flowers, but – since they had been sent weeks before Samantha went missing – it hadn't seemed important to find out who they had come from.

Then I thought about Samantha Claymore's story of where she'd been for the past few weeks. She'd run away to New Orleans. Why New Orleans? Why not Los Angeles or Miami or Seattle or anywhere else? What was in New Orleans? I remembered what

Eddie Haver had told me about her believing her father might still be alive. Could that possibly be true? I had to find out for sure.

I took out my phone and called the station. Teena was still there.

"Remember that file we found on Samantha Claymore's computer at the beginning? The one that needed a password, and that the FBI eventually accessed. There was a list of people called Mandell. Can you bring that up?"

"Why?"

"There were addresses by each name, right?"

"Yes."

"Did any of these people live in New Orleans?"

I waited while Teena went through the file. "I got one," she said. "Jack Mandell. 264 Rosemont Drive."

CHAPTER 60

I flew to New Orleans the next morning. Though the Samantha Claymore case was closed, her father Ronald Claymore had gone missing in Martha's Vineyard five years ago. That had set everything in motion this summer. So I wanted to find out everything I could. It might even help me find out the real truth about Ronald Claymore too. Even if those answers were now fifteen hundred miles away from Cedar Cliffs.

The address was in a town called Metairie in Jefferson Parish, just outside New Orleans. When I got there, I parked my rental car in front of a white clapboard house at 264 Rosemont Drive. I got out of the car, walked up to the front door and rang the bell.

No one answered.

I walked around to the back of the house where a middle-aged man in blue work pants and a sleeveless shirt was digging in the garden. He looked up and smiled when he saw me. His face was deeply suntanned, his hair dark brown and he had a bushy beard.

"Jack Mandell?" I asked.

"That's me. What can I do for you?"

I took out my police shield and showed it to him. "Detective Abby Pearce with the Cedar Cliffs police force on Martha's Vineyard, Massachusetts."

His smile faded.

"I see," he said. "You're a long way out of your jurisdiction, aren't you, Detective?"

"I'm here to talk to you about Samantha Claymore."

"Samantha Claymore? Who's that?"

I'd seen pictures of Ronald Claymore. In the pictures, he had grey hair, was clean-shaven and seemed to weigh more than this man. But there's only so far you can go in changing your appearance. I was pretty sure who I was talking to.

"Do you want to tell me about it?" I asked quietly.

"Tell you about what?"

"Samantha's father died a few years ago in a boating incident. Except it wasn't an accident, it was murder. Samantha figured this out not long ago and has been obsessed ever since with finding out more about the circumstances of his death. She went looking for answers, and put her own life in danger. She's home again and safe now. It's a nice little story, huh?"

Mandell's expression didn't change.

"But I have another theory. Maybe Samantha's father wasn't murdered. Maybe there was an attempt on his life, but he didn't die on that boat. Maybe afterward he decided it was better if everyone thought he was dead. Maybe he's living another life now under a different identity."

"Why would he want to do that?"

"You tell me," I said. "You are Ronald Claymore, aren't you?"

Mandell wiped his forehead with the back of his hand. "I always feared this would happen. Someone like you showing up at my door. Let's go inside and talk, Detective."

We went into the living room and sat down. He looked like he was in shock, like he'd just seen a ghost. Well, in a way he had. His own.

"The explosion that day hurled me into the water," he said. "I was stunned, but alive. I hung onto the end of the boat for a while until it sank. I saw Samantha make it to shore so I knew she was all right. I saw that son of a bitch who tried to kill me survive too. But then again he was prepared – he knew that engine was going to explode. After everyone left the beach, I swam to land too."

"Why didn't you go to the police? Instead of leaving behind your life and millions of dollars?"

"Detective, everyone who has a lot of money spends most of their life trying to obtain it. That's what I did when I was young. I was very successful at it. I built Claymore Cosmetics Enterprises and became rich beyond my wildest dreams. The trouble was I was never happy. I didn't like what I did, I didn't like our friends. So I began to fantasize about having a different life. Becoming a different person. Without all that money to cause me problems." He smiled sadly. "A psychiatrist could have a field day with me.

"So when I survived the explosion – and once I knew my daughter was all right – I decided it was a good time to just disappear. I knew Randall had tried to kill me, and thought he succeeded. So I decided that Ronald Claymore should remain dead to the world."

He told me that he'd been thinking about this for some time. How he'd stashed away money from his company for whenever he thought the time was right to disappear. It was an appealing fantasy, I had to admit. To just walk away from your life and all the problems in it – and start all over again. I thought about what a colleague had once told me back in New York about the most baffling missing person cases. "It's like a flying saucer simply swooped down one day and scooped them up. One minute they're there, and the next minute they're gone. Just poof." Well, Ronald Claymore had pulled that off. Poof, he just disappeared.

"I moved here and became Jack Mandell. I'm an architect now. I read that Valerie had me declared legally dead and remarried. So I got married again too. And you know what, I'm happy as Jack Mandell, much happier than I ever was as Ronald Claymore. After a while, I began to forget Ronald Claymore even existed."

"Until your daughter showed up here and reminded you."

"Yeah, Samantha was the one thing I always felt badly about leaving behind. I figured Valerie would be happy with anyone as long as they had money. But Samantha – well, Samantha was special to me."

"So special that you took a chance and sent her flowers on her sixteenth birthday."

"She was turning sweet sixteen. I wanted her to have those flowers as a special gift even if I couldn't tell her who they were from."

"But she realized you were still alive and tracked you down. This is where she came when she ran away, isn't it? She was here, with you. How did she find you? How did she know you were now Jack Mandell?"

"It doesn't really matter. Let's just say my daughter is very resourceful. More resourceful than I realized when I sent her those birthday roses. She was very confused and upset and afraid when she called me. She said she was in trouble, and she wanted to see me. I sent her cash to make the trip. Then, after she got here, I told her to stay for a while. We got to know each other again. It was nice. But then her mother died. It was on the national news – Claymore Cosmetics Queen Dead. So I bought her a plane ticket and convinced her that she needed to go back to tell you the truth."

Except she didn't tell me the truth.

About her father still being alive.

Which was why she'd been so evasive when I asked her for details about how she'd traveled to New Orleans and then back again to the Vineyard again after her mother's death.

"Why did Samantha lie to us about you being dead?"

"I told her to say that."

"So that you could keep on being Jack Mandell?"

"Yes. That's why I lied too when someone from your department called here early on and asked about the name 'Mandell' being in Samantha's computer file – I said I didn't know anything about it. I didn't want to lose the life I've built for myself here. I like being Jack Mandell. Better than I liked being Ronald Claymore."

I had more questions for him. A lot more.

"Tell me more about why Randall tried to kill you," I said. Even though I was pretty sure I knew the answer.

"I'd been at his house. A number of times. I was unhappy with my life – and I guess it gave me some relief to be around those young girls.

"But one day, one of the girls began to cry. She said she wanted to get away from Randall, but didn't know how. She was afraid. Suddenly, I was disgusted with myself for being there and decided I was going to help her.

"I told Randall he needed to stop or I would tell the police what he was doing. He threatened me with videos he'd secretly taken of me but I said that wouldn't stop me. I had no idea he'd actually try to kill me. I guess I underestimated Peter Randall."

"We all did," I said.

He stood up and walked over to a window. Outside, I could see trees and grass and other little homes like his. It seemed peaceful. I could understand why Ronald Claymore loved this life so much. Claymore had found an idyllic little world to live in. He'd thought he could just drop out, cut his ties with everything and that there would never be any consequences. But in the end his past caught up with him, the same as it does with all of us.

"So what happens now?" he asked.

"You have to come back to Martha's Vineyard. Just like Samantha did."

"Are you going to arrest me?"

"Like you said, I'm out of my jurisdiction."

"You expect me to go back on my own, voluntarily?" He shook his head. "I won't do that. Listen, if you think I'm going to risk everything I have here simply to—"

"No, you listen!" I was angry now. All the feelings that had been building up inside me since I'd figured out the truth came pouring out. "Your answer to life's problems seems to be to run away from them. Well, that doesn't solve the problems, Mr. Claymore or Mandell or whatever your name is. It only leaves someone else who has to deal with them."

"But I have my life here…"

"Oh yeah, you told me. Your life's great now, huh? Well, big deal. How about the life of your daughter who grew up under psychiatric care after losing her father? Or your wife who had to raise Samantha without you and wound up turning into a drug user?"

"I'm sorry." He put his head in his hands. "I really am sorry for all of it. But I didn't know what else to do."

"There's something you can do now. Come back with me and tell the truth."

"But it's been too long. So much has happened. It's too late now to try and make things right."

"Better late than never," I told him.

CHAPTER 61

I had one final thing to do when I got back to Martha's Vineyard. I drove out to Melvin Ellis' house to explain everything to him in person and apologize for the department – mostly me – erroneously believing he was the sexual predator we were looking for, not Peter Randall.

Ellis was stunned by everything, and said he had been ever since the original story broke in the media claiming he was my chief suspect. But he assured me he wasn't planning to take any legal action against either me or the department.

"I'm just glad it's over," he said.

He said he had only met with Bruce Aiken that day in Edgartown because Aiken was trying to borrow money from him – saying he needed it to deal with a cash flow problem in Claymore Cosmetics. And that was also why Aiken had come to his house that day we followed him, because he was pleading for the loan. Like I'd suspected, Aiken had been playing fast and loose with the company finances – and it had all caught up to him.

Was Aiken in Edgartown that first day too because he was looking for his stepdaughter Samantha?

Or was it really a coincidence that it all went down at the same time and in the same place?

Ellis said those two times – in Edgartown and later at his house – were the only times he ever met Bruce Aiken. He also said he never gave Aiken the money because he didn't trust him. He insisted his only role in the entire Claymore case was to offer up the reward money because he felt that it might help to get the girl home safely.

I believed him.

I was wrong about Melvin Ellis.

I'd been wrong about him from the very beginning.

And, as it turned out, that wasn't the only thing I was wrong about.

Before I left, someone else came into the room where we were meeting. Mark Ellis. His son. The man who had lived in my nightmares since that prom night years ago.

"You remember my son, Mark, don't you?" Melvin Ellis said.

"Oh, I remember him," I said.

Actually, I almost didn't recognize Mark Ellis. He'd put on a lot of weight, most of it in the form of a potbelly, and he was losing his hair. He didn't look like a dreamboat anymore. I asked him if we could talk a minute on my way out. He said sure.

"Abby Pearce," he said, once we were outside. "After all these years."

"That's right."

"You look good, Abby."

I didn't bother to tell him he didn't look so good. Or how much pleasure it gave me to see him as an overweight, balding man.

"I've read a lot about you," he said. "You've become quite a celebrity, Abby."

"Not bad for a shy little girl who once thought the biggest thing in the world was to get invited to the prom by you, huh?"

"Oh, that was a long time ago," he said.

"Not long enough."

"Huh?"

"I still remember you raping me that night."

I don't know what I thought was going to happen then. I'd had a lot of fantasies. I'd shoot him. I'd tell his wife and kids and friends what a creep he was. I'd make him apologize for what he did that night. But I wasn't prepared for what happened next.

"What are you talking about, Abby?" Mark Ellis said.

He seemed genuinely confused.

"I'm talking about what happened when we came back to your house – to this house – after the prom."

"Nothing happened."

"Taking a girl's virginity against her will is not nothing."

He shook his head. "All that happened that night is you had too much to drink. You got really drunk and you freaked out. So, I took you home and left you by your front door. You were worried about what your parents would say if they saw you. I didn't want to stay around for that kind of scene, so I left. I told your father the same thing when he came to see me afterward. That's the truth, Abby."

I stared at Mark Ellis.

Was he telling me the truth?

The fact of the matter is I'd never remembered everything about that night.

I remembered the prom, drinking at the Ellis mansion, and going home with blood on my dress. But there were snatches of time in between when I'd blacked out from the alcohol and that I'd never been able to completely account for. What had really happened to me?

"Someone raped me," I said.

"I'm so sorry, Abby. But it wasn't me."

"Then who?"

"Maybe you should ask your father."

"I can't. He's dead."

"It wasn't me," Ellis repeated.

I drove to the assisted living facility on Cape Cod where my mother now lived. I told her I wanted to know what had happened to me the night of my prom. The real story. I said she owed it to me to tell the truth.

So she did.

Finally.

And the truth about that night turned out to be even more shocking than what I had believed all these years.

The person who had raped me was Stan Larsen. Yes, my father's partner at the restaurant in Vineyard Haven. The man I called "Uncle Stan." The man who was like a second father to me growing up – and recently. Right up until now.

I had the chronology wrong. I didn't go to Larsen's house after I was raped. I walked there after Ellis dropped me off in front of my house, afraid to face my parents while I was drunk. Apparently, Mark Ellis wasn't the only one to notice I'd turned into an attractive young woman. Uncle Stan did too. His desires took over in what he called "a horrible moment of weakness." That's what Larsen told my father when he confronted him afterward.

At first, my mother said, my father wanted to turn Larsen over to the police. But Larsen begged him not to. He said that he couldn't face jail, he'd kill himself first. And my father was worried about the ordeal of putting me through a court case. So, he and Larsen made a deal. They would end their business partnership, Larsen would move away, and he would never contact any of us again. And I hadn't heard from him since then, until I tracked him down in California.

We'd never talked about that night in any of our conversations. I'd never wanted to relive the memories of that night.

Larsen must have wondered at first if I knew – but then realized I didn't, and so he kept up the pretense of being my "Uncle Stan."

"Your father always wanted to tell you about it," my mother said. "He could just never find the courage to do it. I guess neither of us could. He carried that secret to the grave. And it cost him a terrible price. It cost him his daughter."

I was angrier at my father – and my mother too – than I had ever been before.

"What about me?" I said. "My father was worried about Stan Larsen going to jail? He was more worried about him than me, his own daughter? How could you have ever justified something like that?"

"There were other reasons your father did what he did. You have to understand that. But it was all so long ago…"

"I want to know everything."

My mother told me then how Larsen had loaned a large amount of money to my father to keep the restaurant going during some tough financial times. My father was afraid the restaurant would go under if Larsen went to jail.

"It would have ruined the restaurant, your father, and our family," she said. "Your father had no choice."

"Oh, he had a choice," I said. "He could have protected his daughter – but instead he protected his goddamned restaurant. This wasn't even about protecting 'Uncle Stan' from going to jail. It was about protecting himself and his business. And I'm the one who paid the price."

"Your father never meant to hurt you. He thought he was doing the only thing he could. He just wanted it all to go away."

"And you?" I asked my mother now. "You let this happen. You could have told me the truth. You're as much to blame as he is."

"It was easier to pretend it never happened. I know now that was a mistake. But the longer it went on, the harder it became to do anything about it. Please forgive us, Abby."

I wasn't sure I could do that.

Forgive her.

Forgive my dead father.

Or forgive Stan Larsen for what he did to me that night.

I deleted Larsen's number from my phone.

And I walked out on my mother without giving her an answer.

EPILOGUE

I'd been wrong about a lot of things in this case. Melvin Ellis and his son, Mark. Stan Larsen. Mayor Peter Randall. Vic Hollister. Barry Wilhelm. Even Teena at the beginning. And, of course, Lincoln Connor.

But, in the end, I did right by Samantha Claymore.

I really believe that.

I'm thinking about this now – and about Bridget Feckanin and the others I couldn't save – as I sit on the beach in Cedar Cliffs. It is early morning. The sun is just rising and casting a magical light on the water. When I was a little girl growing up here, I used to love to go the beach by myself to watch the sun come up. I still do.

Only this time I'm not alone. I'm with Lincoln Connor. Yes, he came back and showed up at my door last night. And, when I woke up this morning, he was still there with me. I don't know what the future holds for me and Lincoln. But it's nice to be in his arms right now.

I spent ten years on the New York City police force and I loved every minute of it – until I didn't love it anymore. That's why I returned to Martha's Vineyard. I needed to take control of my life again. But there was always something missing for me. I felt my job was unfinished. And that I needed to do something to erase the memories and demons of my past. I needed something more. I needed… well, redemption.

I wasn't sure I'd found that redemption yet. But I sure got a piece of it with Samantha Claymore.

Lincoln and I sit there on the beach watching the early morning sun rise and sparkle on the water.

Then I stand up, give Lincoln a kiss and begin walking toward the Cedar Cliffs police station.

Time to go back to work...

A LETTER FROM DANA

Dear reader,

I want to say a huge thank you for choosing to read *Her Ocean Grave*. If you did enjoy it, and want to keep up to date with all my latest releases, just sign up at the following link. Your email address will never be shared and you can unsubscribe at any time.

www.bookouture.com/dana-perry

This book is a change for me in character and setting. After writing two thrillers for Bookouture about the New York City media (where I worked for many years), I tell the story here of former NYPD homicide detective Abby Pearce who returns to her small hometown police force on Martha's Vineyard. When a teenage girl mysteriously goes missing during a bike ride, it sends shock waves through the people of this picturesque resort island where major crime almost never happens. But then, as Abby digs deeper into the baffling case, she uncovers that this isn't the only girl who has disappeared on Martha's Vineyard without a trace.

I hope you loved *Her Ocean Grave*, and if you did I would be very grateful if you could write a review. I'd love to hear what you think, and it makes such a difference helping new readers to discover one of my books for the first time.

Cedar Cliffs is a fictional town. All the characters I write about here and everything that takes place and happens in Her Ocean Grave is fictional too – not based on any real people or events. Martha's Vineyard, of course, is a real place. And I was inspired to set this book there because I have spent numerous wonderful summers in the town of Oak Bluffs – which is the real-life Cedar Cliffs, a beautiful place where crimes like these never happen!

I love hearing from my readers – you can get in touch on my Facebook page, through Twitter or Goodreads.

Thanks,
Dana Perry

 @DanaPerryAuthor

 @DanaPerryAuthor

Made in the USA
Middletown, DE
16 May 2023

30677191R00166